Cutter inched his chair away from the table. The scraping of the wooden legs across the sawdust floor caused the rest of the saloon to grow quieter.

Kelly spotted the handle of a silver pistol Cutter kept holstered on his belt, butt forward. Kelly had never been much of a fan of guns, so he had no idea what kind it was, but it looked intimidating enough. He imagined that was the point.

Cutter said, "People don't talk to me like you just did, mister. Not in my own place. Not even a mad Irishman such as yourself."

Kelly's head snapped around at the insult. "Mad, is it?"

Before he realized he was doing it, Kelly cut loose with the bullwhip and slashed Cutter across his gun hand. The gambler cried out as he recoiled, almost falling out of his chair.

RALPH COMPTON

THE KELLY TRAIL

A RALPH COMPTON WESTERN BY
TERRENCE McCAULEY

BERKLEY
New York

BERKLEY

An imprint of Penguin Random House LLC

penguinrandomhouse.com

Copyright © 2020 by The Estate of Ralph Compton

Penguin Random House supports copyright. Copyright fuels creativity, encourages
diverse voices, promotes free speech, and creates a vibrant culture. Thank you for buying
an authorized edition of this book and for complying with copyright laws by not
reproducing, scanning, or distributing any part of it in any form without permission.
You are supporting writers and allowing Penguin Random House to continue to
publish books for every reader.

BERKLEY and the BERKLEY & B colophon are registered trademarks of
Penguin Random House LLC.

ISBN: 9781984803382

First Edition: August 2020

Printed in the United States of America
1   3   5   7   9   10   8   6   4   2

Cover art by Steve Atkinson
Cover design by Steve Meditz
Book design by George Towne

THE IMMORTAL COWBOY

This is respectfully dedicated to the "American Cowboy." His was the saga sparked by the turmoil that followed the Civil War, and the passing of more than a century has by no means diminished the flame.

———◆———

True, the old days and the old ways are but treasured memories, and the old trails have grown dim with the ravages of time, but the spirit of the cowboy lives on.

———◆———

In my travels—to Texas, Oklahoma, Kansas, Nebraska, Colorado, Wyoming, New Mexico, and Arizona—I always find something that reminds me of the Old West. While I am walking these plains and mountains for the first time, there is this feeling that a part of me is eternal, that I have known these old trails before. I believe it is the undying spirit of the frontier calling me, through the mind's eye, to step back into time. What is the appeal of the Old West of the American frontier?

———◆———

It has been epitomized by some as the dark and bloody period in American history. Its heroes—Crockett, Bowie, Hickok, Earp—have been reviled and criticized. Yet the Old West lives on, larger than life.

———◆———

It has become a symbol of freedom, when there was always another mountain to climb and another river to cross; when a dispute between two men was settled not with expensive lawyers, but with fists, knives, or guns. Barbaric? Maybe. But some things never change. When the cowboy rode into the pages of American history, he left behind a legacy that lives within the hearts of us all.

—*Ralph Compton*

RALPH COMPTON

THE KELLY TRAIL

CHAPTER ONE

At that precise moment on that fine spring morning, William "Bull" Kelly figured he was probably the happiest man in Texas.

He had just made the last payment on the ranch that would forge his dynasty.

As of ten minutes earlier, the ranch he had spent years paying off was entirely and legally his. He had spent a fair portion of his life driving cattle to markets up north. Kansas. Nebraska. Even Montana on occasion. Cattle that had belonged to other men. Cattle that had made other men rich.

Kelly and his beloved Mary had been scrimping and saving every cent for decades to provide for their five sons and keep their own small ranch running. And now the day they had dreamed of together for so long had finally come. He only wished Mary had lived long enough to see it.

He looked up to toward the sky, where he expected

his departed wife to be, and said, "We did it, girl. I only wish you were beside me to see it with your own eyes."

He blinked away a tear and dried his nose on his sleeve as the weight of it all finally hit him. Now the aging Irishman could finally make his lifelong dream a reality. He and his five sons could set about driving the three thousand herd of cattle he had amassed north to the market at Dodge City and sell it to the highest bidder. This early in the drive season—early April—and with cattle going for twenty-five dollars a head, he would make a tidy profit for his boys to start their new lives in the cattle business.

After all of those years of making other men rich, it was finally time to have something of his own. Free and clear of all debts.

With his beloved Mary now gone, his sons' future was all that mattered to him. He knew she would live as long as they did.

Jacob and James and Jeremiah and Joel and Joshua.

Their mother had named them all, as he had been on the trail when each boy came into the world. She had kept their names biblical, and in honor of her own father, John, back in the old country, had used the initial *J* for each boy. Kelly had known her father and did not think the old miser was worth the memory, but Mary did, and her happiness was all that had ever mattered to him.

He hoped she would be happy now.

He wiped another tear on his sleeve and tucked the deed to his ranch into his coat pocket. He knew a man of his age was a fool to be taking three thousand head of cattle north to market in Kansas, but William Kelly had never been accused of being a practical man. He had not acquired the name "Bull" for nothing.

He knew a man in his position should take the easy part of the trail for a change. Maybe riding in the chuck wagon with Concho, his friend and the outfit's cook. But age was only a number to William Kelly. He had seen many a gray-haired old man act like a child and many a boy be more of a man than expected.

His exact age was a mystery, even to himself, but he imagined he was somewhere in his middle fifties. He imagined it was all written down in the parish church back in Ballinamuck, but he had never been curious enough to find out when he had still lived there. And he had no intention of going back after all of these years. Besides, his mind had never been sharper than it was at that moment and he could not remember a time when he felt quite as strong as he did now, not even during all of those years earning saddle sores and sleeping outdoors at the whim of the elements.

Back then, he had been working for someone else. This time, he would be the head of his own outfit and his own herd with his own boys riding with him. He was working for himself and for their future. That was a feeling to savor at any age.

As he walked to his horse, he could feel summer was in the air, but so was the windy chill of a mild spring. The men who owned farms near his ranch fretted about the effect a cold spring might have on their crops. It was a fear he had grown up with. Kelly's father back in Ireland had been a farmer and all of his brothers were still farmers.

But a life tied to a plot of land owned by another had never held much appeal to William Kelly, which was why he had set out early in life to see the world with his own two eyes.

And he had seen enough to fill ten lifetimes. Perhaps too much.

No, he only cared about the grass along the trail being green and tall enough to keep his herd well fed on the way to Dodge City. Kelly knew one drive would not make a dynasty, but it was an important first step in making the Kelly name mean something in this new world called America.

Kelly ignored the ache in his bones as he walked toward the hitching rail, where his black Morgan mare stood waiting. He knew the townspeople were looking at him oddly as he set one foot in the stirrup and climbed atop the large animal.

Many men told him a man of his experience should know better than to take such a large beast on the trail. The Morgan was not as swift as some of the other breeds of horses he could have chosen for the drive. He knew that was true.

But Bull Kelly had never won anything based on being the fastest or the most practical. Everything he had earned in this world had been won through his own sweat and determination. His own instinct.

Determination had kept him alive on the prison ship to the hell that was Fremantle. Cunning had helped win his freedom and had steeled him and Concho during their long voyage to America. His instinct had kept him and the Spaniard alive on the streets of Boston and helped him send money back home to Mary in Texas while he worked the cow trails that snaked their way north from Texas.

Determination for a better future had made him endure all of the obstacles life had thrown down before him. And in his bones, Bull Kelly knew he was destined for greater glory in this life and the next.

The few chuckles of the townspeople died away as they watched Kelly mount the great black mare and bring her around with ease. They stopped laughing altogether when they saw the coiled bullwhip tied to his belt by a tong. Several beasts—and more than a few men—over the years had made the mistake of believing the bullwhip was just a gimmick, but soon learned the error of their belief when he cut loose with it.

Years of practice and bitter experience had made the whip an extension of Kelly's hand. Twelve feet of kangaroo hide with a metal popper on the end gave the weapon a sinister look. His skill in wielding it made it as deadly as any pistol; perhaps even deadlier. For fear or rushing a shot made it easy for a man to miss a shot in a gunfight. Bull Kelly's whip never missed.

The story behind the whip—and the circumstances under which he had obtained it—would have been hard for most men to believe had he ever chosen to tell it. But some things were best kept to oneself, especially the most horrible things.

Kelly rode the big Morgan he had named Morgan for the sake of simplicity down the street toward the general store, where his sons and Concho were gathering the final supplies for the trail ahead. He had hired ten hands to help with the drive. Combined with him, Jacob, James, Jeremiah, Joel, and Joshua, he thought that number would be sufficient. Concho's cooking would be a welcome way for the McCabe outfit to wake up in the morning and wind down at night after a long day in the saddle.

As he approached the general store, Kelly saw four of his boys helping Concho load sacks of supplies into the wagon. Jacob, Jeremiah, Joel, and Joshua could have been twins had ten months or so not separated each of his sons' births. The boys were younger images of him, all standing just shy of six feet tall with lean frames. He was glad they had inherited their mother's fine features and thick black hair but bore the blue eyes he had given them.

They were all good, hardworking boys, too, another quality they had inherited from their mother back while he was riding the trail to support the family. The sight of the four of them there in front of the general store working hard to load the wagon made him proud.

And, much to his disappointment, the notion that one boy was missing did not surprise him in the least.

Kelly pulled up the horse beside the wagon. "How's it coming, boys?"

"Just fine, Pa," said Jacob. At twenty-five, he was the oldest of the brothers and the quietest. "We'll be done here before you know it."

Kelly looked at Concho, who many people mistakenly took for a Mexican. Given that this was Texas, it was a forgivable mistake to make except for Concho. The Spaniard used to fight men for making the assumption, but like Kelly, the years had mellowed him to the point where he allowed most slights to pass.

"Where's James?" Kelly asked his old friend in Spanish. They had always spoken to each other in Concho's native language once Kelly had managed to pick it up.

"Where do you think?" Concho nodded toward a saloon farther down the street. An ancient wooden sign swung above the door in the gentle morning breeze. It was called the Golden Dream Saloon.

Kelly had been expecting that. His second-born was the most capable of all his sons. The best-looking, the brightest, and the most affable. The one Kelly boy who had inherited all of his mother's finest qualities and all of his father's worst vices. A boy like that could get into a lot of trouble anywhere, particularly in Texas, where trouble was easy to find. And James had already uncovered more than his fair share of it at an early age.

Unfortunately, James was also allergic to hard work, an affliction he had developed entirely on his own.

"How long has he been there?" Kelly asked Concho.

"About an hour, give or take," Concho told him. "I haven't heard any fights break out yet, so I think he might be behaving himself this time."

Kelly knew that probably was not true and would not last long if it was. Trouble had a knack of finding his second-born wherever he might be, and James had a habit of embracing it.

"Want me to go get him?" asked Joel, his second youngest.

Kelly knew it would be pointless to send either Joel or Joshua. They idolized their older brother and often sat up well into the night listening to James lie about all of the women he had loved and the dangerous men he had bested in bar fights and brawls. Sending one of them to get their brother would be like sending a field mouse to get a tomcat.

Kelly let up on the reins and urged the Morgan forward. "I'll fetch him and bring him back here. You boys keep up the hard work. I won't be but a minute."

A S HE HITCHED his horse's reins to the rail in front of the saloon, Kelly decided the Golden Dream looked more like a nightmare. The yellow paint had long since begun to crack and peel from years of exposure to the harsh Texas weather. Kelly had been able to smell the place from halfway up the thoroughfare and the stench had only worsened now that he was in front of it. It stank of cheap whiskey, stale tobacco, and wasted hours.

It was exactly the kind of hellhole James loved.

More out of habit than menace, Kelly rested his hand on the bullwhip coiled at his hip as he walked up the steps and pushed his way through the batwing doors of the saloon.

He stood in the doorway and waited for his eyes to adjust to the dimmer light. He looked for his son but could not find him in the sea of faces. Despite the early hour, the place was packed with drinkers at the bar and gamblers at the tables. Working girls with too much perfume to cover their stench and too much face paint to cover up their sins flitted among the customers like bumblebees in a garden.

A gambler at the table closest to the door looked

up at Kelly from his cards. His spotless bowler hat and a brocade vest adorned with a gold watch chain spoke of prosperity. His waxed mustache and trimmed gray beard only served to enhance Kelly's impression of the man as something of a dandy. But his narrow eyes spoke of something more. Something Kelly saw in the mirror when he shaved each morning.

Kelly had never liked it when people looked at him. He had always done his best to blend into a crowd and never draw attention to himself. Attention often got men killed and Kelly still had plenty of years ahead of him.

The gambler squinted up at him. "You lost, mister?"

"Hardly," said Kelly as he kept looking for James.

"I ask on account of it looks like this is your first time in a saloon is all, standing there like you are. The ladies' league holds meetings up at the church around this time of day if you'd prefer their company."

The other gamblers at the table laughed.

If William Kelly did not like people looking at him, he liked people laughing at him even less. "I'm here for James Kelly, mister. Not you. Best go back to your game and leave me about my business."

The gambler smiled. "You the law, mister?"

Another laugh from that table and from others who had come to notice him.

"No. I'm his father. I'm here to fetch him home."

The gambler cashed out his hand and flopped his cards on the table before settling back in his chair. "Well, it seems to me that if your boy is old enough to be in here, then he's old enough to make up his mind on where he wants to be, now, ain't he? Why don't you leave him alone? Let the boy have a good time."

Kelly stopped looking over the crowd and looked at the gambler. "Why don't you mind your own business?"

The men at the table and at the other tables close by froze. The rest of the saloon remained noisy, but no one in that part of the place moved or made a sound.

The gambler said, "Normally I would, except that everything that happens in the Golden Dream is my business, mister. I'm Ace Cutter and you're standing in my saloon."

Kelly glanced around at the cracked wooden floor and the faded felt of the gambling tables. "A grand place, to be sure. I'll be out of your hair in a minute, Mr. Cutter. Like I said, I'm just here to get my boy."

Cutter inched his chair away from the table. The scraping of the wooden legs across the sawdust floor caused the rest of the saloon to grow quieter.

Kelly spotted the handle of a silver pistol Cutter kept holstered on his belt, butt forward. Kelly had never been much of a fan of guns, so he had no idea what kind it was, but it looked intimidating enough. He imagined that was the point.

Unfortunately for Mr. Cutter, Kelly was not so easily intimidated by steel.

Cutter said, "People don't talk to me like you just did, mister. Not in my own place. Not even a mad Irishman such as yourself. I say you'd best head on home and let your boy have his fun. Yes, sir. I believe you should do that while you still have the chance."

Kelly's head snapped around at the insult. "Mad, is it?"

Before he realized he was doing it, Kelly cut loose with the bullwhip and slashed Cutter across his gun hand. The gambler cried out as he recoiled, almost falling out of his chair.

"I'm no madman, Yank. You'd do well to remember that."

"He ain't likely to forget it now," said a rangy man at the same table closest to Kelly. "And neither are you."

The man began to stand, but Kelly brought the hard handle of the whip down on the top of his head, sending him flat on his rump.

More men began to rustle, and Kelly moved to a clear area between the tables and the bar. He cut loose with the whip and snapped it just above the heads of the gamblers around him.

"Everyone who wants to keep his head should keep his seat," Kelly warned them. "I don't want trouble here. I just want my boy. Give him over, or I'll cut the lot of you down like wheat."

"Do as he says," called out the bartender behind the bar. "And consider yourselves lucky. You too, Cutter. That's Bull Kelly you're dealing with. That man could've just as easily taken your hand off with that whip instead of just scraping it like he did."

Kelly did not recognize the fat man behind the bar, but the man clearly knew him. Kelly had tried hard to not acquire a reputation, but sometimes a reputation has a habit of following a man despite his best efforts to the contrary.

"Yes, sir," the bartender continued to observe, "Mr. Kelly's a right surgeon with that damned lash of his. And many is the man now crippled who can attest to that very fact."

Kelly realized the bartender had a brogue. "Where you from?"

The fat barman stood up straight. "I'm a Cork man."

Kelly did not bother replying. He had always believed the best thing to come out of Cork was the road to Dublin. "Where's my boy?"

"Right here, Pa!" he heard his son say. "Quit hurtin' folks."

Kelly looked up and saw James coming down the stairs, struggling to slip his braces over his shoulders. A painted lady still fixing her frilly dress followed close behind him.

Kelly had been disappointed in his boy too many times to be surprised by what he had been up to. "Let's go, boy. Your brothers have been waiting and so have I."

He knew his son had a reputation for being quick with his hands and even quicker with his sharp tongue.

But he also knew James was aware there was a time when he could push his father and a time when he risked the whip if he did.

This was a time not to question him.

"Yes, Pa," he said sheepishly as he moved through the crowd toward his father and past him on the way outside.

Kelly began to coil his whip as he backed out of the place.

Cutter spat in his direction and yelled, "I'll kill

you, Kelly. I swear to God, I'll kill you for what you did to me today."

Kelly grinned at the wounded man cradling his bloody hand. "Many is the man who said so. And I'm still here."

Kelly backed up through the batwing doors and mounted his horse.

CHAPTER TWO

KELLY KEPT THE big Morgan mare moving toward the wagon at a steady pace as James walked beside him in the thoroughfare.

James looked up at his father. "Why'd you have to go and do that for, Pa?"

"Do what?" Kelly said as he rode toward the wagon. "Pull you off a whore so you could get back to work where you belong?"

"You know what I mean," James said. "Why'd you have to go and do that to Mr. Cutter?"

"Mr. Cutter, is it?" Kelly repeated. "I didn't know you held the man in such esteem."

"I don't." James shrugged. "I just like going in there from time to time."

"Well, you won't be going in there again," Kelly reminded him. "I don't let men talk to me like that and neither should you. You're a Kelly, for God's sake. 'Mr. Cutter,' indeed!"

"I was just having a little fun is all." James kicked a rock out of his way. "I won't be back here for a long while, if ever. I figured I owed it to myself to get it all out of my system before we hit the trail tomorrow."

But William Kelly had already known his son's reasoning without his boy having to explain it. He knew the lad better than the lad knew himself. "A hard day's work is a good way of getting something out of your system, too, boy. Helping your brothers loading that wagon, for instance. I've always found fun is more enjoyable after a bout of honest labor."

"Fun," James sneered. "Like you'd know anything about having fun. All you ever do is work and push us to work, then work some more."

Kelly looked at his son. His fine features had been marred a bit by a broken nose that was still healing and a broken jaw from the previous year that the town doctor had not been able to set properly. But neither of these features had taught him a lesson. If anything, they had only served to give him a more rakish air than he already had.

For once, Bull Kelly held his tongue and could not help but have a bit of pity for his son. He had never stepped foot out of Texas but thought himself a man of the world. He thought his father a prude. *If he only knew.*

"There's nothing wrong with fun as long as it's earned, boy," Kelly persisted. "And did you ever stop and think about your brothers and Concho? Don't you think they might've liked a little fun after working so hard on the wagon? Why, the lot of you would have already been done with the loading if you had pitched in and done your share. You all could've been in that cellar you call a saloon together right now, having fun."

"They know even less about fun than you do," James said. "They're all just like you. All work and nothing else."

Kelly laughed. "And if you were more like them, you'd be better off." He decided he had spent enough time on the issue and saw no sense in belaboring the point. "Well, now that you've had your fun, I hope it'll last you for a good long while. We won't be having much time for fun once we hit the trail tomorrow morning."

He could see his son was still annoyed about the whole thing, so he decided to throw a bit of salt on his wounded pride. "And when you start to itchin' from whatever that soiled dove gave you back there, don't come crying to me, for you'll get no sympathy. You can scratch yourself raw for all I care. You'll do your full time in the saddle or, by God, you'll feel my whip. That's a promise."

James rubbed his backside, which Kelly imagined still hurt from the last time the boy had doubted his words. "No thanks. I'll do my bit."

Kelly would believe it when it happened. "See to it that you do."

B Y THE TIME they reached the general store, Concho and the boys already had all the sacks loaded and were ready to go. James climbed up into the saddle without looking at his brothers.

But that did not prevent the boys from having a good time at their brother's expense.

"Will you look at that, boys?" Jacob said. "The prodigal brother has returned."

"From a hard day in the fields from the looks of it." Jeremiah laughed.

"Hard day on a straw mattress is more like it," Joel chided.

Joshua would not be left out of the fun. "Which one was it this time, Jim? The blonde or the redhead Cutter keeps stocked for you?"

"He looks too well rested for it to have been either of them," Jacob observed. "My money is on one of them old steers Cutter peddles in the cribs out back."

Even Concho laughed as the boys took delight at James's expense.

James frowned at his father. "You just going to sit there and let them talk to me like that?"

"They've earned it," Kelly said. "You've already had your *fun*. Let them have some, too."

Concho released the wheel brake and snapped the whip, bringing the four-horse team alive. James spurred his horse and rode ahead of his brothers, undoubtedly in hope of escaping their joshing, but to no avail. They followed right behind him and kept piling on the torrent of abuse.

Kelly decided to ride alongside the wagon. He had to admit the sight of his five boys riding together warmed his heart and made him miss his Mary all the more.

As they began to roll away from the general store, Concho spoke to Kelly in English. He only spoke in English when no one else was around, though Kelly had never understood why.

"I noticed things got quiet while you were in there, William."

"For a reason," Kelly replied as he rode beside the wagon. He felt his friend's reproaching glare. "For a *good* reason. I promise."

"I suppose James was not the only Kelly man who needed to have some fun before the trail," Concho observed.

As they rode past the Golden Dream Saloon, Kelly saw Cutter standing on the boardwalk. He had a sopping bar rag wrapped around his bleeding hand and he was glaring at the small Kelly outfit as it went by. He made a point of glaring at William Kelly in particular.

Concho seemed to notice it. "It seems like you have made another enemy, my friend."

Kelly did not bother to look at Cutter. He had seen that look in the eyes of countless men before and knew the menace that was behind it. "I'd say that means he finds himself in good company." Bull Kelly smiled. "Yes, sir. Better company than he knows."

CHAPTER THREE

Ace Cutter backhanded the doctor, staggering him backward. As it was his left hand and not his right, the blow had not been strong enough to send the man flying. Cutter blamed the lack of power on the loss of blood and the shock of the news the doctor had just given him.

"What did you just say to me?" Cutter yelled.

Doc Post, known in town as Old Doc Post, brought a gnarled hand to the left side of his face. "I told you the truth, Ace." The doctor looked down at his hand to see if there was any blood. There was none, except for that which had come from Cutter. "I told you it would be best if you let me take that hand off for you."

The whores of the Golden Dream who had clustered around Cutter scattered as the gambler got to his feet fast enough to cause his chair to tip back. The rage decreased the pain and embarrassment from the cowpuncher's whip, but Doc Post's words stung worse than the bullwhip had.

"The hell you say," Cutter bellowed. "I came into this world whole, by God, and I aim to go out the same way."

"No one's making you do anything, Ace," Doc Post told him. "Not that anyone's ever been able to, least of all me. You paid me to look at your hand and I'm telling you it would be best if you let me amputate."

Cutter looked down at his ruined hand and grew dizzy. The bleeding had only begun to stop before the doctor had gotten to the saloon. He imagined the old bastard had taken his time, hoping the gambler would bleed to death before he had gotten there. That would be one way Doc Post could get out from under the debt he owed Cutter for enjoying the whiskey and women at the Golden Dream.

Cutter had been glad to disappoint him, but he had not been expecting news like this. "Can't you just sew me up and stop the bleeding? Why do you have to take my hand?"

Doc Post pointed at Cutter's wound. "That's not exactly a scratch you're sporting there and it's not a cut, either. Kelly's whip took a hunk out of your right hand just below the wrist. He took a lot more than skin, tendon, and muscle also. Bone, too, but you'll have to trust me on that score. Looking at it yourself is liable to make you faint."

Cutter saw the look in Doc Post's eyes turn to something else. Something close to pity. And pity was something that Alan Cutter, the gambler they called Ace, had never been able to abide.

He may have shot Doc Post right then and there if he had been able to grab his Colt.

But he could not grab it because his hand was in ruins.

One of the working girls must have sensed the wave of exhaustion that had washed over him, for she rushed to his side and propped him up. He wanted to push her away but found he did not have the strength.

"Just patch me up like I told you, Doc."

But Doc Post took a step backward, ensuring that he was well beyond the arc of Cutter's punch. "Don't you understand? It's not a simple matter of stopping the bleeding and letting you heal for a couple of days. Everything that makes that hand work is gone. The bone is exposed, and it is only a matter of time before gangrene sets in. Maybe only a matter of hours, if it has not yet started. If it does, you may lose the entire arm. You may even die." The doctor shook his head. "I wish I had better news for you, but I don't. That hand needs to come off and it needs to come off right now."

Despite the weakness eating away at his strength from the loss of blood, Cutter remained on his feet, propped up by the women who worked for him.

"Ever see a one-armed gambling man, Doc?" Cutter shook his head. "Me neither. At least none that was any good."

Doc Post's eyes narrowed. "No, but I've seen plenty of one-armed men in my day. Men who went on to make a good life for themselves after the war. And you won't lose the arm if you let me get to work right away. You might be able to keep your arm. Hell, you might even be able to . . ."

"To what?" Cutter yelled. "To do what? Paw at things with a stump? Or get a hook like some damned pirate? Maybe get myself a parrot to complete the look?" The gambler sneered. "Not a chance, Doc. If I can't play cards, I'm no one. I've never been a good enough player to win an honest game and I'm no good with my gun hand gone, so that means I'm good as dead already. So just do what you can about the bleeding and leave me be."

Doc Post hung his head and ran his hands through his stringy hair. "I took an oath to do no harm and I aim to do just that. But I hope you'll reconsider, Ace. I really do. Life is a gift worth living, even for a man like you."

Cutter was too weak to appreciate sentiment. "I may not have had a choice about how I came into this world, old man, but I've certainly got a choice in how I leave it. And I'm leaving it the way I want to. But before I do, I intend on taking one or two of the Kelly boys with me."

"In your condition, you'll be lucky if the walk down the stairs doesn't kill you, much less a ride out to the Kelly place." Doc Post picked up his weathered medical bag and gestured toward Cutter's bedroom. "Get him into bed, ladies, and fill him with whiskey until it comes out his ears. This is going to hurt something awful."

The women began to guide Cutter toward his bedroom when he stopped them. "Why would it hurt? You said there's nothing left to hurt."

Doc Post had neither the intention nor the inclination to give the gambler a lesson in surgery. All of his previous medical advice had fallen on deaf ears and he saw no benefit in trying to explain himself further. "Sometimes, it just hurts, Ace. That's all."

He motioned for the ladies to resume escorting Ace Cutter to bed. This time, the gambler did not stop them.

CUTTER DID NOT know how long he had been unconscious when he finally came to.

A certain dryness about the mouth and eyes told him he was in for one hell of a hangover. He decided to check the whiskey stock when he finally sobered up because there was obviously something in the barrels that had tainted the liquor. He remembered vivid nightmares of pain and gore and blood. Of terrors that had caused him to scream at the top of his lungs and burn his throat. The stabbing pain whenever he swallowed told him his dreams had been so severe that he must have cried out in his sleep.

Yes, checking the whiskey barrel he had drunk from last night was the only sensible thing to do. There must have been some kind of dry rot inside that had polluted the whiskey. Mold and mushrooms were known to be able to give a man wild dreams and visions. He imagined that must be the case here. He did not want his customers getting an extra kick from his booze without paying for the privilege.

He decided to get the jump on his coming hangover by getting up out of bed. Sometimes, the nausea and headache after a night of too much drinking could be staved off by getting a good meal into his belly and some coffee in his blood.

But when he tried to throw the sheets aside, nothing happened.

He swiped his right arm toward the sheets again, and still nothing happened.

Had his arm grown numb while he had been asleep? God knew it had happened before. But as he opened his eyes and began to rise out of bed, he was surprised by hands that gently, but firmly, pushed him back down. One of his working girls, the brunette with the ringlets, called Emma, smiled down at him, though her eyes were red with tears.

"What are you doing here?" Cutter said.

"Don't worry about that, boss," she said. "You just sit there and rest awhile. You've had a rough time of it."

The old, cold feeling of fear crept into his belly as he began to wonder whether his dreams from the previous night had really been dreams or if they had been memories.

He remembered the Kelly boy. He remembered Kelly's old man, the one they called Bull. He remembered that damned whip of his striking his hand.

He remembered Doc Post and—
God.

He looked down at his hand, but Emma lay across his arm and tried to smile. "It's okay, boss." She smiled and caressed his face. "You just rest now and let time take its course." She rubbed his chest. "I can make you feel all sorts of better if you want." She kissed him on the cheek and he could smell the salt of her tears. "That's the best thing about running a saloon. You get everything on the menu for free."

But Cutter was too afraid and too angry just then to think about the pleasure Emma or any woman could give him. He pushed the soiled dove off his right arm and she reluctantly got up.

He raised his arm and gaped in horror at the bloody stump before him.

His right hand was gone just below the wrist. The bandages where his hand had once been were rounded and as white as any sheet in a whorehouse could be.

Emma patted his arm. "See that, Ace? I did that part myself. Doc Post did it once, and when I saw how he did it, I've been changing your bandages ever since. Just like clockwork. Showed the other girls how to do it, too. We've been taking good care of you, Ace. Real good care, if I do say so myself."

But Ace Cutter was not interested in the assurances of a whore just then. He could not take his eyes off the stump that had once been his right hand.

His voice caught as he said, "I told him to just sew me up. Why'd he go and take my hand anyway?"

"He said it was for your own good," Emma quickly told him. "Said there was nothing to sew up since so much of it was gone. Said it was a miracle it was still attached at all. He said he had no choice, really, but he got out of town anyway just in case you woke up and wanted him killed."

Emma picked up a bottle from the nightstand and held it up to him. "He left you plenty of this stuff to make you feel better. I know my letters and everything, but I don't have a clue as to how to say that big word on the bottle."

Cutter did not need to read the label to know what it was. He recognized the bottle. "It's laudanum. For the pain." God, the stump was bandaged so neatly, it was hideous, almost mocking. "It works on all sorts of pain."

"That's what the doc said before he lit out of town,

the weasel," Emma said. "What kind of doctor is more concerned about his own hide than a hurt man in need of his care?"

"A smart one," Cutter said. "For I surely would have killed the son of a bitch for what he's done to me. He should've had the decency to kill me instead of leaving me like this."

Emma wiped tears from her eyes. "Don't go saying things like that. You're still young and strong. And with all of us girls around to help you, what do you need two good hands for anyway? Why, we'll fetch everything you need, Ace. Anything at all."

But Ace Cutter knew there were some things that could not be fetched. Some things could not be regained once they were lost. Like his hand. Like his pride. Being shown up by a cowpuncher in his own saloon had been bad enough. But having to live as a cripple among the people who had witnessed it? To have them whisper about it behind his back for the rest of his life?

He was no stranger to people whispering about him. He had acquired a reputation as a slick gun hand and a top hand at cheating at cards. He had made as much being paid to run cheats out of saloons as he had cheating them himself.

But all of that was in the past now. All of his best days were behind him. All anyone would whisper about him was how he had lost his hand in a run-in with Bull Kelly and that damnable whip of his.

The life he had known was gone for good. No amount of fetching by any whores could bring it back. The life of a cripple was no kind of life at all. It was only a matter of time—maybe a year if he was lucky—

before some other gambler came in and took the place from him. Took his Golden Dream and made it his own. Emma would probably be caressing the new man's face as she was caressing his now. Her devotion to whoever that man was would be just as honest as it was to Ace Cutter now. Women like Emma were not bad. They were survivors, no different than a hawk or a coyote or a snake under a rock. No better than him. Sentiment didn't play into it one way or the other.

She would probably give him that same sympathetic smile as the bouncer kicked him into the street without a penny to his name or a friend at his side. He'd be left to fend for himself in a land that was harsh for men with two good hands, much less a man with only one.

And then what? Become the town drunk? Sleeping it off in stables and doing odd jobs at saloons just to get his next sip of rotgut?

That was no life at all. Not for a man like Ace Cutter.

"How long have I been out?"

"Almost a day," Emma told him. "Everything happened late yesterday morning. You had a rough night, but we saw you through it." She demurred. "Actually, it was mostly me, Ace. The other girls helped, but, well, it was still mostly me."

But Cutter did not care about what had happened. All that mattered was what was about to happen. "That means Kelly and his brood are still around."

"Maybe," Emma said. "I don't rightly know. What difference does that make to you?"

It made all the difference in the world. "I need you to do something for me. Something important."

Emma laughed and rubbed her hand the length of

him. "That's the spirit, Ace. That's what I want to hear. What do you need, honey? Tell me and it's yours."

"I need you to help get me up and get me dressed, including my gun belt. Then I need you to get one of the boys downstairs to get the wagon ready for me."

Emma smiled as if she did not understand what he was saying. "What are you talking about, honey? You're in no shape to go anywhere right now."

"I'm in no shape to stay here, either." Normally, he would have belted her for talking back to him, but he simply did not have the strength, so he had no choice but to be nice to her. After all, no one was afraid of a cripple. "Just do as I asked you, now. It's important."

Emma frowned, but pulled the sheets away from him and helped him out of bed. His legs wobbled a bit as he put his weight on them, but it was no worse than what he had suffered on any of the mornings he had been hungover.

She left him by the bed as she gathered up his pants and shirt and shoes. Everything he owned, everything he was, required two hands. What Kelly had done to him was worse than death, even worse than how Doc Post had left him. Emma would have to button up his britches and his shirt. She'd have to help him on with his boots, too. He had not needed anyone to help him get dressed since childhood. Not even at the end of his longest benders.

But fortunately, he would not have to live with that shame much longer.

He would make sure he finished his business with Bull Kelly. One way or the other.

* * *

BILLY, THE BARTENDER from the Golden Dream, helped Cutter up into the wagon box. Emma and the other soiled doves stood inside the doorway of the saloon, weeping at the sight of their boss struggling with the simple task of climbing into a wagon. It was an indignity he did not intend to suffer for long.

Billy said, "I sure wish you'd let me go with you, Mr. Cutter. It'd make me feel a whole lot better about things."

Despite the throbbing pain in his missing right hand, Cutter was surprised by Billy's loyalty. "I never thought you liked me that much."

"Ain't for you." Billy inclined his head back toward Emma and the others. "That bunch will be caterwauling about you for the rest of the day and night. Crying whores is bad for business, boss. It sets customers to thinking about their wives and why they came to a saloon in the first place."

Cutter was no stranger to saloons or whores, but he was new at the business of running a place of his own. It took a whole different set of skills that he did not possess and did not want to take the time to properly learn. Thanks to Kelly's bullwhip, he wouldn't have to.

Bookkeeping and bartenders and whores were the problems of the living. The way Ace Cutter saw things, he was already part of the dead.

Using his left hand, Cutter took up the reins of the horse that would be pulling the wagon. He released the hand brake and cracked the reins, sending the horse moving.

He did not bother to look back at the Golden Dream Saloon, its sullen bartender, or its weeping whores as he brought the horse around in a slow arc toward the Kelly spread. The saloon was no longer his and the people there no longer worked for him. He was alone now. Alone for the rest of his life, which, if everything went as he planned, would not see the indignity of another sunset.

As he rode toward the Kelly spread, he wondered what hell would be like and took some comfort that he would not be alone there. He would have many old friends waiting to greet him. And the comfort of a Kelly or two by his side. That made the trip toward the Kelly spread much easier to take.

CHAPTER FOUR

JAMES KELLY WAS not a superstitious man by nature, but on that morning, he sat on the porch of the homestead waiting for something. He did not know what was coming but knew something was headed his way. Heading toward the Kelly ranch.

The pinkish hues of the sky had been burned off by the sunrise. Now the sky was clear and blue and there was no sign of an approaching storm. But a feeling in his young bones told him to be ready. It was why the new Colt he had bought when last in town was now on his hip. It was cleaned and loaded that morning. He sipped his coffee and watched as the ranch came alive.

It was his father's ranch, he knew, but he still felt a certain pride in it. He and his brothers may have been born elsewhere, but his entire life had been spent on this land. Every memory he had was of this place. Every part of the men he and his brothers had become was because of lives spent on this ranch. Watching it grow. Watching their mother manage it alone for months at a time while their father was out making other men their fortunes. And now that he finally had enough cattle and men to make the run north, Bull Kelly was going to do exactly that. James and his brothers were going to help him.

James had never wanted to go on a long cattle drive up north, but it was his father's dream. He may have been the rebellious brother, but James Kelly knew he had disappointed his family enough times in his young life. He was intent on making sure this drive went well for his family and for himself. He was in his midtwenties now. Some men his age already had a family and a place of their own. It was time to grow up.

He looked up when he saw a puff of trail dust kicked up on the road to the Kelly ranch. The outfit was all fixed to hit the trail. They had hired on all the men they had needed and settled all of their business in town the day before. There was no reason for anyone to come to call except for one man.

Ace Cutter. The man who had lost his honor at the end of his father's whip.

James Kelly had not expected the gambler to be up and about so soon after his injury. He could not remember the last time he had seen his father wash his bullwhip except to treat the hide. He figured the hooked popper of the whip was probably covered in all manner of diseases fatal to man.

James knew Cutter never strayed far from the green felt of his poker tables, much less into the light of day. It was difficult for James to believe that such a man had the constitution to survive the grime of the infection that was undoubtedly festering in his wounded hand.

Maybe it was the fever from that same wound that had caused the damned fool to ride out here to take on the Kelly outfit all by himself. James could tell by the dust thrown up by the wagon's wheels that he was alone and, judging by the way he struggled to keep the horse running straight, that he was holding the reins with one hand.

Cutter certainly had guts. That much was certain. It should count for more than it did, for James Kelly knew he had no choice but to kill the man. Not his father. Not his brothers. He had brought this trouble upon his family and he would be expected to deal with it. His father would not have it any other way.

James set his coffee mug on the porch floor next to his chair and stood to meet the visitor. The closer he came, the clearer it was to see that it was, in fact, Ace Cutter. He was paler than he had been yesterday at the Golden Dream, but that was to be expected. James had been on the receiving end of his father's whip several times and knew how much it could take out of a man.

But as much as he had tried to work up some pity for the gambler, he could not. What had happened in town was something spur-of-the-moment. Cutter had gone up against his father and paid a terrible price.

Riding out to the ranch, especially in Cutter's condition, took planning. It took resolve. And he had ridden out here with the intent to kill every Kelly man he saw. Otherwise, he would not have come at all.

James Kelly had every intention of making sure he was the last man Ace Cutter saw before he passed over into the next world.

Cutter stopped the wagon about thirty yards away from where James Kelly stood. He pitched back and forth in the wagon as he struggled to pull the horse to a full stop. He sluggishly kicked out with his foot and threw the brake, locking the wheels in place.

James's hand dropped to the Colt on his hip when he saw the gun belt in Cutter's lap.

"Stop right there," James told him. "Don't move."

"I already stopped, you idiot," Cutter slurred. His eyes were dull, and he blinked as if he had trouble focusing. "You can't order me to stop after I've already done it."

"Fine," James conceded. "Then how about you tell me why you're here. I know it's not to bid us a fond farewell."

"Damned right it's not." Cutter stifled a cough that stirred in his chest. "I came here to kill you, Kelly. You and that murdering old man of yours."

James was enjoying seeing the cocky gambler in such a state. The man was not drunk, but he was weaving and slurring his speech like he was. He looked like he might fall out of the wagon at any moment, whether or not Kelly decided to shoot him.

"And just who was it that my old man was supposed to have killed?"

Cutter held up the bloody, bandaged stump of his right hand. "Me."

James tried to hide his surprise at the gory sight. "You got what you deserved. Any man who goes against Bull Kelly knows where he stands."

"And any man that does this to Ace Cutter gets killed."

James Kelly had cleared leather before Cutter even reached for the gun belt. The dying gambler's clumsy movement only served to knock it off his lap and onto the wagon box at his feet.

Kelly laughed, mocking the gambler's lack of co-ordination. "You rode all this way to kill me and mine, and you can't even keep a pistol in your lap." James Kelly laughed again. "And I always heard Ace Cutter was a dangerous man. What a laugh."

The gambler cursed him as he reached down for the gun belt at his feet but fell over after a fit of coughing.

James Kelly threw back his head and laughed again. He enjoyed the way the sound of his own laughter echoed across the flatlands of the ranch. There was a menace to it that he had not noticed before. Had it always been there or was it the sight of this fool groveling at his feet that had brought it out? Either way, James Kelly was sure he liked it.

"God, I wish the rest of town was here to see this," Kelly said. "The great Ace Cutter laid low. The cripple who can't even get his own gun in a gunfight."

"ENOUGH!"

James Kelly flinched as the sound of his father's voice boomed from the house like a thunderclap.

He turned to see his father walking toward him with Concho close behind. "Get away from that man, boy, and I mean right now. You've done enough."

"What the hell did I do?" James asked. "I didn't even touch him. You're the one who took his hand, not me."

Concho motioned for James to step away from the wagon, and much to his surprise, James found himself doing exactly that. Even after all of these years, Concho and his father had a way of making him feel like a little kid.

As Bull Kelly approached the wagon, James yelled, "Careful, Pa. He's got a gun. I saw it."

But his father ignored him as he went to the wagon and took a look at Cutter.

"How is he?" James heard Concho ask in Spanish. He might not have been able to speak the language, but he could understand a few phrases here and there.

"He's bad." Bull Kelly took the pistol from beneath Cutter and tossed it back to Concho, who caught it and tucked it into his belt in the same motion. "Help me get him down from here, both of you."

Concho stepped forward, but James remained where he was. He was not sure he had heard his father clear enough. "Did you just ask me to help him? The same man who came here to *kill us*."

"I didn't ask you to do anything, boy." Kelly got hold of Cutter under his arms and began to pull hm down from the wagon. Concho was there in time to grab his legs before they hit the ground. "Go on," Bull repeated. "Grab hold of him, like I told you."

James could not understand his father's thinking but knew there was no use in arguing with him at times like this. It was better to just do what he wanted and ask questions later if and when the right time presented itself.

"We'll carry him into the bunkhouse," Bull said. "Lay him down in one of three empty bunks in there. Maybe the men can tend to him for a while."

"Men?" James repeated. "We're supposed to be hitting the trail today, Pa. Why, he'll be nothing but a bunch of bones by the time we get back."

"We're not going anywhere," Bull said. "Not until this plays itself out."

James had more questions with each step they took toward the bunkhouse but was too busy trying to keep up with his father's pace to ask him anything. Sometimes, it was just easier to hold his tongue and watch what Bull Kelly did instead of asking him.

That was why he kept his mouth shut the rest of the way and just helped his father and Concho carry Cutter into the bunkhouse.

ONCE THEY GOT Cutter's boots off and had him under the blankets, James figured his father would step away long enough for him to ask his father some questions. But his father surprised him by pulling up a chair and sitting beside the bed they had placed Cutter in. Concho opted to stand behind his boss and watch what happened next.

James stood there, dumbstruck. If he had not been seeing this with his own two eyes, he never would have believed it. Bull Kelly was tending to the same man he had not only attacked the day before but had threatened to kill.

Sensing his father was in no mood to explain himself, James held back and remained out of sight while this strange scene played itself out.

Cutter was perspiring now and clearly had a fever. Bull Kelly reached into a bucket of cold water and placed a damp cloth on the gambler's forehead.

"There you go, Mr. Cutter." His brogue was smooth and soothing, not harsh like it normally was. He was speaking in the way James had heard him speak to his mother back when she was dying.

Cutter's eyes fluttered open and he stopped babbling nonsense. He looked at Bull and seemed to recognize him immediately.

"You?" he rasped. "What are you doing? Am I dreaming?"

"No, Cutter," Bull assured him. "And you're not dead yet, either, but you're well on your way, I'm afraid. You damned fool. You should've just let Doc Post take care of you the way he probably wanted to."

"I didn't want to be taken care of, you bastard." He tried to put some hate into his voice, but he was too weak to do it. "I rode out here to kill you."

"You rode out here to die." Bull took the now-dry washcloth from his head, dunked it in the bucket of cool water, and replaced it on the gambler's head. "You were probably hoping me or one of mine would finish the job I started yesterday. You weren't counting on us taking pity on you and tending to you."

"Keeping me alive isn't pity, Kelly. It's cruel. Crueler than what you did to me yesterday. Finish what you started, damn you, and kill me."

"Never killed a defenseless man in my life," James heard his father say, "and I've no intention of changing at this point of my life. Especially not for the likes of you."

"So you'll just sit here and watch me rot." Cutter laughed, which brought about a round of intense coughing. "You'd like that, wouldn't you? Watching me die slowly."

"I didn't want you to die at all, you fool," Kelly said. "I wanted to get my boy out of there and bring him home with his brothers where he belonged. If anything, he's to blame for what happened between us. As are you for getting mouthy when you should've stayed out of it."

"But not you." Cutter raised his bleeding stump. "Not for doing this to me?"

"That was your own doing," Bull said. "I only cut loose with my whip when you went for your gun. I'm sorry I didn't take the whole hand off when I did it. I didn't think I had hurt you that badly until I saw you in front of the saloon. Guess I let my temper get away from me."

"And now you're trying to make up for it," Cutter rasped. "By tending to me now."

"I suppose so." Kelly took the dry washcloth and once again dunked it in the cool bucket of water before placing it on Cutter's forehead. The cloth was getting drier faster because of the fever now coursing through Cutter's body.

Cutter tried to stop Kelly from putting the cloth on his forehead but failed. "No need to soothe your conscience, Kelly. I'm a dead man anyway. We don't owe each other anything. Hell, I wouldn't do this for anyone who rode out to my place to kill my family."

"You were in no shape to do anything except die when you got here, so quit acting otherwise. I'm not taking care of you for you or for me."

"For someone else, then?" Another round of coughing shook Cutter like a rag doll. "You're doing it for your dead wife, maybe. The one you talk to all the time."

At the sound of his mother being mentioned by this no-good bastard, James reached for his pistol, but one look from Concho froze him. The crazy look in the older man's eyes spoke of horrors to come if he so much as touched his gun.

James decided to leave the Colt in his holster and watch the proceedings from afar.

His father surprised him by laughing. "I suppose I do talk to her quite a bit, now, don't I? And to answer your question, she's a good chunk of the reason why you're in here now with me tending to you. Before her passing, I would've led that wagon upwind from here and left you there to rot. Come check on you again when we got back here later this summer. Doubt there would've been much of you left by then, after the birds and the coyotes and the other critters had their way with you. But tending to my late Mary after all of her suffering changed me a bit. I don't like to admit it, but it softened me some to other people's suffering."

Cutter turned his head and spat blood in the opposite direction. "If this is your softer side, I'm glad I never knew you when she was still alive."

"I said softer to suffering," Kelly reminded him. "Becoming soft in the spine is something else entirely and won't happen anytime soon. Yes, sir. Striking you down before you could shoot me is well within my character. Just ask Concho here. He's known me longer than anyone. Even longer than my dearly departed Mary."

Concho nodded his head, not that Cutter was in any condition to see him do it.

Cutter struggled to raise his head and Bull settled

him back against the pillow. "Easy, lad, easy. Best to do your talking from a relaxed position. Save your strength for the long fight ahead."

"You a Christian man, Kelly?"

"I try to be," said the old trail boss. "Not that life out here gives a man many options to be Christian. Why?"

"Because if you've got any decency at all, you'll end my suffering. You'll have more mercy than I rode out here to show you. You'll put me out of my misery and end this once and for all."

"I wish I could help you, Mr. Cutter, but I already told you, I've never murdered a man in my life. If I'd have killed you yesterday, that would've been fine. Legal even. Maybe more than legal. It would've been justice. But I didn't aim to kill you and I probably should have. You're paying for my mistake now and I'm sorry about that. If I thought you would've wound up like this, I'd have taken you clean. It didn't work out that way. Now we're both paying for our actions. You for trying to draw on me and me for not killing you outright. We're just going to have to suffer through this together."

Cutter let loose with a string of curses that would have made a sailor blush. It was the bluest streak of words James had ever heard strung together. He heard words that he never had before and knew he would have trouble calling to mind again. Cutter called James's father, his grandparents, and his brothers every name in the book. He accused them of things James knew were impossible and slanderous lies.

James had seen his father take the whip to him and his brothers for even looking at him sideways, but now, as he tended to the dying man, he weathered the barrage of curses the way a bale of hay absorbs a rainstorm. He kept tending to the dying man as everything of his being was defiled.

Cutter only paused when another fit of coughing racked his body.

His father again replaced his washcloth on Cutter's forehead. "That make you feel better?"

Cutter even managed a smile. "A little, I guess."

Bull Kelly smiled, too. "Then it was worth it."

Cutter's eyes suddenly grew wide before they dimmed again, and his face went slack. His eyes remained half-open, but James could tell they were staring at nothing in particular.

Ace Cutter was finally dead.

Bull Kelly dropped the washcloth in the bucket and folded the man's hands across his chest.

"What do you want me to do with him?" James heard Concho ask his father in Spanish.

Bull Kelly replied in English. "He's got gangrene running through him and God knows what else. Take some boys and plant him in a shallow grave. Burn the body before you bury him. Don't want anything digging him up and getting sick only to pass it on to some other poor animal. Could create a problem."

He glanced at James. "Take him with you to bury him. Make him do the heavy lifting and the digging, too."

"Me?" James asked. "Why me? Hell, I don't know why you went through all that trouble anyway. You should've just let me shoot him like he wanted to shoot us. Would've taken a whole lot less time and we would've been on the trail by now."

The speed of Bull Kelly had surprised his son many times over the years and this time was no exception. In one fluid movement, his father was off the chair and had his son by the throat. He pulled James close until his face was less than an inch from his own. "You don't know enough about life to mock death, boy. You don't know a damned thing about anything yet. Until you do, don't you dare question my decisions. Ever. Now, you're going to bury that man because you're as responsible for him being dead as I am. Maybe even more so. If you had been with Concho and your brothers like you were supposed to, he would still be alive, and we'd be on the trail to Dodge City. Instead, we're here cleaning up something you started." He shook his son by the throat, making the young man gag. "Again."

He released his son with a shove toward the door. "You do what Concho tells you, or by God, the feel of my whip will be the least of your worries. Now go find some of the boys and bring them in here. And tell them we're not riding out until tomorrow. That's an order."

Concho and Bull watched James adjust himself before he walked off to do what his father had told him.

Bull looked back at Concho. "And don't you go telling me I was too hard on him, either."

But Concho kept looking after the younger Kelly as he walked off to find men to help them bury Cutter. "No, amigo. I don't think you were too hard on him. I don't think he learned anything by what he saw here today. I fear for him and I fear for us. I fear for what he will do."

He looked back at his old friend. "I fear he may never see Dodge City. And I fear we might meet the same fate as Cutter there as a result of it."

Kelly looked down at the dead man. He knew the smell of rot coming off him must be from the arm, but it didn't make him like the stench any better. "Not if I have anything to say about it. And I have plenty to say."

CHAPTER FIVE

At just after dawn the next morning, William Kelly felt the last of the cold night air as the first lines of pink and purple cracked along the eastern sky.

The death of Ace Cutter the day before could not dampen his excitement. Yes, the gambler had delayed the company's trek north to Dodge City, but it had been worth it. He would rather have known Cutter was out of the way than wonder if the gambler might be on his back trail the entire ride up to Kansas. He had not intended on killing the man, but he did not regret causing his death, either. If he had not reached for his gun, Kelly would not have had to defend himself.

But Kelly did not waste time on regrets. He knew how life was in this part of the world. Sometimes a man's life work could be undone in a second. And in that same second, a new life could begin.

Today was the first day of a new life for him and

his boys. Kelly had not felt this much excitement in as long as he could remember. Perhaps not since that day decades ago when he had saddled his horse and ridden away from his family farm and headed over to London. He had been so young then, so eager to leave the rig and furrow behind and see the world.

The journey had been nothing like the romantic notion of his boyish dreams, but no matter how winding his path may have been, it had led him here. To this moment. Watching the first rays of sun rise upon his dream of a better life for him and his sons. The moment when the Kelly name would finally mean something in this new world. He only wished his Mary could have been here with him now.

But she had done more than her part to bring this day about. She had raised their five boys while he spent all those years in the saddle working for other men. Now the future was up to him. He had lost track of the number of cattle drives he had led by now. Ten? Perhaps twenty or more. He had been a leader of men for more than half his life. His sons knew horses and cattle. The ten men he had hired had made the journey several times with many outfits. They only needed someone to lead them. To make decisions and keep order on the journey north to Dodge City.

Kelly knew there were few men in Texas, nay, perhaps the world, who were more accustomed to maintaining order than he.

But he knew he could not do it alone and neither could the men he had hired.

There was one final piece of the puzzle that would have to fall into place.

He climbed atop the Morgan and urged her into

the pasture where the second-most-important member of the enterprise stood alone.

A massive longhorn bull called Hell.

Kelly judged the black bull to be more than two thousand pounds if he was an ounce. Probably closer to three thousand, and every bit of it rage and muscle. His majestic horns were broad and curved upward into dangerous spikes.

Hell was the most horrifying animal Kelly had ever encountered in all his years on the trail. What's more, the bull seemed to know it. Kelly had given the longhorn its name for its nasty temperament and cunning disposition. It was unlike any other bull Kelly had ever seen. It had a way of looking at a man as if it was thinking of ways to kill him.

As he trotted toward the pasture, Kelly could still remember the day he had found the longhorn tending its own herd of about three hundred cows among the shrub brush down near El Paso the previous summer. The damned thing had watched him ride toward it and waited until he had climbed down from his horse before it decided to charge him.

But Bull Kelly had been ready.

The first crack of his bullwhip had caught the bull square in the snout, stopping the charge as quickly as it had started.

The blow had seemed to take some of the fight out of him, but Kelly knew it was not over. The bull rubbed its sore snout in the dusty dirt of the Texas flatlands and snorted.

The second charge had come without warning, but Kelly had been ready. The bull launched itself at him, head down and horns forward at a dead run.

This time, the whip's popper smacked the bull square between the eyes and stopped him cold. The bull slid to a halt on its rump, dazed. Amid a cloud of dust and dirt, it grunted and snorted as it shook its massive head.

Kelly did not hold his ground. He took a step forward and cracked the whip again.

Sensing there was still some fight left in the beast, he waited until it had regained its senses. When it got up, the massive beast had turned its back to him, and Kelly cut loose with the whip one last time. The popper lashed a small cut in its hind leg, just beneath its prized testicles.

The bull had jumped and skittered away like a house cat. Back to its herd.

He knew that last blow had done the trick. The bull now knew who was boss.

Kelly climbed atop his Morgan and forced the bull back toward where the rest of the herd he had gathered stood grazing. Hell fell in line and the three hundred cows with him followed.

There had been other times in the months since when the animal had thought he saw a weakness in Kelly and appeared ready to charge.

But when Kelly uncoiled his whip, the bull remembered what had happened that day in El Paso and resumed its place in front of the herd.

Now, as Kelly rode into the pasture, he passed his son Joel and Baxter, one of the men he had hired to help on the long drive ahead.

The men bid him good morning and he returned the pleasantries.

"Fine day to start a drive, Pa," Joel said.

But as Joel had never been on a drive before, Kelly discounted his son's observation and spoke to the man who knew what he was talking about. "How are we faring today, Mr. Baxter?"

Kelly had always insisted on calling the men he oversaw "mister" when he spoke to them. He had found when he treated working men with a bit of respect, he tended to get more out of them when it counted and when it did not. Little investments like courtesy often paid countless dividends on the long trails out of Texas.

"The men and animals are ready to go whenever you are, sir." Baxter nodded toward the longhorn bull. "Or whenever he's ready, I guess."

Kelly glanced at Hell. "He'll be ready when I say he's ready." He set his Morgan moving again. "And I say he's ready now. You and Joel best spread the word we're starting out."

"Yes, sir," Joel and Baxter replied in unison, and split off to carry out Kelly's order.

HELL LOOKED UP from the grass when he caught the Morgan's scent on the wind. The animal locked eyes with Kelly. It did not lower its head but slowly began to scrape at the ground with its hoof. Kelly knew he would not charge, but it was as if he wanted to remind the human that he was thinking about it.

Kelly took it as a good sign. He had never wanted to break the animal's spirit. A broken bull was no good to him. He had simply wanted to bend him to his will just enough to make him lead the herd when the time came. And that time was now.

Kelly uncoiled his twelve-foot whip and let it trail along the ground beside him as he rode closer. Reluctantly, the bull recognized the sign and slowly walked away from him toward the path that would take them north to Dodge City.

The path to riches and to glory. The path that led to the dynasty Kelly would help his boys forge for themselves and a better life than the one he had known.

Once the bull had reached the front of the herd, the men behind him began to whoop and yell to get the main body of the herd to follow. At first, the cattle were confused by the noise, but when they caught sight of Hell plodding away from them, they quickly fell into line and followed.

Kelly gave the bull a wide berth as he rode around in front of him and took his place at the head. He looked back and saw that Hell was following him at a respectable but constant distance.

Kelly was glad the wind was blowing down from the north. It would carry their scent back to the rest of the herd. The most important part of any journey was those first crucial steps and Kelly decided they were off to a good start.

William "Bull" Kelly and Hell led three thousand head of cattle, all bearing the Square K brand, north to market in Kansas.

The Kelly outfit was on the move. And William Kelly was right where he belonged. Where he had always been.

Out front and alone.

CHAPTER SIX

JAMES CAUGHT UP to Jacob just as the last of the cattle had cleared the ranch.

"Well, the die is cast," James said to his older brother. "The Kelly outfit is bound for Kansas."

"Seems that way." Jacob took a closer look at James. "I heard about the trouble you caused yesterday."

"I didn't cause anything," James said. "Any trouble was between Cutter and Dad. You know old Bull has a knack for finding trouble or the other way around."

"Wouldn't have been any trouble if you hadn't wandered into that saloon in the first place, Jimmy." Jacob was the only person in the world James allowed to call him "Jimmy." It was a right James assumed he had earned, being the oldest and all, even if he was an old lady at times.

"I went in there on my own accord. I didn't have

any trouble with Cutter until the moment he rode up here looking for blood. I won't have that."

"You won't have that," Jacob repeated, and laughed. "Awfully strong words when you're talking about going up against a man who was half-dead from gangrene."

James didn't like the implication of cowardice. "Ace Cutter was no man's bargain and he was armed."

"He was half-dead from bone rot on account of his gun hand being gone," Jacob reminded him. "Save the tall tales for our brothers. They're young enough to believe that nonsense."

James was beginning to lose his temper. "I would've killed him if Dad hadn't shown up when he did and called me off. Hell, I wanted to finish him off several times after he took him in, but Bull wouldn't hear of it. He was intent on doing the Christian thing and seeing to his wounds."

"Is that what you think that was all about?" Jacob shook his head. "Taking care of Cutter didn't have anything to do with Cutter, you blockhead. It had everything to do with teaching you a lesson. Looks like it didn't take."

"And what lesson would that be?"

"The one about being more careful about where you spend your time and who with. About tending to business before pleasure. About not being so damned greedy all the time. He wanted you to see what happens to a man like that. He was teaching you a lesson, stupid. Unfortunately, it looks like it didn't take." Jacob shook his head again. "Damned shame."

"A lesson?" James turned it over a bit in his mind.

"Why do you think Bull didn't pull the rest of us in to help tend to Cutter if he wanted to keep Cutter alive? He did it because he was trying to teach you a lesson, blockhead. He wanted to show you what happens when you're thoughtless. He wanted you to see what could happen when a man loses sight of what's important in life. And if you don't shape up damned soon, you're liable to be laying in a bunkhouse somewhere in just as bad shape as old Cutter was. Maybe even worse."

James did not know if that had been his father's real aim with Cutter, but if it was, it was an awfully complicated way of teaching a man a lesson. It was the wrong lesson, too, for James Kelly never intended to end up like Cutter or any other saloon squire. He intended on making all the money he could off this drive and buying himself a stake in as many saloons as he could. That way, he figured he would always have some money rolling in. Putting it all in one place was crazy. Only people like Cutter did that, and look at where it got them. James Kelly was smarter than that. Smarter than people gave him credit for. He would show them all one day, especially Jacob and his father.

"Don't go worrying about me, big brother," James said over his shoulder as he chased after a stray cow that had bolted from the rest of the herd. "You keep your eye on your own trail and we'll be just fine!"

CHAPTER SEVEN

THE FIRST WEEK and a half on the trail had been nothing short of glorious from Kelly's perspective. He had ridden a lot of trails in his day and moved a lot of cattle, but this first drive entirely for himself was off to a great start.

The weather had been warm, but not roasting as he feared it might have been. The grass was tall and green and plentiful. The men had done a good job of keeping the herd moving, and by Kelly's reckoning, they had made a solid twenty-five miles a day. The outfit was still in good spirits and his sons had all lived up to every expectation he had of them.

He was happy to see that even James had been pulling his weight. If his hurried coupling with the whore back at the Golden Dream had left him any worse for the wear, he had hidden it well from his father's watchful eye.

Even Hell had cooperated with the enterprise. The

bull seemed just a bit more docile on the trail than he had been in the pasture. Kelly imagined twenty-five miles a day would be enough to tucker anything out, even this great beast.

Kelly sat atop the Morgan as he watched his herd ford a narrow stream. It had been all flatland until then and this was the first major obstacle in their path. But man and cattle seemed to be taking it in stride. It was still a long way to Kansas, but Kelly could not help but feel pride in the way that everything had progressed thus far.

He looked up at the heavens to his beloved Mary and said, "It's all going beautifully, my love. I sure hope you're proud of these boys. Hope you're proud of me, too."

"Talking to Ma again?" James surprised him by riding up on him. Kelly had always prided himself on being a difficult man to surprise and began to wonder if the trail was not beginning to have the same effect on him as it was having on Hell. He hoped not.

"Just pausing to share the moment with her is all," Kelly told his son. He had never felt shame in talking to his wife. He took comfort in the belief that she was with him more now that she had passed on than she had been when she was alive. "I think she's pleased."

"She's got plenty of reason to be." James crossed his arms on the saddle horn and watched the herd ford the stream. "Things couldn't be going better. Why, we haven't lost a single head the entire trip."

But Kelly already knew that. He had made it a point to question the men around the campfire at the end of each day. It served to remind them that he was still the boss, and knowing he might question any one of them over supper kept them sharp in the saddle during the day. "It's still a long way to Kansas, boy, but I'm pleased we've had a gentle start."

"Good old Pa." James laughed. "Ever the optimist. I hope you won't whip me for saying this, but I thought you were crazy when you came up with this idea after Ma died. So did the others. We thought it was just the sadness of her passing making you do this. After all, none of us have ever been on a cattle drive."

Kelly kept his eyes on the passing cattle. "I've driven men and beasts for most of my life in one way or another, boy. There's far more to me than grief."

"Can't blame us for thinking that way, Pa. We've only heard about the drives you've been on. We've never really seen you do it."

Kelly knew the boy was right. He had no call for being defensive. "You may not have seen it, but you've profited from it just the same. My driving kept a good roof over your heads all those years. Food in your mouths. Schooling in your minds." He glanced at his son. "Well, in your brothers' minds leastways."

James smiled. "I know it cost you a lot, Pa. We always knew you wanted to be with us instead of with those cows. I suppose that made you not being around much easier to take. I guess what I'm trying to say is, we're all grateful to you. For this. For all of it. I can speak for the others when I say thank you for everything."

Kelly glanced sideways at his boy. "What do you want?"

James frowned. "What's that?"

But his father was onto him. "You're not the sentimental type, James. You never were. You got that from me. Just like you get that bit of a quiver in your voice when you're working up to telling me something unpleasant from your mother."

"Aw, Pa. Just wait a minute!"

But Kelly was an impatient man. "Either you've got bad news to tell me or you're about to ask for something. I know it's not bad news, so I can only imagine it'll be a request of some kind. Might as well spill it now so we can sort it out."

James shrugged. "Well, now that you mention it, there *is* something . . ."

"Thank God I'm already sitting down. I don't think I could stand the shock of it were I standing."

"Well," James continued, "it's just that I know that we've been making great time on the trail. Some of the boys think we're even ahead of schedule."

"I believe we are," Kelly agreed. "And I have every intention of making better time still. The sooner we get to Dodge, the sooner we'll beat the rest of the outfits to market and command top price on these cattle."

"That's what the boys say, too. So, I was thinking . . ."

"No."

James looked away. "I ain't even asked you yet!"

"Whatever it is that required such a buttering-up job in advance must be mighty bad," Kelly said. "So, whatever it is, the answer is no."

But his son persisted. "It's just that we're making such great time that I thought it might be a good idea for us to take a little break is all. Let the boys have a little fun along the trail. Now, as I understand it, there's a town not too far from here. A nice, quiet little place called Bledsoe and—"

"I knew it." Kelly shook his head. "I just knew it. I didn't know where or when it'd happen, but I knew it would happen eventually. We're within smelling distance of a town and you want to go."

"Come on, Pa. What could a little fun hurt?"

"You? Probably none." He nodded toward the men leading the herd across the stream. "These boys out here? Plenty. They're not as good at your idea of fun as you are, boy, and I'll not have our progress impeded and undone by a bunch of hungover cowboys too drunk to stay in the saddle. The answer is still no. In fact, it's hell, no."

But James was a stubborn young man. "I'm not saying we all have to go, Pa. Why, I was thinking of taking Baxter and maybe you with me. He's worked awful hard and it might do well to reward him a little by letting him have a good time."

Kelly knew his son had never been one to take no for an answer, so he decided to make himself as plain as he could. "And just what were you planning on using to pay for this good time you're planning on having? We haven't any money, boy. All of it went to paying off the ranch back home so we're free and clear from here on in. What little we had left went toward buying provisions and paying the men."

Then the depth of his son's plan dawned on him. "That's why you want Baxter to go with you. He's got money and you don't. You plan on using him to stake you to whiskey and women. Maybe buy you a seat at a lousy card game while you're at it." He had to admire his son's cunning. "Ah, it's a sly bastard you are, James Kelly!"

"That's not it at all." James grew indignant. "Baxter's a hard worker, Pa. I just wanted to show him a little of what you might call appreciation for all that hard work he's done."

"He's the best hand in the outfit," Kelly countered, "and he'll get all the appreciation he needs when we pay out at the end of the drive. And need I remind you that we're still in Texas, boy, and have a long way ahead of us. But don't worry. Dodge City's enough of a town for any man, even for a man with your considerable appetites, if you could defile such an elegant word to call them that."

Kelly went back to looking over the passing herd. The matter, as far as he was concerned, was decided. "My word is final, James, and the answer is no. Now be on about your business."

Although he might not have been looking at him, he could feel the anger rising in his son like heat off a stove. "I'm not a boy anymore, Pa. I'm a full-grown man and I can do as I please."

"You're my son and a member of this outfit." He pointed at the cows fording the river. "This herd's as much yours as it is mine or your brothers'. You have a piece of all that beef out there. Tend to it and make it pay for you. When you draw your cut at the end of it, you can do as you please. Until then, what I say goes. My word is final, and my word is no."

The boy muttered a curse to himself as he brought his horse around and crossed the river.

Kelly knew his word might be final in his own mind, but not to his son, so he called after him as he rode away. "And don't go defying me, either. If you do, you'll feel my whip before the entire outfit, by God! Mind that, boy, when the urge strikes you later."

He knew James had heard him. The whole outfit had probably heard him, but James continued to ride across the stream without looking back.

Kelly let out the breath he had been holding and glanced up at the sky toward his Mary. "That one is a handful, darling. I hope the good Lord is showing you extra kindness for all the trials he must have put you through all those times I was away."

He paused, as he often did when speaking to her, waiting for some kind of reply. But none came. It never did, at least not in any form he could recognize.

He went back to watching the men drive the herd across the river. Things *were* going well, weren't they? Perhaps that was all the answer he needed. He hoped it would not change between here and Dodge City. But Bull Kelly had never been a hopeful man.

JAMES KELLY SPENT the rest of that day riding the herd hard. He chased down strays and brought calves back to their mothers. He pushed his horse and himself further than he thought they could go in a bid to ride the growing restlessness out of his system. But it was no use.

He was beginning to get the fever to go a bit wild again. Not the way he used to when he was a bit younger. Not even the way he had back at the Golden Dream. This was a different kind of feeling, a restless, boxed-in kind of feeling he had never known before. He had never been this far away from home and a town before.

But now, for the first time in over a week, he knew he was close to one. So close he could almost smell it.

Bledsoe.

It did not sound like much of a town, and from what he had heard from the other men in the outfit who had passed through there, it lived up to its billing. It was a sad little burg, maybe ten buildings in all, but that was ten more than James Kelly had seen in what felt like quite a while.

He didn't need much to break the monotony of trail life that was eating away at his soul. Just a nice town with a saloon and maybe a game of cards and a willing woman to pass the time with.

If the trek northward had taught him anything, it was that he did not share his father's enthusiasm for the trail. For long days in the saddle and short nights spent on hard ground. Concho's cooking was fine as far as it went, and he imagined a good cook was tough to find in this business.

His father and brothers seemed to love sleeping around a crackling fire and tending cattle beneath the stars, but James had other comforts in mind. The kind of warmth in his belly provided by good whiskey and the general warmth of a woman in his bed. As he looked at the herd he tended with the rest of the outfit, James realized that he would use these animals for everything they were worth, then get what he could out of them. Trail life might not be for him, but he planned on making the most of the money he earned from it. Let his father build his cattle empire. James Kelly planned on building an empire of his own.

That was why he waited until the last of the herd was brought up from the rear and secured for the night before he put his plan in action.

He rode up to the perimeter of the chuck wagon to make sure everyone was accounted for. A good fire was already started, and Concho was working on dinner for the outfit. More beans and chili and tortillas, no doubt. All of it good and more than enough to keep a man alive on the trail, but not enough to fill the hunger growing in his belly. The hunger for whiskey and action.

He rode by so the men would see him and his father would not panic later when he realized what his son had done. He would not be surprised by it and he would not be happy about it, but his father's wrath was worth it. His anger would be tempered once he knew his son had just gone to town like he had threatened and was not lying in the darkness hurt or dying.

When he decided enough of the men had seen him to make some kind of report to his father, James Kelly loped around the herd, then headed into town. Toward Bledsoe.

ALTHOUGH HIS BONES ached from another long day in the saddle, Bull Kelly made a point not to grunt when he sat beside the campfire after nightfall. None of the men were complaining about their own aches and pains and he could not afford to set a bad example. He imagined he was old enough to be the father of all the other men in the outfit. He did not want to bring attention to that fact by griping about saddle soreness. He had to be above all of that, for his sake as well as theirs.

He gladly accepted the warm plate of rice and beans and biscuit that Concho handed him. The night was promising to be cooler than he had expected, so the warm food was welcome. As was his custom, he made sure he ate only after the last man in the outfit had begun to eat.

"How do you think we fared today?" Kelly asked Concho in Spanish.

"Twenty-five miles," his friend told him. The old Spanish pirate had always been able to judge distances better than any man he had ever known. "I thought the stream might have slowed us down a bit, but even the wagon made it through just fine."

Kelly broke apart the biscuit and used it to sop up some beans and rice. "Won't always be such a smooth trail."

"Let us be grateful for what we have today, William," Concho reminded him. "Tomorrow can take care of itself and will be here soon enough."

Kelly grinned up at his friend. "How'd you get so smart?"

The cook shrugged. "I suppose trailing around half the world with you all these years helped me pick up a few things."

"Not me, amigo," Kelly reminded him. "You got yourself into plenty of trouble long before we ever set eyes on each other." Preferring to not dwell on the unpleasantness of their shared past, he decided to change the subject. "The boys are doing well, aren't they? My boys, I mean."

"Mary raised five fine men," Concho said before looking away too quickly.

Kelly caught it and grabbed his friend's arm before he went back to the wagon. "I know that look. What is it? What's wrong?"

In all of the thousands of miles their friendship had taken over the years, no matter where they were or what they did, they had never lied to each other. Not once. Not even a small bending of the truth. That trust was part of the reason why their friendship had endured for so long. That was why he knew Concho would not lie to him now.

And the expression on his old friend's face told Kelly all he needed to know. "James went to town, didn't he?"

Concho nodded reluctantly.

Kelly set the plate aside before he threw it. "Damn that boy. When?"

"Just before dinner was ready. He snuck out without telling anyone. I only know he's gone because I saw him riding away. He's not supposed to be tending the herd tonight, so I can only think that, since he's not here, he must have gone to town."

Kelly looked at the men around the campfire and was glad to see Baxter talking to Jeremiah and Joel and some of the other men. "Looks like he went alone, doesn't it?"

"Looks that way," Concho said. "Jacob and Joshua are tending the herd and they would not go with him without your permission. All of the other men are here."

Kelly was going to curse his son again, but realized it was pointless. He thought of something much more productive. "How long's the ride to town? Bledsoe, I think it's called."

"An hour or more," Concho told him, "but please do not go, my friend. Stay here with us. The men need you to be fresh for the trail tomorrow, not chasing after James. He's a grown man and must face the consequences of his decisions."

"He defied me, Concho. I told him he couldn't go to town and he went anyway." Kelly looked at his friend. "And don't go saying he reminds you of me when I was his age. He's nothing like I was."

"He's not half the man you were back then," Concho told him. "You were brave and careless with your own life at times, but never reckless like him. He is not a thoughtful man, William. He is the type of man who can only learn by failing. He is too old for the whip to do him any good now. Yes, even your whip. He has learned nothing from his broken nose and jaw. I am afraid only life can teach him now. We must let life do its work. We have known many men like this, haven't we?"

"Those men weren't my son, by God!" Kelly realized he had shouted, and even though it was in Spanish, he did not want the others to know he could show emotion. Not even anger. He was their leader and he did not have the luxury of showing his feelings.

Concho laid a hand on his shoulder. "James is too old for your punishments, my friend. If you beat him now, you will only drive him away from you, perhaps forever. He has your wandering heart, but not your stomach for it. In time, he will have no choice but to see his own weaknesses, but for now, there is nothing anyone can do. Not even you."

Kelly knew his friend was right. The old pirate was always right.

He picked up his plate again and resumed his dinner. "I hope he enjoys himself tonight. I hope he makes it count, because it'll be the last whiff he has of peace until we reach Dodge City. And that, amigo, is a solemn promise."

J AMES SLOWED HIS horse to a trot as he reached the outskirts of Bledsoe, Texas. It was a nice night, and despite his excitement at the prospect of fun, he decided there was no reason to rush it. He did not want to be seen galloping into town like a tenderfoot on his first night away from home, even though that was exactly how he felt. He wanted to ride in calm and peaceful, like he had been there before and would be again. He knew a man without a cent in his pocket had to rely on airs to make the proper impression.

He had thought about asking Baxter to lend him some money but had decided against it. Baxter would have wanted to come along, and Pa had been right. Baxter was the best hand in the outfit.

And if Baxter had lent James some money, the old man would have laid into both of them with that bullwhip of his. That would not do, either. James was the one hankering for a good time. He knew he would face the wrath of his father soon enough. He saw no reason why Baxter should have to pay for it, too.

James slowly rode down the main street and took in the length of town, if Bledsoe could be called a town. It appeared to James to be nothing more than a jumped-up old ranch with five buildings on either side of the main street. Each building was more crooked than the next and all of them dark save for one at the far end of the street.

After he'd spent so much time on the trail from home, the harsh yellow light shining in all the windows resembled the warm glow of a home fire to him. The sound of the tinny piano and raspy laughter that came out of the place told him this was Bledsoe's idea of a saloon. Only time would tell if James agreed, as he saw himself as something of an expert when it came to saloons.

James tied his horse's reins to the hitching rail out front and walked up the crooked steps to the creaky boardwalk in front of the saloon. The place was as run-down as the Golden Dream had been, but at least it sported a fancy door with leaded glass. He hoped that was a good omen for the kind of time he could expect inside.

But once he opened the door and entered the place, he realized he had been mistaken.

A little old man banged away at an upright piano as a painted woman old enough to be James's grandmother wailed away in some language his young ears had never heard before.

The bartender was a sullen, skinny man who looked as if he had not shaved for weeks. He looked like he had not slept much, either, for he had propped himself against the back wall and fought to stay awake. He barely stirred when he saw James walk in, and promptly went back to sleeping on his feet.

The rest of the place had three card tables, but only one of them was occupied. Two men who bore the familiar mud and dust of ranch work sat across from each other, staring at the cards they held with little enthusiasm. A bottle of whiskey stood between them on the table.

Both men perked up when they caught sight of the stranger who had just walked into the saloon.

The broader and darker of the two looked up from his cards and smiled. "Well, would you look at that, Marty? We've got ourselves a stranger."

The painfully thin man called Marty made a show of blinking his eyes as if to focus them. "I believe you're right, Billy. I certainly believe you're right."

"Evening, boys." James flashed the same smile that had won him a seat at many a card game over the years. "Glad I got here before the rush."

The old woman at the piano cackled. The man kept banging on the keys. The bartender snorted and tried to find a different part of the wall to lean against.

"This is the rush, friend." Marty gestured at one of the three empty chairs at their table. "But we've got room for one more if you'd like us to deal you in."

Billy said, "Take a seat, friend. We're always happy to take a stranger's money."

James rubbed his hands on his pants leg. He had not been expecting the kind of noisy fun he could have had back home at the Golden Dream, but he did not like the setup. He was a stranger here and he had hoped there would have been at least a few more people in the place so he could blend in more. And he had been hoping for some younger, more appealing female company.

"Don't be shy," Billy added. "We don't bite." He

opened his mouth, revealing less than half of a full set of teeth. "I promise. Just a friendly game of poker to pass the time is all."

James looked at the empty chair and at the whiskey bottle on the table. It had hardly been touched and he had ridden a long way to get here. Given the punishment he knew awaited him back with the herd, he hated to see it go to waste. Besides, he knew he would already catch hell from his father for defying him, so why not enjoy himself in the process?

James inched toward the chair. "Don't mind if I do, but I've got to be straight with you boys. I'm kind of short on money at the moment. If you could spot me the opening hand or two, I'd be grateful."

The two men looked at each other.

Marty spoke for both of them. "Who said anything about money? Just a friendly game is all. A bunch of cowhands passing the evening over a bottle of whiskey." He tried to hide his interest as he said, "You *are* a cowhand, aren't you, mister?"

"Maybe up here from down south apiece?" Marty added.

James was beginning to relax. These two certainly seemed friendly enough. And the whiskey certainly looked inviting enough.

He decided there was no harm in sitting, at least for a little while. "I certainly am, boys. And if this drive goes as well as my old man says it will, we'll be fixed for life."

"Sounds like you're a prosperous man," Marty said as he pushed the chair out for James to take a seat. "Sounds like a man we'll be glad to know."

Billy added, "Sounds like the kind of man we can

tell our grandkids about. Brag about how we knew you way back when and all."

That sounded just fine to James. In fact, he liked the idea the more he thought of it. He gladly sat down and accepted the glass of whiskey Billy had poured for him. "The name's James Kelly, and after this drive is over, they'll be naming a town after me."

"You don't say?" Billy looked at Marty as James took his drink. He quickly filled their glasses, then James's. "Tell us all about it. How many head you moving?"

And while young James Kelly sipped their whiskey, he was all too happy to tell them all about his father's outfit.

And the strangers were only too eager to listen.

CHAPTER EIGHT

BULL KELLY FELT himself being shaken awake from a fitful sleep. When he opened his eyes, he could just make out the outline of his youngest boy, Joshua, against the backdrop of stars behind him.

Kelly sat up as he shook the sleep from his eyes. "What is it, boy?"

"It's trouble, Pa," Joshua told him. "Bad trouble. Two men rode into camp holding James at gunpoint!"

The news brought Kelly to his feet without any help from his son. "Two of them, you said?" Kelly asked as he buckled his belt. "Who are they? Ever see them before?"

"I didn't get a good enough look at them in the dark," Joshua admitted. "I was standing watch over the herd when I heard some riders coming up the trail. When they got close enough, I could see two men riding alongside of James. But when I saw they

had their guns aimed at his belly, I knew there was
trouble, so I came to get you right away."

Kelly cursed his son again as he grabbed up the
whip that he always kept coiled beside him. He knew
something like this would happen the moment Concho told him that James had defied him by going into
town. "Any idea where your brothers are?"

"I saw them riding out to meet the men while I
came to get you," Joshua said. "I didn't wait to talk to
them. I figured you'd know what to do."

Joshua might not have been the smartest of his
sons, but he had always been the most sensible of the
bunch.

"Lead on, boy," Kelly said. "On foot, if you please.
And quiet, too. No call to give this rabble any notice
of our approach if we don't have to."

"It ain't all that far, Papa," Josh said as he began to
lead his father in the near darkness. "Just tell me what
you want me to do when we get there and I'll do it."

"I don't want you to do anything," Kelly told him.

His years on the trail had helped him see better at
night than most men and he took the lead, making
sure his son did not trip over anything and give away
their position.

"You'll do absolutely nothing when we get there.
Just let me do all the talking my own way. And be
ready for whatever happens. Stay back and out of the
light as much as possible."

"Sure, Pa." Kelly heard Joshua pull his pistol from
its holster and cock it. "I'll be ready."

Kelly admired the boy's bravery as they moved
through the darkness. "You ever shoot a man before,
son?"

"Can't say as I have. But there's a first time for everything."

Kelly knew this was no time for a lesson. "Then put it away. Killing a man is hard enough in the light of day. The darkness doesn't make it any easier. Do like I told you."

He was glad when he heard the gunmetal slide back into leather.

At least one of his sons knew how to obey him.

K ELLY PULLED JOSHUA to a stop as soon as he saw the three riders standing by the large campfire near the chuck wagon. Every single one of the cowhands in camp was on his feet and watching the strange men. Kelly was glad to see all of them had the good sense to get out of the circle of firelight. Targets in the dark were much harder to hit, especially if the shooters were on horseback.

Kelly saw that James and his mount were penned in between two strangers. The stockier of the two men had a pistol aimed at James's belly. His son's scraped face and swollen eyes told Kelly these men had given his boy a good working over before they had decided to bring him out here. He would worry about the reason later. For now, he needed to get his son out of the fix he had found himself in.

"We want Kelly!" one of the strangers called out. "We're here to see William Kelly. The man in charge. You'd best get him out here now if you care what happens to his boy!"

Remaining in the darkness, Kelly pushed Joshua to the right while he broke off slowly to the left toward the men. He had no intention of revealing himself to them. "I'm William Kelly."

The thinner of the two men said, "You the same William Kelly they call 'Bull' Kelly? The cattle driver out of El Paso?"

"I'm Kelly," he repeated as he crept ever closer to them. He saw no reason to say more than that.

One of the captors laughed. "Sounds to me like we'd best be on our toes, Marty. We've found ourselves up against a dangerous man. There's no bull to Bull Kelly, or so they say."

"That's what I hear," the other man replied. "Heard he's a real artist with that whip of his. Heard he took old Ace Cutter's hand clean off down in El Paso a couple weeks ago. Don't place much stock in it myself, even if Ace was ever all that."

Kelly did not care what either man thought. Stories like that only served to give a man a reputation. And a reputation did not do a man much good out on the trail, except to put a target on his back.

"Let my boy go," Kelly called out as he inched closer. "Let's talk like men, the three of us together."

"You step out into the light and we'll do all the talking you want," said the man on the other side of James. "I don't like talking in the darkness, much less to a man I can't see. Feels like I'm talking to a ghost."

Kelly turned his head as he spoke, to hide his true position. "Let my boy go or you'll be finding yourselves ghosts before you know it."

"In case you didn't notice, we've got your boy, boss man!" the man shouted. "Now, you either come out where I can lay eyes on you right this instant or you can watch your boy die from where you're hiding."

Kelly let the whip uncoil, quietly dropping twelve feet of kangaroo hide to the hard Texas dust. He gripped the handle tightly. "If you wanted James dead, you'd have killed him in whatever hellhole you boys found him in. You came here to talk, so get to talking and get this over with. I've got a nice dream waiting for me back where I was sleeping."

The two strangers looked at each other around James. Kelly was glad to see his son was sitting stock-still with his head low and his swollen eyes closed. The boy was smart enough to know what would be coming next.

He was making himself as small a target as possible.

"I know how fond you old-timers are of your beds," said the man who had been doing most of the talking. He was a compact man in his thirties. A capable-looking man, as Kelly's dearly departed Mary might have described him had she been there. "Your boy here owes us a hell of a lot of money."

"Cash money," the other added.

"Does he, now?" Kelly drew closer to the men in the darkness, dragging the hooked metal popper on the ground behind him. "Well, you boys find your-selves in honored company. My son owes money to just about every important man from all the way down to El Paso. Down to Mexico, even." He forced a laugh as he inched closer. "You two should pull a jug and toast yourselves for hooking such a popular man."

But neither of the strangers laughed or moved. The man who had been quiet most of the time, a thin bald man with deep lines on his face, called out, "We didn't ride all the way out here to drink with you cow-punchers. We came here to get what we're owed."

Kelly imagined his wife would have described this one as looking "poorly."

The man kept talking. "We came here to get paid on account of your son telling us that you had the money to cover all of his debts."

"Money and then some," the other man added. "Three thousand head and more by what your boy's bragging."

"That's a lie!" James cried out before the poorly-looking man cracked him in the jaw with a hard-right hand. Kelly's son almost fell to the ground but kept his place in the saddle. Kelly knew James, for all of his many faults, had always been a capable horseman.

The capable-looking man spoke next. "Your boy has suffered enough for one night, Kelly. Whether or not he suffers any more is up to you. But I don't aim to keep scraping knuckles on him, either. I need these hands to make my living."

"And where might that be?" Kelly asked as he moved ever closer in the darkness. Just a little closer and he'd be in range to lash out with his whip. He just had to keep them talking, keep them distracted while he got into position. "You boys pimps in some whore-house in town? Or bouncers who roll drunks for spare change?"

"The both of us work the Diamond B," the man told him. "The B stands for Bledsoe. Andrew Bledsoe. The same town we met your boy in." The man suppressed a laugh. "Ever heard of him?"

"I have." In fact, Kelly was sure every man who had ever taken to the trail in Texas had heard about the Diamond B and the Bledsoe family. Andrew's grandfather had built his brand in a wind-scoured wilderness fit for nothing but the scorpions and tumbleweeds and Comanche who called the place home. But Old Man Bledsoe had found water when he had drilled deep enough for it and found a way to turn the land green. He had found a way to make a dirt farm fit for breeding cattle and, over the years, had turned a dust bowl into one of the most prosperous ranches in that part of Texas.

"I've got no trouble with Mr. Bledsoe," Kelly told them. "Don't want any trouble with him, nor with you two, neither. Just like I know you boys don't want any trouble with me. You say you've heard of me, so you know I'm a fair man. Let my boy go, put away your guns, and come down from those horses so we can talk this out like civilized men."

"After what we've done to your boy here?" The poorly man laughed. "You think we can expect a fair hand from Bull Kelly?"

The other one said, "Why, you'll gun us down the second you get the chance."

"My boys haven't gunned you down yet, mister," Kelly said. "With you boys gabbing in the firelight like you have, a blind man could've shot you down had he wanted to. Me and my men aren't killers. We're cattlemen same as you, so just do as I told you. Put down the iron and climb down out of the saddle and we'll talk this over like civilized folk. I'm anxious to have my boy's wounds tended to as soon as possible."

The capable man gave Kelly the answer he had been expecting. "I'm afraid we can't do that, old man. We're comfortable right where we are, and we've

grown to like your son's company. So how about you
come on out where we can see you and we'll tell you
how much he owes us. Whether or not you get him
back depends on how much money you've got. And
by money, I mean cash on the barrelhead, mind you,
or gold. I won't take payment in cowhide."

Kelly decided he had drawn close enough in the
darkness to force things a little. He gripped the handle of the whip tighter. "I told you to put those pistols
away and we'll talk. Last chance."

The capable man thumbed back the hammer on
his pistol and was about to press it against James's
belly. "And I said—"

In a single move that was as much instinct as second nature, Kelly brought back the whip and flicked
it toward the capable man's gun hand. He did not
have to think about it. He did not even consciously
aim at the hand. He had simply looked at where he
had wanted the popper to strike and let fly.

The popper had shattered the man's gun hand just
as the sound of the whip cracked through the air. The
man's gun fell to the ground and fired, striking the
poorly man's horse in the leg.

As the wounded man fell from the saddle, his
horse ran away. The poorly man struggled to keep his
wounded, frightened mount under control.

But though his hands were bound, James had
found a way to keep his horse still, for there was no
way of knowing where his father's next strike would
come from in the darkness.

Kelly stepped forward, tracking the poorly man in
the darkness until he was close enough to cut loose
with the whip once again.

The curved edge at the end of the popper bit into his target's back, easily tearing through the man's vest and shirt to slash the skin below. The stricken man cried out as if he had been shot.

Kelly jerked the whip back and swirled it in the air without allowing it to touch the ground before he sent it snapping out again, hitting the poorly man in the face. The force of the blow was hard enough to make him drop from the saddle. He landed on the other side of the fire from where his companion had curled himself into a ball.

With both men now unmanned and unarmed, Kelly's crew rushed out from the darkness and tended to the wounded James. They all took great care in easing him off his horse and getting him clear of the campfire.

For if there was one thing the men of the Kelly outfit knew for certain, it was that Bull Kelly was not through with these men.

Kelly stepped out of the shadows, trailing the whip behind him. He looked down at the gunman cradling his hand as he tried to get up. A stern boot in the back from Kelly forced him back on the flat Texas earth.

"Looks like you were wrong, Mary, darlin'," Kelly said aloud to the sky. "This one's not a very capable man at all."

"Mary?" cried out the man pinned to the ground. "Who the hell is Mary?"

Kelly dug the heel of his boot in the small of the man's back until he cried out. "My wife, you heathen bastard. Are you willing to talk now or to I have to take more sand out of you?"

The man beneath Kelly's boot struggled to speak. "I already told you why we're here. That damned cheating son of yours owes me money. He lost it to us fair and square in a card game and now he says he can't pay."

Kelly did not doubt the man was telling the truth. James had lost a great amount of money over the years during a great many hands of poker. Kelly had always been able to cover his son's losses before, but given how all of his money was tied up in the drive, he feared he might not be able to do so now. "How much does he owe you? And if you lie, I'll know it."

"Fifty dollars."

Kelly called out to his son somewhere in the darkness. "That true, James?"

"Yeah," came his son's reluctant reply. "It's true, Pa."

Kelly swore under his breath. On the rare occasions when his son won, he always won small. When he lost, he always managed to lose big.

And although he knew the answer to the next question, Kelly had to ask it for his own sake. "Do you have fifty dollars, James?"

His reply was slow in coming. "No, but they agreed to stake me to it. I signed my name to a voucher and everything."

The man beneath Kelly's boot said, "And it sounds like it ain't worth the paper it's printed on. Just like I thought."

Kelly put more weight on the man's back. "My people always pay what they owe, boy."

The man pinned beneath Kelly's boot managed a laugh. "This is rich. Mister, you just crippled me and took a hunk out of Marty's back over there on account of your son being a deadbeat. Mr. Bledsoe's not going to like you treating us this way."

"Think he'll like hearing that you two held an unarmed man hostage?" Kelly asked. "Think he'll be happy about you not bringing him to the sheriff when you could've? They have law in town, don't they?"

Kelly applied just enough pressure to the small of the man's back. "Don't lie to me now."

"Yeah, there's law in Bledsoe," Billy said. "But—"

"But you decided you'd ride out here and see if James's old man was as dim-witted as his son." Kelly began to slowly pull the whip into a coil. "Thought maybe the sight of you holding my son at gunpoint would turn me into a blithering idiot, didn't you? Figured maybe you'd get more out of me face-to-face?"

But the man beneath his boot didn't say much of anything.

Until Kelly let the popper drop and strike the man on the temple hard enough to make him cry out. "Don't lie. And don't hold out on me, either."

"Yeah, that's what we thought," Billy admitted. "So what? You know how much of a loudmouth your boy is. You ought to use that thing on him once in a while. Teach him some damned manners. Some sense, too. If we wanted a little extra money, we deserved it on account of putting up with his nonsense all night."

Billy struggled to get a better look at Kelly, but the boot kept him pinned to the ground. "And you can use that whip of yours to pluck the skin clean off my bones if you want to, mister, but deep down, you know I'm right."

Kelly jerked the popper from the man's head and

let it fall away from them. "As a matter of fact, I agree with you. James was wrong for gambling with money he didn't have and for leading you men to believe I might have it."

"He didn't tell us that," Billy said. "We just figured you did."

Marty cried out from the other side of the fire, "Just like you can figure on being dead by this time tomorrow, old man. Mr. Bledsoe ain't gonna like what you've done to us. Not one bit."

But Kelly had other things on his mind just then besides Bledsoe. With his foot still on Billy's back, he closed his eyes and raised his face to the heavens. "Mary, my love, it's times like these I wish you were still beside me. I always followed the course you set for me and it never steered me wrong."

He knew what he had to do next, of course. He had known it the moment he had heard James was being held as a hostage. But talking to his Mary in difficult times such as these had always managed to make him feel better somehow.

He took his foot off Billy's back and stood between the two strangers. "James doesn't have fifty dollars, boys, and I'm afraid neither do I. Why, I think you could shake out the whole outfit by the ankles until they were blue in the face and I doubt you'd come up with thirty."

"Then you've got bigger things to worry about than Mr. Bledsoe getting to you," Billy said. "We played with him on credit, figuring he was good for it. If you don't make good on his bet, pretty soon everyone from here clear up to Canada will know your credit's no good. They'll know Bull Kelly and his punk kid don't pay off like they should."

"What'll they think of the great Bull Kelly then?" Marty added, before moaning from the pain in his back.

"They'll say no such thing because it's not true," Kelly told them. "I meant what I said when I told you I don't have the money on hand. Which is why I'd like to make you two a proposition."

Billy had rolled over on his backside, holding his ruined hand to his chest. "I already told you I ain't interested in no fifty dollars' worth of cattle. I'd just about break even on the price Mr. Bledsoe would charge me to run my stock with his and I'm not going broke to pay for money I already earned."

"No one said you should." Kelly dug his left hand into his pocket, found what he was looking for, and allowed the coins to drop at his feet. "That's twenty Yankee dollars right there. Pure gold. It'll get you more than fifty if you spend it in the right places."

Billy scooped up the coins with his good hand and tucked them in his shirt pocket. "What about the rest of what he owes us?" he asked. "The other thirty we've got coming?"

Kelly was getting to that. "My boy will also give you that brand-new Colt he's been toting around along with that fancy gun belt he prizes so much. Doesn't look like they're doing him much good anyway."

"Pa! You can't!" James cried out from the darkness.

"I can and I will!" Kelly glared at his son until he was satisfied there would be no further discussion.

"Add his horse into the bargain and you'll have yourself far more than what he owes. Damned near double by my counting. We'll call it even for your busted hand and the cuts on your friend's back over there. What do you say?"

Marty bit through his pain as he said, "I say any man who's got twenty in gold has fifty. And that's what I'll have."

Kelly could feel his temper beginning to slide away from him. "I'm giving you what I have, boy, which is more than I can afford. A wise man should know to quit when he's ahead."

"Don't give in to him, Billy," called out the skinny man. "Make the crazy Irish bastard pay."

Kelly's head snapped around at the insult. "Crazy, am I?" He cracked the whip in Marty's direction. The hook end of the popper wrapped around his neck. Kelly pulled him flat on the ground. "Why am I crazy? For not whipping you boys to death or for talking to my dear Mary above us?"

Marty gagged as Kelly began to pull him closer toward him.

Closer toward the fire.

"You heathen bastard," Kelly said as he continued to pull. "You know what we do to heathens where I come from? We roast them alive."

Billy grabbed Kelly's leg with his good hand. "Please, mister. Don't do it."

Kelly kept pulling the man toward the fire. "What'll it be, then? Have we a deal?"

"What if I say no?"

"Then we'll be having ourselves a grand bonfire

this very night. There's not much to your skinny friend here, so we'll have you on there in no time."

Billy grabbed Kelly's leg tighter. "You can't do that!"

"Watch me."

The man pounded the dirt with his good hand. "Fine. You've got your deal, mister. Anything you say. Just let him go."

Kelly stopped pulling and looked down at the man. "You're certain? No griping about the raw deal you got when you get back to your ranch? Swear it."

"Yeah, I'm certain. I swear."

Kelly shot slack through the whip and released the hold on Marty's throat before pulling it back across the fire. "I hope you're a man of your word. Because if you're not and make trouble for us, I'll have no choice but to finish what I started with this whip. And when I do, you'll be begging for the fire before I'm through."

Billy spoke through gritted teeth. "I promise we'll take your deal and go."

"And never come back?" Kelly pushed.

Billy glowered up at him. "Never."

Kelly looked down into the man's eyes and, even in the flickering light of the campfire, found truth in them. Yes, Mary had taught him that trick, too. She would have liked this boy if he had not threatened to kill their son. He decided he would like him, too.

He began to pull his whip into a coil once more. "Then I believe we have a deal, witnessed by all the men of my outfit."

Kelly called out to his son. "Jeremiah! You there, boy?"

"I'm here, Pa. All of us are here, even Joshua."

"Very well. Fetch your brother's gun and belt and bring his horse over here for these men to take with them when they leave us."

"The saddle, too?" James cried out.

Kelly ignored him. "The whole rig, Jeremiah. No exceptions. Your brother has to learn he can't gamble with money he doesn't have. Come now."

Kelly stood between the two wounded men until Jeremiah led out the horse from the darkness. It was a fine bay gelding Kelly knew James had grown fond of since he had acquired it the year before. The loss of it would sting him for a long while. He only hoped it made his son think twice about pulling another stunt like this anytime soon, though he doubted it would.

Billy scrambled over to Marty and began to help his friend to his feet. Neither Kelly nor any of his men made a move to help them.

Billy had to hold Marty as he retched when he finally got to his feet. It was no easy feat for a man with only one good hand.

He looked across the fire at Kelly. The shadows of the flame made him look uglier than he already was. "I guess you're really everything they say you are, mister. I used to think it was all talk, but now we know different."

"Talk's cheap." Kelly put the whip on his belt and thumbed the thong over it to hold it in place. "Scars speak volumes. Keep that hand bandaged and clean. You'll get some use back in it in a month or so. By this time next year, it'll probably be close to normal, if you're lucky."

Marty had finished his dry heaving and managed to stand as upright as his scraped back would allow. "That's all talk, Billy. If he was as good as that with a whip, he would've killed us by now."

They all looked as Marty's wounded horse cried out as its leg finally gave way and it collapsed to the ground. The amount of blood on its hind leg proved there was no hope that the animal might survive its wound.

In one fluid motion, Kelly uncoiled his whip and slashed it at the dying animal. When he pulled the whip free, he had taken a good chunk of the horse's throat with it.

The animal was dead a second later, if not sooner.

The two men from the Diamond B did not move as Bull Kelly slowly approached them. He pulled the whip into a loose coil until the bloody popper was in his hand.

He slowly wiped it on Marty's shirt. "What is it you were saying about my skills with a whip, lad?"

Marty retched again but did not throw up.

Kelly motioned for Jeremiah to bring James's horse closer to the men.

To Billy, Kelly said, "If you need help climbing aboard, one of my boys will help you."

But the man managed to do it on his own with his good hand. His eyes glinted with greed as he patted the soft leather of the gun belt draped on the saddle horn.

Kelly had seen that look in men's eyes before and knew where it led them, too. In a year, maybe two, this man would find himself dying on a barroom floor or in an alley with a knife in his belly. By then, the Kelly outfit would already be starting a new life in Nebraska with their pockets bursting with gold from the cattle they had brought to the railhead. They'd be deciding on whether or not to put down roots up north or make another run south before calling it quits.

The harsh Texas landscape and the events of that evening would be a distant memory by then, and the Kelly family could finally enjoy the living in the wealth he had toiled so long to attain.

But as Concho had reminded him at dinner, they still had to get through today first.

Marty rubbed his chaffed neck. "What horse am I supposed to ride?"

Joshua led the capable man's horse from the darkness. "You can ride your friend's horse back to wherever you came from, mister. I was able to catch her after she ran off. She's not hurt. She's just a bit spooked is all."

Marty jerked the reins away from Joshua and cried out in pain as he pulled himself up into the saddle. Kelly knew the pain from the gashes in his back would only grow worse as the days went on. He would probably fail to keep the wounds clean or find any of his friends back at the ranch who were willing to do it for him. The cuts would most likely be infected in a day or so. After that, Kelly imagined he would be dead in a week or so. He only hoped the outfit was too far away by then for any of the men from the Diamond B to bother riding after them.

Still, Kelly knew Mary would want to give the boy some advice. "If you've got a doctor back at the Diamond B, you might want to have him take a look at those wounds. A bit of whiskey on them will clean them out. Keep them bandaged and you'll heal fine. I made sure I didn't cut you too deep."

Marty looked down at Kelly through the pain coursing through his body. "You cut deep enough, mister. Deeper than you know."

"Scars are God's way of teaching us a lesson, boys. I'd say you both learned plenty tonight. Now, on your way."

He cut loose with another crack of his whip and the mounts, eager to get away from the pain they knew often followed that sound, wheeled away from it and ran at a gallop in the opposite direction.

Kelly brought his whip into a coil and secured it back onto his belt. He slowly walked out of the circle of light and stood in the darkness, watching and listening to the men he had just set free ride away.

He was glad the rest of the outfit had gathered around James, leaving Kelly alone in the darkness of the cool Texas night.

He had no doubt the thought of vengeance would cross the minds of Billy and Marty at some point between the camp and the bunkhouse of the Diamond B. But a life spent on the trails and in cow towns had shown him that the harshest lessons were the longest learned.

He knew those two men would not be back that night. A broken hand and a scarred back and stretched neck would assure him of that. A whip was a stern taskmaster indeed. He had learned that long ago, too.

No, he would not have any further trouble with the men he had released. But their friends were a different story. He wondered if Mr. Bledsoe was the kind of man who let affronts to the dignity of his outfit pass without notice. He wondered if Andrew Bledsoe was the type who demanded satisfaction for any slight.

He cast his eyes to the heavens and the stars twinkling above. "Did I do right by letting those men go, my love? Perhaps I'm getting soft in my old age."

No, Kelly decided. Letting them go was the right thing. Killing them would have been going too far.

And if he was wrong, he would deal with it then. He gripped the handle of the bullwhip tightly. *We'll be ready for them, won't we, darlin'?*

ASSURED AS HE could be that the men he had allowed to live were actually on their way back to the Diamond B, Kelly walked back toward the campfire, where the men were looking at James's wounds. The men, including his sons, were standing around helpless while they watched Concho apply some kind of pasty mud to James's swollen face.

"How bad is it?" Kelly asked Concho in Spanish.

"I've seen better." The old Spaniard shrugged. "I've seen worse. He'll live, but he won't be pretty anymore. He was always too pretty. Maybe this will be good for him."

Kelly wasn't so sure. His second-oldest boy was a stubborn one and scars tended to make a man more appealing to a certain kind of woman. The kind of woman who James naturally appealed to.

"Will you two quit speaking that chicken language," James yelled as some of Concho's salve stung his wounds. "Can't ever understand a word you're saying to each other."

"Maybe that's the point?" Kelly said.

"Well, it shouldn't be the point," James said. "I know you're talking about me and English ought to be good enough."

"You've spent your whole life in Texas," Kelly said, "and never picked up an ear for Spanish." The father shook his head. "You're a man of limited horizons, my son."

"I'm a man who's shy a good horse and a fine Colt pistol," James whined. "A fine saddle, too. You gave them a lot more than I owed them, Pa. Why'd you do that? Me and the boys had them outnumbered."

Kelly looked at the men in his outfit. His boys, Jeremiah and Joshua and Joel and Jacob. Concho. A stocky man who went by the name of Brick and a fifteen-year-old kid named Greenly. Baxter, and the seven men currently out tending the herd. Together, they were barely adequate cowhands and none of them was much of a fighter with a gun or their fists. They were not meant to be. If Kelly had needed gunmen, he would have hired gunmen. Instead, he needed men who could move his beef to Dodge City. Gunmen weren't much good for that. They were good at causing trouble, and trouble was the one thing Bull Kelly had always tried to avoid.

"You've been in more fights than any man in the outfit, boy, and look at the face on you. Do you think any of these men would do any better than you?" He made a point of looking at the men as he quickly added, "No offense meant to anyone. You're all good men, just not the fighting sort."

They all said that no offense had been taken.

"I'm paying these men to move cattle for us to have a new life, not to fight your battles. I gave those

Diamond B boys more than this outfit could afford just to save your hide. You'd better pray to the good Lord above they don't come back tomorrow with their friends looking for trouble. For if they do, I might be inclined to let them have you, especially if they bring the law with them."

For once, James had no response.

And William Kelly decided he had done enough talking for one evening. "It's late, boys, and we've an early start before us in the morning. Get some sleep. Especially you, James. You'll be riding drag for a while. I don't want to see hide nor hair of you until I send for you." He turned and began to walk back to his bedroll. "Your mother and I are mighty disappointed in you, son. Mighty disappointed indeed."

He imagined the men in the outfit thought he was slightly daft for talking about his dead wife as if she were still alive. Good. It never hurt for the men to think he was just a little crazy.

Just as it was good to remind them what he could do with a whip from time to time.

CHAPTER NINE

A NATURAL EARLY RISER, Andrew Bledsoe was already on his porch, enjoying his second cup of coffee, when he watched two riders pass beneath the wooden Diamond B gate that spanned the road. It was not much of a gate, Bledsoe admitted, nor was the Diamond B much of a ranch. At least it was not much to look at. The fact that he had more than five thousand head of cattle just over the next rise and well out of view was a point of pride for him. No one needed to know his business unless he decided he wanted them to know it. And such people were few and far between.

Like his father and grandfather before him, Bledsoe had never allowed the opinions of others to play much of a role in his thinking. He had always preferred to keep his own counsel and had always been glad of it.

He did not like the look of the riders approaching his ranch. They were slumped forward in their saddles and seemed very much the worse for wear. They were still too far away for him to tell for certain, but they looked like Marty and Billy.

He vaguely remembered Rance, his foreman, had mentioned something about the two ranch hands having his permission to go into town the night before. The town his grandfather had built and saw fit to name after himself. The town he had been quick to abandon when he grew bored of the politics and other menial matters that always came along with a town. The collection of ramshackle buildings may have still borne his family name, but that was all the connection it shared with the Diamond B as far as Bledsoe was concerned.

But something about the approaching riders troubled him greatly. His men knew better than to ride up the main road when they came back late from a night on the town. Even hungover and often still drunk, they usually had the good sense to use the back road. He would make it a point to make sure Rance doled out a particularly harsh punishment for these two. He did not expect much from his men, but he did demand they respect the brand. For respect, once lost, was difficult to regain.

The future of the Diamond B was an open question as far as Andrew Bledsoe was concerned. It was one of the biggest ranches in that part of Texas, but the distinction meant little to him. He was beginning to wonder whether or not the next drive to market should be his last.

At thirty, he was still unmarried and, at present, had no real prospect for a wife. Perhaps he should sell off the entire spread and be done with the whole business. Start anew somewhere else doing something else. Everything came to an end eventually. The Diamond B was no exception.

He had been pondering the end of the ranch for the past two summers and knew he was quickly approaching a crossroads. If he did not sell his ranch soon, he just might find himself stuck here for the rest of his life. And what kind of life would that be without a wife and children to complete it? What kind of place was the Diamond B to raise a family?

Ranching no longer had the same hold on his heart that it had once had. He had begun to grow resentful of the cattle that had made him rich. He resented being tied to the land they grazed on. He grew tired of housing and feeding the men who worked for him and made all of this possible.

Perhaps the time had come to use this ranch to forge a new destiny of his own choosing. Maybe take his money and move up north, where the weather was more hospitable and the company far more refined. He would be sure to find a woman in Dodge City or points west. Perhaps even San Francisco.

The only real virtue of the Diamond B was that all of it belonged entirely to him. The ranch house he called home was not a particularly remarkable or beautiful building. It had a single level and a porch that wrapped around all four sides of it. The roof still did not leak very much on the few times it did rain.

The interior of the house was sparsely furnished, just as it had been when his father had lived there and his father before him. The Bledsoe family had been on this land since it had been deeded to them by Mexico way back in the early 1800s. In gratitude, the

Bledsoes had been decidedly neutral when the war for independence came and had not raised a finger to help either Sam Houston or Santa Ana. They heartily cheered independence, of course, but only after independence had been won. Never unduly risking their neck for the concerns of an outsider had been an unofficial motto of the Bledsoe family and one he intended on continuing until his dying day.

But now, as he watched the two riders come ever closer, he began to grow worried. At least Rance was riding out to meet them. He imagined the Diamond B's foreman must have seen them as he came by the ranch house to give Bledsoe his daily report. He looked none too happy about their condition and Bledsoe wondered if this would be one of the few times Rance enforced a little discipline around here.

Andrew Bledsoe drank his coffee as he watched Rance confront the men in the middle of the road. Rance had been a bad man in his younger years. He was rumored to be one of the worst outlaws in Indian Territory before Bledsoe's father had found him shot to hell, nursed him back to health, and gave him a job. He had turned out to be a second-rate foreman of a third-rate ranch, but overall, he did a good enough job so the ranch always made more money than Bledsoe expected each year. He kept Rance around mostly for his past with a gun. To his way of thinking, having a former killer around was better than having no killer at all.

After a few moments talking to the men on the road, Bledsoe watched Rance ride back up the road as the two riders continued behind him at an achingly slow pace.

Bledsoe's gut told him this was not just another case of some cowhands coming home late after a good drunk. There was something more going on here. Something wrong.

Being an incurious man by nature, Bledsoe was not apt to jump on his horse and ride out to see for himself. Instead, he was content to wait until Rance rode over and told him whatever he had to report.

William Rance had been with the Diamond B nearly as long as Bledsoe could remember. He imagined they were both around the same age—thirty years old—and where the rancher's easy living set him on the soft side, Rance looked like a man who rode a horse for a living, with his bowlegs and broad shoulders. Bledsoe made sure the top hand received extra money each Christmas by way of thanks for keeping the ranch running well enough for Bledsoe to spend his mornings on his porch and his evenings counting his money.

"Morning, boss," Rance said as he reined up next to the porch.

But Bledsoe's concern about the riders caused him to set pleasantries aside for once. "What's wrong with those two? Isn't that Billy and Marty?"

"It is, sir," Rance replied. "And it's trouble. Trouble of their own making."

Bledsoe motioned for Rance to move out of his line of sight as he watched the two men amble past the porch toward the bunkhouse. "Those men look like they've been in a stampede. Did we have a stampede last night, Rance?"

"Not us," his foreman told him. "Those two made the mistake of locking horns with the wrong man."

He shrugged it off. "It happens sometimes. I'll be sure to lay down the law to them once they heal up some."

For the first time in a long while, Bledsoe found himself growing curious about something that concerned the Diamond B besides money. "What man did that to them? And why?"

Rance pushed his hat farther back on his head. "Trust me when I tell you it's hardly worth your trouble, boss. They just crossed paths with a rattler and got bit. Like I told you, I'll handle it."

Bledsoe did not appreciate Rance's stonewalling. He wanted answers, not opinions. "If it involves my ranch, I want to know about it."

Rance did a poor job of hiding his surprise at his employer's sudden interest in anything about the Diamond B. "Well, since you asked, I'll tell you what they told me. They said they got into a card game in town with a guy who looked like an easy mark. Some cowpuncher on the trail north to Dodge City. Turned out the guy was better at cards than they thought he was and ran up a pretty good number on them. He took out a marker to go all in on the last hand but lost to Marty over there. When he didn't have the money to pay, they decided to take the boy back to where his old man's outfit was camped for the night. Things with the father got out of hand and Billy and Marty got roughed up pretty good. There's probably more to the story than that, but that's just about the gist of it."

Rance had been right. Bledsoe did not give a damn about the details, but he did care about the herd heading north. "Whose herd is it?"

His foreman looked around. "You might want to

skip knowing that part, Mr. Bledsoe. Won't do you any good or change things any."

Bledsoe was beginning to grow frustrated with his ramrod's newly found independence. "I don't like this new habit of yours where I have to pull information out of you, Rance. When I ask a question, I expect an answer right quick."

Rance let out a long breath before answering. "The herd belongs to a fella named William Kelly. He's the same one that doled out the beating to the boys."

Bledsoe turned the name over in his mind. "William Kelly? Means nothing to me."

"Maybe not," Rance told him, "but the name Bull Kelly probably does. Made a name for himself driving cattle up to Nebraska and Kansas from these parts. I think your daddy threw his lot in with a few of the herds he ran north once or twice."

Rance had been right. The name William Kelly meant nothing to him, but Bull Kelly was a different story. "He's the whipcracker, isn't he?"

Rance nodded. "The very same."

"Doesn't use a gun, from what I remember."

"He'll use one if he has to," Rance said, "but he prefers that bullwhip of his. Pretty accurate, too. Any cut from it's liable to make a man sick. He never cleans the end of it. Damned thing's got so many germs on it, makes a Tijuana whorehouse seem like a hospital."

Bledsoe had heard that, too. It made men afraid to even look at the whip, much less get struck by it, out of fear they would catch something. "And that's what he used on Billy and Marty last night."

Rance said it was. "I wouldn't hold out much hope for either of them surviving the fever they'll get from the cuts, but we'll do the best we can by them."

Bledsoe slowly turned his coffee mug on the arm of his chair. "Two men down because of a lousy interloper. I don't like that. I don't like that at all."

"I don't know anyone who'd call Bull Kelly an interloper, sir," Rance argued. "He's a good man, and from what I know of him, an honorable one. He's got a name for being tough, but fair. He even made good on his boy's debts. Gave them gold and horses and tack I figure comes to twice what his boy lost in the card game. Over a hundred dollars by my reckoning."

But Bledsoe was still turning the whole thing over in his mind. Why? he wondered. What did he care about two ranch hands getting a beating they probably had coming? Was it the beating or was the beating just an excuse for him to go after something more? Like Lelly's herd, maybe. If he had as many cows as Bledsoe hoped, it could mean the payday he had been looking for to get away from that place once and for all. "Sounds like he's generous with his son's debts. Generous with his beatings, too."

"Serves those two fools right if you ask me," Rance said. "Marty and Billy should've called in the sheriff if they wanted the Kelly punk to pay up. Instead, they rode out to the herd outgunned and alone to put some fear into the old man to pay up. They won't be doing anything so foolish again, I'd wager. Why, just look at the two of them slinking back to the bunkhouse like a couple of beaten dogs. Have you ever seen a sorrier sight in your life?"

Bledsoe pitched forward so he could look back to-

ward the bunkhouse. Billy and Marty looked the
worse for the wear. He doubted they would cross
swords with the likes of Bull Kelly anytime soon.
They probably would not be able to pull their weight
for a few days, if they were ever any good to him
again. He would have to carry them until then, feed
them for free without compensation. If they got better, they might not be any good to him. They might
die. Either way, Bledsoe was out two men and hiring
replacements would cause him more trouble than he
wanted to go through. The effort, however minor,
would put him out.

The idea of Kelly thinking he could do something
like this without giving it a moment's thought both-
ered Bledsoe. He found it almost insulting. "How bad
are they hurt?"

"Billy almost lost a hand and Marty's got a bad
gash in his back and a scarred throat from being
dragged close enough to the campfire to get himself
singed."

Bledsoe looked at his foreman. "Did Kelly's whole
outfit join in or was it just Kelly?"

"Bull Kelly's a whole outfit unto himself, Mr.
Bledsoe. He's a surgeon with that old bullwhip of his.
Why, I've heard tell of him holding off many a stampede all by himself just by cracking that thing and
turning the herd. In the middle of a lightning storm
no less."

Bledsoe remembered hearing all of the stories
since he was a boy. He remembered his father had
been quite taken with Kelly's exploits. He had tried
to hire the trail boss a couple of times, but the stubborn Irishman had always turned his father down

flat. He said he had dreams of running his own cattle one day with his sons and setting himself up in a family business. Bledsoe wondered if that dream was coming true for him now. "You said he's riding for himself these days?"

"That's what I've heard and what the boys just told me," Rance said. "He's called his brand the Square K. Guess the *K* stands for Kelly. I've heard talk for years now that he's been planning on making a run north with his boys. Guess the old man's finally gotten around to it."

"Yes," Bledsoe said as he pondered what had happened and planned for what might happen soon. "And he's doing it at our expense, too."

Rance sat taller in the saddle. "How do you figure that, Mr. Bledsoe?"

An interesting idea began to take root in Bledsoe's mind. He tapped his coffee cup against the arm of his chair as it began to flower. "Marty and Billy won't be ready to sit a full day in the saddle for weeks, if fever doesn't catch hold of them." He looked at his foreman. "We run a tight operation, don't we, Rance? The notion of two men being unable to work will put quite a strain on how we run this place."

Rance seemed to give it considerable thought before answering, "Not really, sir. I would never say Billy and Marty are the best hands we've got. Sure, the boys in the bunkhouse like to have them around on account of the fact that they make them laugh now and again, but I don't see us suffering much from them being laid up for a week or so. I'll see to it that your housemaid tends to their wounds for a couple of days. By then, we should have an idea about how long—"

Bledsoe fixed his top hand with a hard glare. "You'll do no such thing. Rita works for me. Her duties are in the house, not tending to a couple of drunken cowboys who were dumb enough to let an old man with a whip get the better of them."

Rance held up his hands in surrender. "Have it your way, Mr. Bledsoe. I'll just ask Miguel to look after them. He's already in charge of the stables and I'm sure he'll be able to find time to tend to the boys."

"And neglect the other duties we pay him for?" Bledsoe shook his head. "Not a chance."

The idea that had begun to flower in his mind was blossoming now and he liked what he saw. "No. Billy and Marty will have to take care of themselves. We can't spare anyone to play nursemaid to them. Especially now."

Rance set his hat properly on his head as he took a few moments to choose his words carefully. Bledsoe imagined he would give him an argument in that roundabout way Rance always argued with him. Not straight on, but as though he was agreeing with him.

"Since you feel that way about it," Rance said, "I say we pay off Marty and Billy and let them head on into town so the doctor can see to them proper-like. Those wounds will heal if they get treated, but those boys will die if they don't. They're no good to us dead and you've got a right to fire them for what they did. But they don't deserve to die for what they've done, either."

Bledsoe's eyes narrowed. "And let everyone in town know that the Diamond B could be hampered by a crazy old man with a whip? Why, our name would be ruined in a week. Just look at how quickly word of

Ace Cutter's demise spread north. How long do you think it would take for our shame to ride way north of here? Clear into Dodge City and beyond? What do you think that will do to the ranch's good name?" The more Bledsoe spoke, the more he found himself being whipped into a frenzy. What had started as a simple excuse to take a man's cattle from him was on the verge of blowing up into indignation. "This isn't only a matter of pride, either. Just how much do you think we'll get for our cattle when the buyers think we can be undone by a single man?"

Rance rubbed his face as he tried to keep his own temper in check. "Sir, there's no shame in losing to the likes of Bull Kelly. He's not an old man and he's more than just some loner with a whip. He's ridden the trails twenty or more times in his life in all types of weather under all types of conditions. It takes a special kind of man to do that kind of work. The kind of man who's best left alone." He swallowed hard before adding, "I know what you're thinking, Mr. Bledsoe. You're thinking about riding out after him, aren't you? I sure hope not, but if you are, I hope you'll reconsider."

But Bledsoe had already passed the point of reconsidering anything. There was more at stake here than just a couple of wounded ranch hands. More, even, than that nonsense he had spouted about the honor of the Diamond B.

There was something else at play now, something that not even a lazy man such as he could pass up. More than just the cattle, too.

It was the chance to ruin a man's dream and benefit in the process. Dreams he himself had only come to have recently. There was suddenly more sand in the bottom of the hourglass than the top. Why risk trying to make more of what he had when he could get it instantly by taking Kelly's cattle. Perhaps he would even make a name for himself in whatever new life he chose.

He pressed Rance for answers. "Those two idiots of yours have any idea about how many cows Kelly is driving?"

"Billy said the Kelly kid told them that his father was moving more than three thousand head north to Dodge City. I asked Marty to confirm it, but his brains are still a bit scrambled from the beating he took. I wouldn't place much stock in what either of them tells us." Rance's brow furrowed. "Why you ask, sir?"

The news was better than Bledsoe had been expecting. "Three thousand head is nothing to sneeze at. It would almost double what we have here. Depending on the quality of his stock, we could get a tidy sum if we were able to fold his herd into ours and bring them to market."

The more Bledsoe thought about the possibility, the more he liked the idea of it. If he combined what the heads would bring with selling his ranch to someone up north, he would not only have enough to start over in New York or San Francisco, but to do so nicely. Perhaps start that family he had been thinking of recently.

Bledsoe looked at his top man. "We have enough men who could handle that many cattle, don't we? Say six thousand or more."

"To tend here in the pasture," Rance said, "but a

drive of that size is something different entirely." He leaned forward in the saddle. "But I'm telling you there's no chance of it happening. None at all. We'll never get our hands on that cattle as long as Bull Kelly's got any breath in him. And there's no one in this outfit with the sand to take it out of him."

"Patience, Rance," the rancher assured him. "Don't be so hard on yourself. I think you and the boys will perform admirably, especially with the promise of all the gold that's to be had at the end of it all."

Rance shifted uneasily in the saddle. "Gold doesn't do the dead much good. Besides, we have no call to go after Kelly, Mr. Bledsoe. Not legally or any other way. He paid off his son's debt. Paid even more than he had to on account of the inconvenience."

"Yes," Bledsoe agreed. "He paid Marty and Billy what he owed them, but not me. He owes me for two cowhands he put out of commission for a week or more. And he owes this ranch for ruining its honor."

Rance scratched the side of his face and frowned. "Billy and Marty ain't worth the trouble of avenging, sir. Especially when that avenging means going up against a man like Kelly. He fought like hell when he was moving cows for other people. He'll be even worse when defending his own."

Rance was a decent enough foreman, but Bledsoe had no intention of sharing his real plans with him. Rance only needed to know enough of his plans to carry them out. "This has nothing to do with the kind of man Kelly is. It's about the kind of man I am. It's about the kind of ranch the Diamond B is going to be if it's going to have any respect in the future."

Rance cleared his throat. "Sounds to me like you're talking about a lot more than fighting for a brand, Mr. Bledsoe, and I don't care if you fire me for saying it."

Even after all these years, Rance still had the ability to surprise him every once in a while. No, Bledsoe would not fire him. But he would not waste time arguing with him, either.

The rancher got out of his chair and stretched his legs. His mind was made up. He felt energetic and strong for the first time in as long as he could remember. He had been sitting for a long time. Not just out on the porch that morning, but for years. The prospect of actually doing something, of fighting for something, felt good to him.

"I want you to go and round up nine of our toughest men, Rance. I want you to have them armed to the teeth and ready to ride out with us in ten minutes. Make sure you don't spare the ammunition, either. I want them ready for battle." He looked in the direction of where Billy and Marty had come from only a few minutes before but it seemed as if this happened a lifetime ago.

"I plan on paying a visit to Mr. Kelly," Bledsoe said, "and when I do, I aim to get a lot more than a horse and a pistol for my trouble."

Rance cleared his throat. "We don't really have any tough men, Mr. Bledsoe. Not like the ones you'll be needing to go up against the likes of Bull Kelly."

Bledsoe stared at Rance until the cowhand got the point. "If you're not up to the task at hand, you can draw your wages now and let me find someone who is."

Rance let out a long, slow breath. It was clear to

Bledsoe that Rance still had plenty more to say on the matter, but as was his way, he would ultimately do what he was told. There was a reason why he was still a foreman and a reason why Bledsoe was the one in charge.

"I'll see who I can scrounge up," Rance said, "but in the meantime, I'm asking you to think this thing over long and hard before we ride after them. Hell, Mr. Bledsoe, I'm begging you not to make us go. We've got all the cattle we need, with a bunch of calves ready to come in soon. Why, if the timing is right, we might even be able to make a run of our own up to the railhead in Kansas or Nebraska before the summer's over."

"A run with Kelly's cows would be closer to seven thousand head." Bledsoe liked the idea the more he thought of it. His family legacy might have been against taking risks for strangers, but when it came to lining their own pockets, some risks were acceptable, even welcomed. "You just worry about getting the men ready. Let me worry about the rest. I want to head off Kelly's herd as soon as possible."

Andrew Bledsoe turned on his heels and walked back into the ranch house. He was far too consumed with thoughts of future riches and glory to see the look of concern on his foreman's face.

CHAPTER TEN

B Y THE TIME the sun was up, the Kelly outfit was already back on the trail and moving north toward Nebraska. Hell, the damnable longhorn bull, trailed behind Kelly and his big Morgan at a fair distance.

The bull had largely behaved himself since the outfit had hit the trail from El Paso. He had bluffed a charge a few times in Kelly's direction, but had not fully committed himself. It was as if he was testing the human's tolerance, to see what he could and could not get away with. Like he wanted to see how far he could go before he risked being struck by the whip once more. On that morning, the big bull seemed content to lope behind Kelly at a constant pace, the rest of the herd trailing behind him.

It was a glorious Texas day with a clear blue sky as far as a man could see. Being atop the massive Morgan, Kelly could see farther than most.

He kept a sharp eye on the horizon as he led the herd northward. The events of the previous night still troubled him greatly. He could not help but worry that someone from the Diamond B might ride out after them seeking revenge. He was sure Billy and Marty were still too sore from their encounter with him to have any appetite for trouble, but they didn't speak for the rest of the men on their ranch. Kelly knew that all it took was one hothead looking to settle a score to cause an endless mess of trouble. In his experience, it was second and third parties that tended to cause the most trouble.

Despite the reputation he had earned over the years, whipping a man had never come easy to Bull Kelly. The act of doing it had left as many scars on him as on the men he whipped. Maybe even more. He comforted himself with the notion that he had never whipped a man who did not have it coming, at least as far as he was concerned. His targets were probably of a different opinion.

Back in El Paso, Ace Cutter deserved what he had gotten in the Golden Dream Saloon and the death he suffered afterward. He also deserved the dignified death he had received. Marty and Billy deserved what he had done to them the previous night. But it did not make it any easier for him to take, perhaps because he had felt the sting of that very same lash so often so long ago. He hoped the unavoidable regret he always felt after a lashing never left him and always feared it would.

He hoped he had seen the last of any man from the Diamond B Ranch, but something in his bones told him it was far from over.

Kelly had once known Jack Bledsoe, Andrew's father. He had brought several Diamond B herds north with him on many drives over the years. He had always found the rancher to be a pleasant, almost passive man. He could not remember a time when the elder Bledsoe had argued about the price Kelly had sold his cattle for and had often given Kelly a bit extra for the effort.

He had even tried to hire Kelly to work his spread on several occasions, but Kelly hated the idea of being tied to one ranch that was not his own. He preferred the notion of being able to pick the men he worked for and the number of head he drove. He loved the freedom that life on the long trail gave him, the money it offered, and the long winters he could spend at home with his Mary and his young sons.

Although he had known Jack Bledsoe, Kelly admitted he did not know his son, Andrew, very well. In fact, he did not know him at all. The younger man had taken over the Diamond B about five summers ago after his father died. A heart attack, Kelly seemed to recall it was. But in all that time, young Andrew had never asked Kelly to drive a single cow for him and Kelly had not sought to solicit the business. His services were always in such high demand that there were no shortage of ranchers asking him to bring their cows to market.

No, Kelly did not know the kind of man Andrew was and kept a watchful eye on the trail because of it.

Kelly turned in the saddle when he heard a rider approaching from behind. He was glad to see it was only young Greely coming for one of his daily chats.

He knew some of the men in the outfit chided the

youngster for trying to gain favor with the boss, but Kelly also knew that was far from the case where Greenly was concerned. The redheaded young man had a curious mind and always seemed to learn something by listening to Kelly's stories. Kelly liked to believe that something of a friendship had developed between them that was beyond him being the trail boss and Greenly being a cowhand. Kelly decided Greenly might even turn out to be a good man one day, if he stuck with the outfit long enough to benefit from listening to Kelly's wisdom on a daily basis.

"Fine morning, ain't it, Mr. Kelly?" Greenly said as he brought his horse beside his boss.

"It certainly is," Kelly agreed. "And you should've said, 'Fine morning, *isn't it*, Mr. Kelly.' Not ain't. *Ain't* isn't a word, son."

"Yes, sir." The boy blushed. "You told me that before. Guess I forgot."

Kelly didn't want the boy to take it too harshly. "Not to worry. You're still learning, lad. Takes a while to get used to speaking the Lord's English properly."

Greenly looked at his boss, confused. "I thought it was the King's English, sir."

"Not to an Irishman." Kelly frowned. "We have no king except He who rules us all from His throne above."

Kelly laughed at his own nonsense. He had not been in Ireland in decades and never had the urge to return, but the idea of being a subject of a foreign king still rankled him to this day. It was why he preferred to think of himself as an American, but his brogue was a constant reminder that he came from somewhere else.

Kelly was eager to change the subject. "What lessons would you like to cover today?"

Young Greenly had been slow to ask questions when they had first set out on the trail north to Kansas, but in the days since had grown comfortable enough with Kelly to speak his mind freely. "Well, I've been wondering a lot lately about you and what you done in your life, Mr. Kelly. I mean what you *did*, last night to them cowhands, I mean. I never seen anything like that before."

Kelly had imagined that was what the young man wanted to talk about. Violence and perceived bravery were particularly appealing to boys of Greenly's age. He could remember a time when they held the same fascination for him.

"You're barely fifteen," the trail boss reminded him. "You haven't seen much of anything in your young life, though I appreciate the compliment. And, to correct your grammar, you wanted to talk to me about what I *did* last night to *those* cowhands. And you should say, '*I've* never seen anything like that before.' Like I keep telling you, good grammar is always an asset to everyone, especially in this line of work."

The boy winced at another round of corrections. "Yes, sir."

"No need to go and hang your head about it. You're still learning and there's nothing wrong with making mistakes. Mistakes mean you're trying to be better. No man should ever be criticized for trying to better himself. Just remember that people underestimate men like us because of the line of work we're in. Speaking properly will surprise them. It'll make them think of you in a different light. Surprise, in that regard, is always a good thing."

Young Greenly seemed to give that considerable thought before saying, "You don't always use the right words, though, boss."

"I'm Irish," Kelly reminded him, "and we speak with a music all our own. You're an American, so it's best to speak properly, given the unfortunate accents God saw fit to give you."

"I'll try to keep it in mind," Greenly said. "Can I ask you something?"

Kelly imagined he knew what it was but decided to allow it anyway. "You never have to ask if you can ask something, boy. Just come out with it and see where it gets you."

"Well, it's about what happened last night."

"Go ahead."

"I know I don't know much, but I never saw anyone handle a whip like you, sir. I was wondering where you'd learned to do something like that?"

Kelly laughed. He had lost count of the times the boy had asked him that question along the trail. His old bullwhip had held a fascination for Greenly since the youngster had joined up with the outfit back in El Paso. He had always found a way to work a question about it into their conversations.

Perhaps it was the result of the regret he felt over the whippings of the previous night, but William Kelly decided it was finally time to relent and give the boy a bit of the history he craved.

It was a story his own sons had grown tired of

hearing over the years. He would enjoy an audience with a fresh set of ears.

He patted the whip that was coiled on his right hip. "My old fried here is one of a kind in this part of the world. I got it during my time in Australia many years ago. It's made of kangaroo hide, which is twice as durable as cowhide, if you can believe that."

"Kangaroo?" Greenly asked. "Those jumping animals you talked about?"

"One and the same. Think of them as deer, except they hop about on their hind legs and have long heavy tails. They're ridiculous-looking beasts, but dangerous, too. Many a man's been killed by cornering one. They can cave in a man's skull with one swipe of their paw and hardly take notice of it. Luckily, their hide is as tough as they are, which makes for a good whip."

"Sounds like it. But what were you doing all the way in Australia, boss?"

That was a longer story that could take another trail ride or two to tell. But knowing the boy would only keep asking, Kelly decided to give him some version of the truth.

"I ran afoul of some men in London and soon found myself on a ship bound for the prison colonies. I was supposed to spend the rest of my life in that damnable place, but as I am here, I clearly had other plans."

Kelly could see his answer had only served to fill the young man's head with even more questions. But as Kelly predicted, he decided to ask about his favorite topic first. "That where you bought the whip?"

Kelly felt himself grow dark at the memory of how he had come to own it. "That's where I *acquired* the whip, boy. Now, there's a good word for you to use every once in a while. *Acquired*. Means to get something. Try it on for size sometime. Makes you sound fancy."

The boy repeated the word, then asked, "How'd you acquire the whip, sir?"

Kelly's eyes narrowed as the fateful day returned to his mind as clearly as if it had just happened at breakfast that same morning. "I acquired it by finally taking it from the man who often used it on me."

Greenly looked like he might fall out of the saddle. His horse felt its rider's confusion and fussed a bit before the boy managed to bring it back under control and ride alongside Kelly.

All the while, Kelly had kept a steady pace.

"You, sir? You mean you let someone whip you?"

"I was a prisoner, boy. I didn't have much choice in the matter. Until one day I did." He threw a thumb back toward the longhorn leading the herd of three thousand cattle behind him. "I suppose I wasn't that much different from old Hell back there. I had learned that there's only so much whipping a thing can take before it rears up and does something about it. That's why I make a point of only using this whip when I have to. On man and beast alike."

"But you're not like Hell, Mr. Kelly," Greenly said. "You're free."

Kelly liked the way the boy thought. "Yes, lad. I'm free all right. Me and Concho. No one will ever put either of us under the whip again."

"You mean Concho was in Australia, too? With the kangaroos and such?"

"That he was. And when I left, he left with me.

We've been friends ever since. It's the only good thing that came out of that damnable experience."

"Sounds like it," Greenly said. "That and the whip."

"A whip is only a tool, boy," Kelly told him. "It's only as good or as bad as the man using it. Though I'll confess that a whip does come in awfully handy in this line of work. It keeps order and discipline among man and beast alike. Those are the hallmarks of every successful enterprise in the world, lad. Order and discipline. If you have those two things, you can do almost anything."

Kelly looked over at the boy to make sure he was paying attention to him.

"Sounds like you and Concho had a hard time of it down in Australia. And in the time it took you to get here from there."

Kelly had no intention of boring the boy with the details. He had no intention of boring himself, either. It had all happened so long ago that repeating it would serve no purpose. He wanted to encourage the young man's curiosity but saw no reason why he should torture himself by indulging in an examination of horrors past. It wouldn't do either of them much good.

Kelly summarized it by saying, "There's nothing wrong with hardship as long as you make it count for something. Life finds a way to shape all of us as we move through it in one way or the other. The best we can do is let it do its work and live with the results. The worst people are those who try to fight it and become something they're not. They make it bad not only for themselves, but for everyone around them.

That doesn't mean you let people walk all over you, boy. And it certainly doesn't mean you sit on your backside and bemoan your lot in life. Life is what you make of it. Take what you are and do the best you can with what you have. Do that, and you'll be happier in the long run. Remember that, and life will be much easier for you."

Young Greenly swallowed hard. "I'm not likely to forget it, sir."

Kelly noticed the Morgan's ears perk up just before the big horse shied away from the trail. He knew that meant she must have caught the scent of something farther upwind. He looked around at the ground, thinking the animal might have caught sight of a rattler or something hiding in the shrub brush, but did not see anything that might cause such alarm in the big animal.

That meant Morgan must have sensed something out in the distance before them, perhaps just over the next rise.

"Something wrong, Mr. Kelly?" Greenly asked.

Kelly was not sure, but he had every intention of finding out. "I need you to ride back and tell the boys I want them to rest the herd for a bit. Tell them I'll be riding ahead alone to scout the trail for a piece, but they're to stay with the herd."

"You want us to stop already?" Greenly asked. "But we just got 'em started a little while ago."

He would have belted Greenly for talking back to him had he been one of his sons. But his sons all knew better than to talk back to him. Greenly was just a naive kid who did not know when to ask questions and when to hold his tongue. "Just do as I tell you. And be quick about it."

The boy said he would and quickly brought his horse around to ride back at a good gallop to tell the rest of the outfit.

Kelly put the spurs to the Morgan and brought the big animal to a trot toward an unseen future.

CHAPTER ELEVEN

KELLY SAW THE reason for the Morgan's alarm as soon as he cleared the next rise.

A line of eleven men was spread out across the trail before him.

The man in the middle sat taller than the others, atop a gray.

"Well, would you look at that, darlin'," Kelly whispered to his departed wife. "Some visitors have come to call. What do you think their intentions might be?"

He glanced at the sky, as if waiting for a response from the heavens. And, as usual, no response came.

"Yeah, I don't know, either," Kelly admitted. "Guess we ought to find out together, shouldn't we?"

Kelly thumbed off the thong holding his whip on his belt as he rode toward the group at a respectable pace. He wanted the Morgan to have plenty of wind left in her lungs by the time they reached the men on the trail. He had no idea how the meeting might go and did not want to be atop a tired horse if things went poorly.

The closer he got to them, the easier it was for Kelly to see that the horses were well fed and tended to. In fact, some of them looked too well fed and appeared to be sluggish. None of the men bore the same pale patina of dust and grime he and his own men had acquired after over a week on the trail. That told Kelly that they had ridden only a short distance to meet him.

Since they were sitting out in the open like this, he doubted these men were highwaymen or rustlers.

That told Kelly they were probably the last people he had wanted to see. They were the men from the Diamond B.

Now that he had a fairly decent notion of what he was up against, he readied himself for the nasty conversation that was sure to come. He was sure they had not ridden all the way out here just to discuss the weather.

Kelly slowed the Morgan to a trot when he got close to the men and held up his right hand in welcome. He had learned long ago to treat every man as a friend until they proved they deserved to be treated otherwise.

"Morning."

"Glad you didn't say 'Good morning,'" the man in the center of the line said, "because I don't think there's anything good about it."

Kelly brought the Morgan to a stop less than twelve feet from the leader. He decided a bit of charm might take some of the sting out of the man's voice. "I'm sorry to hear you feel that way, being that it's such a beautiful morning and all. Are you and your men hungry? Want some coffee? We've got plenty back at the wagon if you're interested."

The man in the center moved his horse forward a few feet. *Even closer*, Kelly thought. *Good*.

"Mister, we're not the least bit interested in your damned coffee."

Kelly ignored the leader's tone. "Have it your way, but you don't know what you're missing, boys. I've got me the best cook on any trail in Texas and that's a fact. If you're not here for coffee or grub, do you mind if I ask why you're here?"

The man in front leaned forward in his saddle. "Do you know who I am?"

Kelly made a show of looking the man over, though he had a fairly good idea of who he was. He bore a resemblance to Jack Bledsoe, though his chin was weaker and his eyes were much sadder. But he decided to keep playing the role of good-natured Irishman for the moment in the hopes he could calm down the angry man and avoid a confrontation. "Can't say I have the slightest idea of who you are. Guess that calls for something of an introduction. My name is William Kelly. Some people call me Bull Kelly."

"I know who you are," the man said. "You're the one who likes to take chunks out of my men with that whip you're toting on your hip."

Kelly feigned sudden recognition. "Ah, then I take it you must be Mr. Bledsoe of the Diamond B."

"You take it right, Kelly."

"Andrew Bledsoe, then. I'm pleased to make your acquaintance, sir. Many's the cow I brought to market for your pa. I hope you'll accept my belated condolences on the passing of your beloved father. He was a fine man, sir. The kind of man they don't make anymore."

Bledsoe ignored the talk of his father. "Me and my men didn't ride all the way out here to talk about dead men, Kelly. I'm here about what you did to my men last night. I've got two men too banged up to work because of you. One's got a busted hand that might never heal and the other's got gashes on his back no white man should have."

"Cut him to the bone from what I saw," said one of the men in Bledsoe's line.

"Hacked off another man's hand, too," said another.

"You boys have it all wrong," Kelly assured them. "I laid into the skinny fella pretty good, I'll admit, but not deep enough to show bone. Just enough to make him change his mind about killing my boy. As for the other one—Billy, I believe—if I had wanted his hand, I would have taken it clean off him with my whip."

He did not give Bledsoe a chance to respond. "But let's not quibble about particulars, boys. It was a regrettable incident all around. One that could have been avoided had your men brought the law in to settle things. If they had, my boy would be in jail right now, where he belongs for welshing on a bet. A place where, I might add, I'd be apt to leave him for the remainder of the drive. If your men had turned him over to the sheriff like they should have, they would be tending your fine herd this very day. Yes, sir. Your daddy always did have the best cows in this part of Texas. Always said so, too."

Bledsoe seemed immune to compliments as he looked disapprovingly at Kelly's belt. "I see you don't carry a gun."

"Never had much cause to use one," Kelly said. "Found I was always better with my hands."

"And that whip you're toting."

Kelly smiled. "When necessary, sir. Only when necessary."

"And last night, you thought it was necessary to whip my men like they were a couple of mules?"

"When they were holding a gun on my boy? Yes, sir. I do. It was regrettable, but necessary, I'm afraid. But I hope your men told you that we came to an agreement on that before they left my camp. I saw to it that they were as well compensated for what happened as we could manage, being out here on the trail and all. Why, it could be said they came out ahead in the bargain. I saw it was only just, considering they had to tolerate my son's horrible behavior at the poker table."

"Oh, they told us all about it," Bledsoe said. "Or at least they told my foreman, Rance, over there. They were well compensated."

Kelly's eyes narrowed a bit. "Then why are you here?"

"Because you still haven't compensated me for the loss of my men."

Kelly could sense the tension rising in the line of riders and in Bledsoe, too. Since Kelly did not want things to take an ugly turn, he decided to continue to play the role of the affable Irishman. He was alone on the trail with a few thousand head of cattle and a long way to go until Kansas. He wanted to avoid any more trouble if he possibly could. If he had to eat a little dirt in front of these men to avoid it, it would be worth it.

"My son is a curse, Mr. Bledsoe, that's for certain. He's been a terror since the day he was born. He caused no end of trouble for his dearly departed mother; God rest her soul. And to me, too, when I wasn't out riding the trail for men like your dearly departed father. James has a terrible talent of finding a way of getting into trouble no matter where he goes. I thought time away from El Paso would help curb his wild ways, but here we are, aren't we?"

"I want compensation, Kelly."

"As do I," Kelly said. "Which is why I'm disappointed that your men decided to take matters into their own hands instead of calling in the sheriff to lock him up after they beat him. But they didn't do that, did they? No, they got greedy and it cost them."

"It cost me, too, Kelly. Cost me two men to tend my herd."

"You have wayward men and I have a wayward son." Kelly shrugged. "But you can always fire them and hire on some new men. Dare I say it, maybe even better men. As for me, James is my son and my cross alone to bear."

Kelly saw Bledsoe grip his reins tighter and his mount tensed. "Save the blarney for the idiots you pay to hear it, Kelly. You owe me and the Diamond B a debt, one my men and I are here to collect."

Kelly tried one last gambit to keep things from getting violent. He had already spilled enough blood for one drive, and he didn't want to spill any more if he could avoid it. "I can see you're angry, Mr. Bledsoe, but as a rancher, I know you're a practical man. So, from one practical man to another, why don't we talk about how we can make this right for all concerned."

"Seeing you laying in the dirt with a belly full of lead would be a good start," Bledsoe said. "Taking your cattle and running them with mine would put us just about even, to my way of thinking."

Most of the men behind him laughed. Only one did not. A serious-looking man who looked to Kelly as if he had seen his share of blood in his time. He pegged him for the ramrod of the outfit. The man Bledsoe had called Rance.

While the men laughed, Kelly seemed to consider Bledsoe's statement. "That's a mildly interesting proposition you've made, Mr. Bledsoe, and a considerable one. But I'm afraid I'll have to ask my wife about it. I always ask her opinion on such important matters."

The men of the Diamond B—including Bledsoe—stopped laughing as they watched William Kelly look up at the sky and say, "Mary, darlin'. If you're not too busy at the moment, I'd like your counsel on a matter of some importance."

While the men from the Diamond B looked confused, they did not see Kelly's right hand grab hold of the whip handle.

After a moment, Kelly nodded to the heavens before looking back at Bledsoe and smiling. "She's a wise woman, my Mary is. Wiser now that she is in the next world than she was while she was here. I'm a lucky man to have her with me always."

"Is that so?" Bledsoe did not bother to hide his laughter as he said, "What did she say?"

"She pointed out some things that were obvious to me the moment I met you boys but failed to come to mind. Things like the men you brought with you are all cowhands and not accustomed to fighting. What's more, your mounts are fat and soft and used to ranching, which means they're probably not accustomed to the sight or smell of blood. They're liable to kick up quite a fuss when this whip takes out your throat and throw the line of them into great disorder. Your men will be at a worse advantage when I ride over you and set to working on them. They'll get off some shots, sure, but I'm sure I don't need to tell you that it's nearly impossible to hit anything from a panicked horse."

Bledsoe wasn't smiling anymore. "You think one man with a whip can take down eleven armed men?"

"No way to know for certain." He let the whip uncoil. All of the mounts shied when the popper struck the dirt. Kelly knew it sounded too much like the quirt the cattlemen used to tame them. "But it won't matter to you. You'll be dead by then."

Kelly saw Bledsoe eye the whip and the man holding it. "No one's that good."

"I think your men from last night would say otherwise, Mr. Bledsoe."

Kelly watched Bledsoe's hand tremble as he weighed the odds. It was clear that everything in the rancher urged him to go for his gun and put down the mouthy Irishman who had shamed him in front of his boys.

But it was also clear that he was troubled by what Kelly had said and the way he had said it. Bledsoe had seen the condition of his men when they had ridden back to his ranch. They had been cut to ribbons by this man in the dark. Under the light of the harsh Texas sun, matters could be far worse.

Bledsoe's eyes hardened and his hand grew still.

And Kelly knew his mind was made up.

Kelly tried one last move to avoid bloodshed. He dropped the act and said, "Don't do anything stupid, Bledsoe. I'll ride with you and my boy to town to hand him over to the sheriff if you want. He can face his judgment before the law. That's fair."

"I don't care about what's fair," Bledsoe sneered. "I've got my own law out here."

As the rancher's right hand dropped to his gun, Kelly cut loose with his whip. The popper cracked as it swiped across the rancher's face and took his left eye with it.

Bledsoe screamed as he pulled back on his horse's reins, man and mount howling in pain as he spilled backward from the saddle. The mount screamed, too, causing the cow horses lined up behind it to fight the bits of their riders.

Kelly spurred the Morgan over Bledsoe and rode into the chaos of horses and men from the Diamond B Ranch. He cracked the whip into the crowd and raked deep across the back of a cowhand, causing him to scream out in pain.

Kelly slung the whip down and raked another man across the front. The popper tore into flesh and down into his horse's neck. The animal buckled, bringing its rider down to the dirt with it.

When a gunshot rang out from his left, instinct and habit caused Kelly to snap his whip in that direction. The curved end of the popper snagged in a rider's hand before Kelly yanked it free, taking a good chunk of the man's wrist and hand with it.

Men and horses were in wide-eyed panic. The smell of blood and gunpowder mixed with the sounds of screams from man and beast filled the air as more shots rang out and the horrible snap of Kelly's whip cracked along the flatlands.

When it was over, six of Bledsoe's men and one horse lay bleeding or dead in the Texas dust. Only four of the men, who'd had the good sense to break free from the melee, were left unharmed and intact. Kelly saw one of those men was Rance, the foreman of the Diamond B. The man had more sense than his boss.

William Kelly brought the Morgan about and faced the men who had clustered together a fair distance away. "Any of you boys want to jump in with your boss here? Who else wants to fall before my lash today?"

Four men and horses shied away from the Irishman whose clean-shaven face was caked in dirt and blood.

"No fight in any of you?" Kelly yelled at them.

The men said nothing, but did nothing, either.

"Well, don't just sit there like a bunch of idiots!" Kelly yelled. "If you're not in the fight, dump your irons in the dirt. Do it now before I ride over there and take my lash to the lot of you!"

The men quickly got rid of their pistols and held up their hands. Rance was the last of the men to do both.

Kelly noticed the right side of one of the riders' pants leg was wet. He had obviously lost control of his bladder during the fight. Kelly singled him out for what was to come next. "You! Climb down and come over here to take the guns from the rest of these men. Pile them up over there."

The frightened man did as he was told but was moving too slowly for Kelly's liking. He cracked the whip, bringing it within an inch of the man's head. "And be quick about it, or by God, I'll take out your throat!"

The man moved with greater speed now, pulling the pistols from the holsters of his fallen friends and throwing them as far away as he could manage.

The horse who had pinned its rider beneath it had regained its footing and began to run away. "You. Grab that mount, boy."

The frightened man managed to snatch the horse's rein and bring it under some sort of control. The rest of the horses had scattered far and wide and were probably halfway back to the Diamond B Ranch by now.

Kelly looked down at the hurt and dying men lying all around him. He had not been able to see the damage he had wrought while the battle was happening, but now that things had quieted down some, he could see it all clearly enough.

The man who had been crushed by his horse was at such an angle that it was impossible for him to still be alive. Another had rolled up into a ball as he held his belly where the popper had sliced him. Kelly knew the man would not last the night.

The man who had lost his hand to Kelly's whip was cradling a bloody stump. Kelly had taken the hand cleanly, as he had wanted. Another three men were trying to get to their feet as the wounds to their backs and shoulders and chests bled freely.

Kelly figured that the three who had scrapes on their backs and chests might live. The man who had lost his hand and the man with the belly wound would surely die, likely from the infections that would take root in their festering wounds over the next several days.

But Kelly knew that every man who had ridden for the Diamond B that day would remember what happened to the men foolish enough to cross William Bull Kelly. He hoped that would be enough to end this foolishness once and for all.

Much of that would depend on the man who had led them here.

Kelly brought his Morgan about and found Bledsoe where he had left him, sitting in the dirt, whimpering as he held his hands to stem the bleeding from his ruined eye. "You blinded me, you filthy Irish bastard! You blinded me!"

Kelly cut loose with the whip, snapping it less than an inch from the rancher's face. Bledsoe shrieked and fell on his back.

"I'm not a bastard," Kelly said as he brought the whip back. "Make that mistake again and I'll take your other eye out of your head. Now, tell me it's over."

"Is what over?" Bledsoe yelled.

Kelly grabbed his whip tightly. "Your quarrel with me, damn you. Is it over?"

With his remaining eye, Bledsoe looked at the carnage that was spread out around him. Three men dead or dying. Three more limping away with bloody shirts and clothes. The remaining men too far away on horseback to do any good. Rance was holding them back. Bledsoe would deal with them later. "There's no one left to fight. You've either hurt or killed most of my men."

Kelly cracked the whip, making Bledsoe cry out again. "Damn it, man. I want to hear you say it! I want your men to hear you say it! Tell them it's over."

The rancher spat as he tried to use his free hand to push himself up into a sitting position. "Yes," he said quietly.

Kelly snapped the whip and brought it across the rancher's legs. "Say it loud enough so all your men can hear it, or I'll take a leg, too."

"I said it's over!" Bledsoe's shriek echoed across the flatlands. "By God, you demon, it's over."

Kelly pointed at the cowhand who had wet himself. "Get your boss here on that horse you're holding." He looked at the rest of the Diamond B men. "I want the rest of you to ride out of here and don't look back, you hear? Go back to wherever you came from and stay there. Take your wounded with you if they can ride and leave your dead where they are. You can come fetch them up tomorrow when we're long gone from this place. But any man who comes back while we're here will face my whip. I've done it once. There's no reason to think I can't do it again. You remember that when thoughts of vengeance creep into your mind tonight."

The frightened cowhand struggled to pull the horse behind him toward where Bledsoe was. The smell of blood had spooked the animal. The man's wet britches didn't make the task any easier.

Kelly had one final word for Andrew Bledsoe. "I hope you're a man of your word, Bledsoe, because I assure you that I'm a man of mine. Hear me when I say that if you or yours come near me or mine again, the loss of an eye will be a pleasure compared to what you'll suffer under my whip then."

Kelly pulled the great Morgan backward as the cowhand helped Bledsoe struggle up and into the saddle one-handed as he covered his wounded eye.

When the rancher was finally in the saddle, Kelly could not resist the urge to visit one last indignity upon him. He cracked the whip, causing Bledsoe's horse to take off at a gallop back toward the ranch. The rancher was barely able to hold on to the saddle horn with his one good hand while he covered his bleeding eye with the other.

The three remaining riders waited for the wet one to take his horse before they began riding double with their wounded comrades.

One of them hung back from the rest of the group. Kelly recognized him as the one Bledsoe had called Rance, his top hand. He remained for a moment while the others fled back to the Diamond B. Perhaps it was to get another look at the man who had laid his ranch so low. Perhaps so he could fix Kelly's image in his mind for a later date.

Kelly was not certain of anything except that Rance and his men were on the losing side. What's more was they knew it. Kelly could tell this man was not used to being on the bottom of the pile and was thinking about doing something about it.

But Kelly knew he would not do anything about it that day. For today belonged to him, and in Texas, today was all that mattered because it was all that anyone really had. Rance had been smart enough to hold himself and his men in reserve while Kelly cut down his boss and his comrades. He would not be dumb enough to force the issue now.

Slowly, the foreman of the Diamond B turned his horse and followed the others back toward the ranch.

Kelly held his ground until he saw that Rance and the others were well out of sight in the distance before he turned the big Morgan and began to ride back toward his herd.

He was not surprised to see Concho standing alone at the top of the rise, watching over all that had happened.

"How much of that did you see?" Kelly asked his friend in Spanish.

"I saw enough," Concho said.

"Then you saw plenty."

His friend nodded. "Just like Fremantle."

Kelly was not so sure of that. "Fewer men this time. Much less blood."

"Same result," Concho reminded him.

But Bull Kelly had not needed to be reminded of that day from so long ago. The day he had finally regained his freedom.

He looked back at the two dead men lying in the dirt. The man with the gash in his stomach had succumbed to his wounds and had been left behind by his friends. The man who had been crushed by his horse was still as dead as he had been a few moments before. Bledsoe's men had somehow managed to take the man with the missing hand with them, though Kelly didn't understand why. Any effort to save his life would be wasted.

"Do me a favor," Kelly said to Concho. "Gather up

the pistols I had them surrender and hand them out among our men."

"You're expecting trouble from them?" Concho asked.

"I didn't like the way that foreman looked at me before he rode off," Kelly admitted. "He's not apt to let this go. I want to be ready in case they come back. And if they come back, it'll be tonight. I'd prefer the boys to be ready for anything."

"Consider it done," Concho said. "And what about tomorrow?"

Kelly liked how his friend always thought a day in advance. "Tomorrow, I want to put thirty miles or more between us and this very spot. I know it'll mean some awfully hard riding for us and the animals, but I don't want another run-in with the Diamond B if we can avoid it."

"Thirty miles won't be far enough to escape trouble," Concho said. "Not the kind of trouble you started here today."

"Not after I did what I *had* to do here today, my friend," Kelly said. "Those boys were going to kill me."

Concho shrugged. "The difference between words won't be enough to change what happens in the future. You did not stop anything today, William. You only kept the fire from going out."

Kelly looked in the direction the men from the Diamond B had ridden. He was glad they were already tiny black dots on the shimmering horizon of the flatlands. "If Bledsoe's as smart as his old man used to be, he'll be smart enough to leave us alone."

Concho looked in their direction, too. "And if he's not as smart as his father?"

"Then I'll feed him and his men to the same fire we started today."

"I hope it does not come to that, my friend. For all of our sakes."

The cook spurred his horse and rode down the rise as he reluctantly began to collect the guns, just as Kelly had told him to do.

Kelly rode back toward his herd, intent on getting the outfit moving as quickly as possible. He was sure the men would have plenty of questions about all of the blood on his face and his clothes and whip. He imagined young Greenly would have the most questions of all. But for once, they would not find Bull Kelly in a talkative mood.

There was far too much work to do to waste time talking. They had to get moving and fast.

CHAPTER TWELVE

THE MEN OF the Diamond B had ridden few miles from the cow camp before Rance noticed that Bledsoe had sagged in the saddle, barely holding on with one hand on the saddle horn.

Rance moved his mount next to Bledsoe and grabbed hold of the rancher's arm to keep him from tumbling to the ground.

"Everybody hold up a minute," Rance yelled to the fleeing group. "Mr. Bledsoe needs some tending to."

He pulled his horse up short and Mr. Bledsoe's mount along with it. He climbed down and slowly eased his boss out of the saddle, placing him on the ground as gently as he could manage.

The wound from Bledsoe's eye socket was too gory for him to look at for long, but he forced himself to look at it for his boss's sake. Rance was no doctor, but he had seen how fast a bleeding wound could cost a man his life.

Rance tore off the sleeve of his own shirt before pulling out his knife to cut it in half. Even from this distance, he could feel the heat already radiating off his boss's body. He could tell Mr. Bledsoe was already out of his mind with fever.

"What are you stopping for, you cowards?" Bledsoe yelled to the hurt and wounded and scared men who had crowded around him. "There's no reason to stop now. Get back on your horses and go after them. Hit them now when they'll least expect it. We have the element of surprise. That's the way, boys. That's the way."

Rance tried to hold his boss still as he packed the wound with half of his sleeve. "Just stay easy, sir. You've been hurt really bad. I aim to save you, but you need to hold still while I go to work on you."

"Hold still?" Bledsoe winced as Rance wrapped a piece of his sleeve around the left side of his head to cover his eye. "How do you expect me to hold still, you fool? Did you see all of the men he killed? How many of us he wounded? How do you expect me to sit still while I have a band of murdering outlaws on my doorstep?"

Rance ignored his boss's rantings as he wrapped the rest of his sleeve tight around Bledsoe's head. The bandage might not have looked pretty, but he hoped it would be enough to decrease the bleeding until they got back to the Diamond B. He hoped one of the men they had left behind at the ranch to tend to the cattle knew how to handle a wound like this. If they did not, Mr. Bledsoe would be in a hell of a fix. He wondered if Rita, the house cook, or Miguel, her husband, might know how to take care of Mr. Bledsoe's wound.

But Rance was not so sure there was much that could be done for an eye wound. He imagined it either stopped bleeding or it did not. He had seen plenty of men live with one eye, so he wondered how serious it was to Mr. Bledsoe's health.

Physically, he would probably live. But mentally was something else entirely. For the first time since he had come to the Diamond B, Rance sincerely began to fear for the ranch's future.

He might not have liked Bledsoe very much, but he had taken enough of the man's money over the years to feel some kind of loyalty to him. And if not to him, then to the ranch he owned. The ranch that had saved his life a long time ago.

If there was a way to keep Mr. Bledsoe alive, Rance would find a way to do it.

Although the remaining men had stopped riding, none of them had dismounted, not even those riding double. It was as if they were afraid to climb down from their horses. One of them said, "Can't you hurry up with those bandages, Rance? I want to get as far away from here as I can. That old man back there is plumb crazy."

Another said, "If that old coot comes riding out after us, snapping that whip of his like he can, he's liable to cut all of us to ribbons now."

"Some of us are hurt pretty bad, too, Rance," said another. "I'd sure like my cuts tended to."

Rance cursed them under his breath. "The man who pays your wages is in a bad way, boys. If you're not going to help me, then just stand there and be quiet."

"None of us would be in this shape, including him, if it wasn't for his stupid idea to rile up Kelly in the first place."

Since coming to the Diamond B years before, Rance had worked hard on controlling his temper, but he turned on the men now. "Then get going, you bunch of cowards! This man pays your wages. He owns the roof over your head. If you can't fight for him, the least you can do is stand watch over him while I fix him up so that he's fit for travel. The man lost an eye!"

"And we lost men," said another. "Good men. Friends of ours. Some of us are cut deep. Randy over here lost his hand. And for what? All on account of Mr. Bledsoe not having the good sense to leave that crazy old man alone."

Randy held up a bandaged hand that had already begun to bleed through the piece of shirt he had wrapped around it. "We know where our wages come from, Rance, but he's not going to have a ranch left, much less hands to work it, if we don't get ourselves back home and patch ourselves up. I know he's hurt, but I've got wounds that need tending to myself."

Rance cursed everyone and no one. He cursed Mr. Bledsoe for getting the men in this fix. Men who were not ready to go up against the likes of Bull Kelly. He cursed himself for not being able to find a way to talk Bledsoe out of it in the first place. He cursed that madman with the whip and the trouble he had stirred up for the Diamond B.

But he knew the men were right about having

wounds of their own that needed tending to and saw no reason why they should suffer any more than they already had. "The rest of you better head on back to the ranch. I'll take care of Mr. Bledsoe myself and be along in a bit."

One of the men asked, "You sure you can get him back in the saddle alone?"

"I'll drape him across if I have to. Now get going, all of you! The sooner you bunch get yourselves patched up, the faster you'll be able to tend Mr. Bledsoe's cattle and keep the Diamond B in business." He stood as he took off his hat and swiped one of the horses on the backside with it. "Go on! Move!"

Rance did not wait to watch the horses run off before he returned to Mr. Bledsoe's side. In his delirium, the rancher had tried to undo the bandage Rance had just wrapped around his head, but he passed out before he could undo it. Rance feared his boss had died until he saw the man's chest rise and fall in a jagged breath.

He placed his hand against Mr. Bledsoe's forehead and felt he was burning up. Rance had not seen the whip up close, but he could tell Kelly had not cleaned it on a regular basis. Only God knew how many germs were on the end of that thing. Any number of poisons could be coursing their way through Mr. Bledsoe's body at this very moment. If an infection took hold, it could go anywhere in his body, even to his brain. That would surely kill him.

There was not a moment to lose.

Rance tied the bandage as tight as he dared and pulled Mr. Bledsoe to his feet. He didn't know if it was instinct or if his boss was more aware than he appeared, but Rance took it as a good sign that Bledsoe put his foot in the stirrup on his own power. But there was no way Rance could count on the rancher staying in the saddle on his own power and he knew he would have to ride double.

After helping his boss get set, Rance grabbed the reins of Bledsoe's horse before he climbed into the saddle behind him. He spurred the horse toward the Diamond B. The trail horse followed. With two riders on her back, the mare would not be able to move at much more than a trot, but it beat walking.

Rance only hoped they would get back to the ranch in time to keep Mr. Bledsoe from dying.

CHAPTER THIRTEEN

NONE OF THE men of the Kelly outfit looked happy when Concho began to hand out the pistols he had collected from the men of the Diamond B.

"I've already got a pistol, Pa," Jeremiah said, "and I hardly ever use it. What do I need another one for?"

"Because a loaded pistol's a good thing to have whether you need it or not."

Kelly had a Navy Colt tucked in a sash around his waist. He had never been much for using guns or rifles, so he did not own a holster. And the thought of taking a holster off one of the men he killed made him feel like a vulture. "We might have trouble coming our way for the next few days, boys. I figure it might do us some good to have extra lead at hand to shoot back with should the need arise."

"Trouble." Joel pointed at James. "Trouble *he* brought down on us.

Joshua joined him in sneering at James, whose

eyes had swollen shut from his beatings at the hands of the Diamond B men and turned an ugly shade of purple. Kelly knew the boy could still see, but not well enough to warrant giving him a gun.

"James had his fun," Joshua said, "and the rest of us have to pay for it. Same as always."

"That's enough," Kelly yelled at his boys. "That's enough from all of you. It doesn't matter who started what or why. What's done is done. All that matters is how it ends and who ends it. I intend on us being the ones who bring this to a close if there's a close to be brought to it at all."

He looked at each man in the outfit. His sons and the men he had hired on for the drive. He looked each of them in the eye as he said, "I know this is more than some of you thought you were signing on for, but every drive I've ever been on has had some bad breaks here and there. Blood has been spilled and men have died. Men I've killed. If you don't want to ride with us any longer, you can draw your wages now and head on back to El Paso without a word said."

"Draw against what, boss?" Baxter asked. "You didn't have much to start with, and after paying off those two from last night, you've got even less."

Kelly had already thought of that. "I'll have to ask you to take my marker on that. You'll get a quarter share of what we sell this beef for at market, which is fair considering we're only about a quarter of the way there."

Some of the men grumbled and exchanged glances as Kelly continued. "I know it's not the best, but it's the best I can do for now. If any man wants to leave,

I won't hold it against him. But now's the time, and I won't hear of anyone leaving once we get rolling again. Not tonight, not until we get to Dodge City."

He kept looking at each man in turn, but none of them said a word. None of them even moved.

Kelly forced a smile. "You're good lads, the lot of you. It's settled." He spoke to James. "When you were playing poker with those two Diamond B boys, you get any idea of how close their ranch is to here?"

James slowly shook his swollen head. "I wish I knew, Pa, but I don't. I guess I'm the one who did most of the talking. But given how fast they rode out to block our trail this morning, I'd say their ranch has to be pretty close by. I didn't see any gear on them, so they didn't camp out overnight. I know we put thirty miles between us and them since this morning, but I'd wager we're still probably pretty close to their ranch."

"You'd wager?" Joshua laid into his brother again. "Your wagering is what's gotten us into this mess."

"That's enough," Kelly yelled.

"Hell, I'm the youngest. I'm supposed to be the dumb one. Not you. Some big brother you turned out to be."

James simply stood by the campfire and looked into the flames.

Kelly stepped in front of Joshua. "You're beginning to sound like you're whining, lad. You know I don't abide whiners in my outfit, especially when they're blood." He took a step closer to the boy. "You a whiner, son?"

Joshua stepped back and looked at the ground. "No, Pa. I'm not whining."

"Glad to hear it, because you're in the same fix as me and every man in this outfit." He looked at all the men again. "None of us asked for this trouble, but here it is, knocking on our front door. If we live through this night, chances are it means that Bledsoe and his men have learned their lesson and will leave us alone. They'll have to ride sixty miles after us by the time we make camp tomorrow night. Bledsoe's shorter on men today than he was yesterday and he still needs to leave behind men to tend the cattle he's got. What's more is he has lost an eye and is in a poor way. That's not the kind of thing a man just patches up and gets over quickly."

"You showed him, Pa," Jeremiah said, to cheers from the entire outfit. "You showed all of them what happens when a man crosses Bull Kelly."

"I didn't show him anything," Kelly said over the cheers of his men. "I showed him up in front of his men. I hurt his pride more than I hurt his body. I'm not proud of that and none of you should be, either. A man is at his most dangerous when his pride has been hurt. So, if they decide to come after us, to-night's the night they'll do it. We'll have to make sure we're ready for them if they do. All of us. Together. Not bickering like a bunch of old hens in a chicken coop."

He looked his men over. "I know most of you aren't Kellys, but you're Kelly men riding with the Kelly brand. It just so happens we don't have much of a brand just yet, but we'll get around to that once we reach Dodge City. But whether you be blood kin or hired men, we're all one now. We've all got the same dreams of heading out of Texas and starting a new life somewhere. For me, it's putting all them years I spent on the trail to good use by spending what time I have left with my boys. Some of you might want other things. But none of us will get anything that we want unless we stick together and fight off this bunch with everything we have the best as we can. Do you understand me, boys?"

"We're with you, sir," Baxter said. "If they're foolish enough to come at us, we'll be ready. I think we ought to post a double watch tonight to make sure they don't try to run off any of our herd while we're sleeping."

"Sounds like sound thinking to me. Baxter, I'm putting you in charge of handing out assignments. We'll all take double watches except for James. He can't see all that well in his current state, but I'll be up most of the night anyway, so I'll shoulder his responsibilities."

But James would not hear of it. "I'll stand watch just like any man here, Pa. I can still see and, what's more, I can hear." He looked at his father. "But they won't come, Pa. You hurt more than their pride today. You took them down and hurt them bad. That's a sting that'll last a long time."

The outfit whooped and hollered and patted James on the back. Kelly was glad to see their spirits were high, but he doubted any of them knew what they were talking about.

Kelly had seen the look in Bledsoe's good eye and had recognized it for what it was. He had seen the way Rance had looked at him before riding away. Kelly knew he had done more than beat them in a fight and killed some of their men. Bledsoe had lost more than an eye that day. He had lost his pride in front of his men. No man whose family has forged a ranch out of the wilderness would allow some foreigner to ride through his land and make a fool out of him.

He doubted Bledsoe would let that go. But if the possibility made his men feel better about the night ahead, so be it. "We don't know what the night will bring us, lads. All we know is that we need to be ready for it, come what may. If you hear them coming, don't be brave. Let off a shot so we know they're here. If they start shooting, find cover and shoot back when you can. We've few bullets between us, so make every shot count. Only shoot if you have something to hit. Firing blind will only make things worse."

"What if they stampede the cattle?" young Greenly asked.

"Get out of the way if they do. I know none of you are gunmen, so the pistols are only to be used if you absolutely need them to save yourselves. Don't fight for the cattle. I mean that. I wouldn't trade a herd twice this size for a single life among you." He looked at his second-oldest son. "Not even James's sorry existence."

He was glad all of the men, including James, took it as the joke he had intended. Laughter was the best medicine for the fear that ailed the outfit now.

"Be about your posts, men," he told them, "and keep a sharp eye in the darkness." He looked up at the darkening, cloudy sky. "I'm afraid we can't count on much help from Sister Moon up there, but trust the ears of your mounts and the mettle of your friends. With God's help, we'll all wake up tomorrow and put thirty further miles between us and the Diamond B."

He thanked the men for their attention and went back toward the spot he had chosen to place his bedroll.

"Pa," James called out to him, and trotted after him, wincing as the effort of it made his sore bones ache. "What do you really think is going to happen tonight? With Bledsoe, I mean."

Kelly let out a long breath he had been holding for the sake of the men. James was wild and reckless, but when it came to horses and cattle, he was as steady a hand as any trail boss could hope for. "I think Bledsoe had someone patch up that eye of his and he's charging right for us as we speak, with fresh mounts and as many men as he has left."

"After the number he lost today," James said, "between the hurt and dead, I can't imagine he could scrape up more than half a dozen men willing or able to come back here."

"And I'd wager the ten he rode out here with today were likely the best of the bunch," Kelly added. "But sense doesn't always factor into things like this, boy. Not when pride's involved. Pride can make a man do some awfully foolish things."

"We'll fight them if they come, Pa. We'll fight them with everything we got. No one's going to take a single head from the Kelly herd if we have anything to say about it."

Kelly looked out on the mass of cattle grazing in the near distance beneath a gray sky. It would be dark soon and that's when the real terror would begin until the sun rose the next morning.

Kelly knew he should feel pride in his herd. He should feel some sense of ownership over them. A willingness to fight to the last to keep them alive. To keep what he had built for himself for once.

But to him, the smelly things had always merely been a means to an end. Cows and bulls were a commodity simply to be brought to market and sold for the highest going rate, just like the gold and silver he had dug out of the ground in Arizona and New Mexico so long ago.

These cows were to be turned into money so he could make all those years spent away from his family actually mean something in his final days.

And he knew his grip on it all was a tenuous one at best.

"Bledsoe doesn't need a lot of men to wreck us," Kelly said. "It only takes one man with a pistol to set an entire herd to running."

"We ran them pretty hard today, Papa," James reminded him. "They're mighty tired and more than a bit hungry. They're less apt to bolt than you might think."

James pointed over at Hell. The longhorn bull was separate from the rest of the herd, standing on a higher rise looking over them all. "If that mean old bastard sticks, the rest of them will stick, too. And so will we."

Kelly did not like hearing his son talk this way. "I meant what I said back there in front of the others, James. If there's shooting, I want everyone to get out of the way and let it take its course. That means you, too." He took hold of his son's arm. "I'll not lose a single man over a head of beef and I'll be damned if I lose a son because of it. We're still close enough to home that we can head back and round up another herd to drive north if we need to, but I can't replace a man, least of all a son."

James flashed the grin that had broken the hearts of ladies all over Texas once upon a time but was ruined now by the scars that crossed his face. "You want us to run. Like you ran from Bledsoe today? Come on, Pa. You can't fool me."

Kelly surprised his son by snatching him by the shirt and pulling him toward him as though the boy was a rag doll. "I only did what I had to do to stay alive, boy. Bledsoe would've gunned me down dead if I hadn't hit him first. His men would've killed me had I given them the chance. That was different. You're different." He pulled the young man even closer, his jaw tight. "You're not me and a gun's not the same as a whip, especially in my hands. When I said I expect you boys to run if they come, I mean it. You've never killed a man, James. It's not as easy a weight to carry around as you might think."

He had not meant to be so rough with the boy, but the glint in his son's eyes scared him. He gently let him go and smoothed down his son's shirt. "Glory's for the living, James. It doesn't do the dead much good. You'll heed me, now, and you'll see to it the others do, too, won't you? For me?"

James slowly backed away from his father. "Of course, Papa. Leave it to me."

Kelly watched his son walk back to join the others. James was a full-grown man now, but still had the wild dreams of a boy seeking adventure. Like Kelly himself had once been on his family's small farm back in Longford. Back when the world was one big adventure just waiting to be had. Back before life had shown him her true and ugly side. Before London. Before Fremantle and everything that had happened in between.

William Kelly looked up at the darkening sky and closed his eyes. "Ah, Mary, darlin'. How I wished we could have raised them up together. You did the best as you could, God knows, but they've too much of me and not enough of you in them. I should've been making a life with you instead of spending all those years trying to pay for it."

He suddenly felt older than he ever had before as he trudged back to the bedroll he had set out for himself away from the bulk of the herd. He would be helping to stand watch that night and decided to grab a few hours of rest beforehand.

And as he walked back to his bedroll, he could not help feeling alone and small beneath the uncaring Texas sky.

CHAPTER FOURTEEN

"G ET OFF ME, woman," Bledsoe shouted at Rita. "I've got me some killing to do!"

The Mexican maid recoiled from the bed as she set the bowl of bloody water on the dresser.

Rance figured the pretty young Mexican cook was recoiling as much from Bledsoe's rage as she was from the sight of his horrible wound.

"Get out of here and let me do it myself," he bellowed after her as she ran from the room.

Rance had been impressed by the young Mexican woman's grit. He would have laid even money that she would have gotten sick when she undid the bandage around Bledsoe's eye. But she had not gotten sick. She stuck by him and did her best to tend to him while he raved about all of the horrible things he was going to do to Bull Kelly. It would have been downright terrible had there been any weight behind it.

But as he heard the rancher continue to rant and

rave about the revenge he would take on the Kelly outfit, Rance was beginning to think that Bledsoe had already begun to lose his mind.

He watched Bledsoe push himself out of bed and get to his feet. He stumbled over to the mirror at his dresser and began to examine the socket where his eye had once been. Rance had to look away.

The few glimpses he had caught of the wound told him that Kelly's whip had done an effective job of stripping the socket bare. He had no idea how the Irishman had been so precise with a whip, but there was no doubting his skill.

"Damned Mexicans," Bledsoe cursed. "I ought to take a whip to her for all of her prodding and poking."

"She was just tending to your wounds, boss," Rance said. "She's a good woman and Miguel's good with the horses. He's got a gift. Don't go taking your anger out on them."

He saw Bledsoe glare at him with his good eye. "I suppose you'd prefer me to take it out on you, then?"

"Not particularly," Rance said. "No need for you to take it out on anyone. You ought to be in bed, resting and getting better."

"Resting." Bledsoe began tending to his wound. "What good will resting do? Will resting help me grow a new eye? I'll rest when I'm dead."

Rance had to admit he had never seen a man so close to death rebound so quickly. The boss had lost an eye and more blood than Rance thought a man had in him. He had suffered from a raging fever since before they had gotten back to the Diamond B. Yet, despite all of that, not only was Mr. Bledsoe already on his feet, he was mad. Fighting mad.

Before Rance was able to coax him back into bed, where Rita could tend to his wounds, Mr. Bledsoe was getting ready for something. For what, he did not dare wonder.

Rance watched him replace the packing Rita had used on the wound and readjust it. It looked so painful, but Bledsoe seemed to have already grown accustomed to it. He supposed a man could get accustomed to an awful lot of unpleasantness if he found himself without a choice in the matter.

Bledsoe surprised him by saying, "I want you to saddle me a fresh horse. Now."

But Rance stayed where he was. "Sir, you're in no shape to stand, much less ride."

"And I'm in no shape to just sit here like a dying calf while that Kelly bastard is roaming free on my land." He held the back of his hand to his own forehead. "My fever has broken, at least for now, but I'm sure it'll be back. That's why I need to ride now while I still can. I could be dead by morning or in a day or two. By then, they'll have gotten too far away for us to catch up, even if I am still alive."

Rance did not know whether to admire his boss or pity him, so he decided to just tell him the truth. "You might be feeling better right now, boss, but you've lost a hell of a lot of blood. You need to let your body rest and heal up. It's got nothing to do with you being strong or weak. It's got to do with you having enough blood in you to stand on your own two feet without falling over. It's bad enough if it happens while you're standing. You could break your neck if you fall off a horse."

"I've been riding horses since before I could

walk," Bledsoe said as he re-dressed his wound. "I don't need you to tell me anything about riding. And I'm not aware of your degree in medicine, Rance." He laughed. "Besides, I should think I know myself better than you or anyone else does."

But Rance realized Mr. Bledsoe did not really look like Mr. Bledsoe anymore. He looked like an angry, broken version of the man he had seen drinking coffee on his porch just that morning.

He had lurched around the ranch house stooped over and sore from the fall when Kelly's whip had knocked him from his horse. Rance could not be sure, but he looked like he had broken a couple of ribs in the fall, maybe even a shoulder.

The gaping hole where his eye had once been now only served to make him look even more horrifying. It was almost impossible to look at him now without gagging, but he had no choice.

"I never claimed to be a doctor," Rance said, "but I've got plenty of common sense. You weren't ready to go up against Kelly when you were at your best and you're not going to be able to take him now that you're hurt."

He was prepared to receive the full brunt of Bledsoe's rage, which he knew from experience could be considerable. But Bledsoe seemed to be too preoccupied with his wound to allow emotion to interfere. "You let me worry about me and you worry about getting my horse saddled. And where do I keep my spare cartridges for my Winchester? If you don't get them for me, I'll just walk over to the bunkhouse and borrow some from the boys."

Rance reluctantly opened the cabinet door where

the shells were kept and tossed a box of them on the bed.

"I would stay out of the bunkhouse right now if I were you, Mr. Bledsoe," Rance said. "You're not all that popular with the men."

"I'll get plenty popular with them again once payday rolls around," Bledsoe said as he set about unrolling a new bandage. Rance admitted the rancher was a bit easier to look at now that he had packed his eye socket. "And after they help me win back the honor of the Diamond B that we lost today, they'll be singing songs about me around the campfire. You, too, Rance, if you're up for it."

He looked at the reflection of his foreman in the mirror. "But judging by the look on your face, I'd say you'd prefer to stay here in front of a warm fire with a blanket across your legs instead of fighting like a man."

Rance looked up at his boss, hardly able to control his disappointment and anger. "You want to talk about men, sir? Men got hurt today. Three died. Our men. Your men. *You* got hurt today. You lost an eye and got busted up when you fell. I don't even know what's keeping you on your feet right now. Maybe God, maybe the devil himself. I don't know which. But I do know that there's no good that can come out of you riding out after the Kelly outfit tonight."

"I'll suffer more if I don't go, Rance. And that's the truth of it."

The more he heard Bledsoe talk, the more he feared his boss was no longer just raving. He was serious. "Leave Kelly and his men be, sir. We've tangled enough with them for one day. In a week, we won't even remember they were here."

Bledsoe turned and glared at Rance with his good eye while the missing one remained half-bandaged and bloody. "Maybe you'll be able to forget and maybe the men's wounds will heal, and memories will fade." He pointed at his missing eye. "But this won't fade, Rance, and it won't heal even after it stops bleeding. No matter how far Kelly rides away from here, no matter how much I might want to forget about what he did to me, I will never forget because I'll have to look at this every single day for the rest of my life."

He turned back toward the mirror. "Hell, I don't know if I'd want to forget it even if I could. No man has the right to ride onto my land and do something like this to me. No man, do you hear? There's only one language a man like Bull Kelly understands and that's loss. He took my eye away from me, so I'll take his cattle. And I'll take more than that if I can."

Rance had been looking down at the floor during Bledsoe's tirade. Not because he was difficult to look at, but because he could not bear to see a man who had once been so proud lose himself in such senseless rage.

There was only one other way he could think of that might stop Bledsoe from throwing his life away on an empty cause. "If I can't make you listen to reason, maybe I can make you understand facts. This ranch lost almost half of its men today, sir. Half, either dead or hurt or shaken up by what happened out there. Let that number sit with you a spell. They're either dead or laid up so bad, they won't be able to ride for a week or more. Randy lost a hand and probably won't live out the night."

"Many's a man who has worked cattle that has lost

a hand," Bledsoe said as he began wrapping the bandage over his eye. "Daddy had Stumpy, who lost his arm in the war, and he was his best worker."

Rance remembered Stumpy, who had been like a father to him when he had first joined the ranch years before. "He was good enough to ride roughshod over cattle but wouldn't have been much good in a gunfight. He sure as hell would not have been someone I'd take along going up against the likes of Bull Kelly. And remembering Stumpy doesn't change the fact that half of your men are down—hurt, sick, or worse. Even the four of us you ordered to hang back don't have the stomach to ride after Kelly in the light of day, much less now in the dead of night."

"Is that your way of telling me you're scared of Kelly?"

"Damned right I am. Why, he did things with that whip I didn't think possible. And he showed more guts than any man I've seen in a long time, maybe ever."

"Then stay here. I'll take the men who didn't ride with us today and do what needs doing."

"It's not just about tonight, sir. It's about your ranch. The men who weren't with us will be run ragged while tending to the cows we already have. Even if we were able to grab Kelly's cows, we just don't have the men to tend to them right now, so why bother taking them?"

Bledsoe waved him off and kept wrapping the bandage flat and tight against the left side of his head. "I reckon I've got enough land for twenty thousand head if I want it. Even with every last cow Kelly's got, we'll be well below that. They can free-graze until our men are healthy enough to tend to them. Wherever the herd goes, they'll most likely be on my land anyway, so what's the difference?"

Rance could tell by Bledsoe's tone of voice that he had thought this over and his mind was made up. He tried one last tactic before admitting defeat. "I told you before, these men aren't fighters, sir. If they wanted that kind of life, they wouldn't have signed on to punch cows like they have. You're asking a draft horse to run a race against purebreds."

"No," Bledsoe said. "I'm ordering men I pay to do what I tell them to do. And tonight, I'm telling them we're taking the Kelly herd. And that's all I have to say on the matter, Rance."

"Rearing cows is a lot different than fighting men, sir. That's a different kind of work."

Bledsoe flattened the bandage against the side of his head. "The kind of work you used to do once upon a time, if I remember correctly."

Rance saw no reason to remember things he had done decades before. "Things I haven't done in years, and for good reason. Those reasons are why I work for you."

Bledsoe turned away from the mirror and admired his handiwork. "I always did have a knack for patching up wounds. It's like the old saying goes, Rance. If you want something done right, do it yourself."

He reached for his Winchester that had been left leaning against the wall and took the box of cartridges Rance had thrown on the bed earlier. "I know you were a bad man once, Rance. I'm asking you to be one again, if you haven't lost your nerve. And I don't think you have." The rancher smiled at him. "I

think the only thing you're afraid of is that you might
fall back into your old habits. Might get to liking it
again. Perhaps too much."

He began feeding fresh rounds into his rifle. "Well,
don't worry about that, Rance. There's plenty of work
around here to keep you busy enough. No fear of you
slipping back into your wicked ways. We'll keep you
on the straight and narrow."

Rance had heard enough. He grabbed Bledsoe by
the arm and looked him in the eye. "You lost, sir.
You've paid a terrible price, but it doesn't mean the
end of us. Everyone goes up against someone better
than him eventually. I know I did before I came here
and it damned near cost me my life. Today, it cost you
an eye. Be grateful it wasn't worse. But it can get
plenty worse if you tangle with Kelly again with the
group you've got. It'll mean killing and none of these
boys can live with that. Not even you." He let go of
Bledsoe's arm. "Losing's not an easy thing to live
with. Believe me, I know."

Bledsoe shook some blood back into his arm and
began feeding more cartridge into the Winchester.
"You're a good man, Rance. Daddy always said that
taking you in was one of the best decisions he had
ever made, and he was right. But he wouldn't be able
to rest easy if he knew his boy had taken the loss of
an eye sitting down. I couldn't live with it, either. I
know killing a man is no easy thing, but it's war-
ranted in this case."

Bledsoe patted Rance feebly on the arm. "I'm already a dead man, Rance. I'll ride out alone if I have
to. I want you to saddle my horse like I asked you and
get me as many able-bodied men to ride with me as

you can. Even if it's one or two. I want them ready to
go within the hour. If you don't get anyone, then it'll
just be you and me. And if you decide not to come,
I'll understand. But I'm going, Rance. Either Kelly
dies tonight, or I die. I guess I don't care much about
what happens anymore. Best be on about your business. You've got a lot of work to do."

Rance slowly walked out of Mr. Bledsoe's bedroom and quietly shut the door behind him.

For the first time since coming to the Diamond B
as an angry young pup, Rance was not sure about
what he was going to do next.

Saddle his horse and find some men, he thought to
himself. It was a crazy idea, but Mr. Bledsoe's mind
was made up and there was no talking him out of it.
Even if he won, it would probably mean the end of
the Diamond B Ranch as Rance knew it. If it was going to end, then it might as well end the best way it
could.

He walked outside and headed toward the bunkhouse to do exactly that.

CHAPTER FIFTEEN

JAMES KELLY IGNORED his aching wounds as he stood watch over the herd. The heat of the day had faded quickly after sundown, leaving the north Texas sky streaked with deep purples and pinks and oranges that were almost too beautiful to describe. The cattle quietly rustled about as they fed on grass. A calf skipped between the legs of the cows. It was moments like these that reminded him how lucky he was to be out here with his family.

The throbbing from his swollen face and cracked ribs reminded him of his foolishness. Like a bad hangover after a night of whiskey, the pain reminded him of the bad decisions he had made. But unlike a hangover, his wounds would not fade after drinking enough water and sleeping it off. The damage he had suffered would be with him tomorrow and for long after his bones and face had healed. His wounds ran deeper than his body. They had reshaped his soul.

Before his run-in with the boys from the Diamond B, James had always thought of the drive as his father's idea and the herd as his father's herd. He had thought of the money they would make from selling it all as his father's money, of which he and his brothers were to get a share whenever his father saw fit to give it to them.

But since surviving the beating, he had come to see the herd as more than just cattle. He saw it as a way to prove to his father that he was worthy of leadership. Worthy of being called a man. His mother often said a proper beating would do him some good and, as usual, she had been proven right.

This was more than just another cattle drive heading north to market. And these cattle were different from any other cattle. All of this was James Kelly's way of proving that he was no longer just the wild son of a legendary trail boss. It was his chance to prove to his father—and to himself—that he had finally grown up. That he was now a man ready to take on a man's responsibilities. Jacob might have been the oldest Kelly son, but all of the brothers had always looked up to James. Even Jacob. He had always known that, just as he knew he had always been his father's favorite. The wild one in any herd usually gets the most attention.

But everyone had to grow up sometime, and James Kelly figured his time was right now. He had gone to town and paid the price for it. Not only him, but the two men who had beaten him had paid a price. Earlier that day, men had died beneath his father's whip.

And all of it because he had decided to go into town one night for a bit of fun. That night had proven to be the most expensive night of his life, for it had cost men limbs. It had cost men lives.

At first, James had been angry at his father when he learned about how he had cut down the men of the Diamond B. How his whip had taken Bledsoe's left eye. He had silently cursed his father for refusing to be reasonable and for always being willing to scar a man for life over a slight, either real or imagined.

But as the reality of all that had happened finally set in, James realized his father was not the problem. His father was nothing if not consistent. His earliest memories of Bull Kelly were of a loving but strict father. A man who had taken his sons to town with him for supplies and ignored the taunts he drew from drunks he had fired on the trail.

If another man had done it, a son could be forgiven for believing his father was a coward. But James Kelly realized he had never thought that about his father. No matter how many jeers he ignored or fights he had walked away from, Bull Kelly never turned his back on the men who hated him. He faced them down until their anger boiled away or the whiskey drowned their courage and they moved on. Even as a boy, he knew fear and he had never sensed it in his father. Ever.

Even when Mama died, Bull Kelly showed more grit than anyone in the family. He had mourned in his own way and remained strong for his sons. James had thought his father had lost his mind when he first heard him speak to her as if she were still there. But he realized it was the only way this man could cope with the loss of his beloved wife.

James knew his father was not to blame for what

had happened over the past two days on the trail. If anything, James was to blame. And his blame was not just due to wanting a break from the trail and a night on the town. His blame was for putting men against a force like Bull Kelly. Men had died because of James Kelly. And James Kelly would have to live with that. Which was why he decided, from now on, he would need to be the kind of son his father wanted him to be. The family looked to him as a leader. Yes, even Jacob. It was time he started acting like one.

When his horse's head jerked up, he knew she had caught the scent of something new on the wind. Nelly was normally a placid animal, but an alert one. Maybe it was a wolf or a deer, but they had not encountered many predators on the drive north. Not the four-legged kind, anyway.

He drew the rifle Concho had given him and laid it across his saddle horn. Something was out there. Something that did not belong. And with the threat of the Diamond B boys still in the air, having the rifle at the ready was not the worst idea he had ever had.

A single shot echoed throughout the flatlands.

The cattle herd began to stir, but James held Nelly in place. Could be one of the men riding watch had shot whatever had spooked his horse. But when a second shot was followed by a third, James knew it was not that simple.

Something was happening. Behind him and to his right.

He brought Nelly about and spurred her on in that direction. If he was going to help his father lead this bunch, it was about time he started acting like it.

CHAPTER SIXTEEN

A S WILLIAM KELLY suffered another night of fitful sleep, his past rode back to him on a tide of blood.

Images and memories buried long ago blurred together in a fever dream of the horror and violence that had once defined his life.

He was back on the gray streets of London choked with people and horse wagons and filth and soot. Ragged men huddled in doorways. Merchants selling fruit and goods he did not have the money to buy. Women older than his mother offering him other things from dark alleyways. The public house where he slaved away as an errand boy, doing every filthy job the proprietor of the place told him to do. The police cracking his skull as they arrested him for killing a man he had never even known. The rotting jail and that stage play they had called a trial that convicted him for a crime he had not committed.

The chains—the unending horror of rattling chains—
that bound him and the other men for countless hours
over countless days, even when they loaded him on the
prison ship bound for Australia. The hell that he had
endured in the belly of the vessel as it was tossed and
thrown by the sea as it made its way down to Fremantle,
Australia.

Even in this, his nightmare, the only sound louder
than the rattle of chains was the sound of the whip
cracking and the men screaming. The whip was
wielded by the ship's jailer, who the men had taken to
calling Old Bones. He was more than a jailer. He was
their tormentor, more evil and vile than anything hell
could threaten. A tall, gaunt man every bit as wretched
as the men he lorded over. He looked like Death itself
to the prisoners chained together in the hold of the
ship. Kelly remembered looking forward to the next
beating, hoping the next would be the one that ended
his life and set him free. He envied the man who had
died next to him and remained chained to him for
three days. The poor soul had remained there until
the stench had grown too much for even Old Bones to
take and they finally threw him overboard.

On the entire voyage down to the land at the end
of the world, Old Bones took pleasure in punishing
these forsaken men with stories of how a prisoner
could win his freedom after a few years of hard labor
in the penal colony. That is, if the snakes and the spi-
ders and the disease that awaited them did not kill
them first. But even that meager hope Old Bones offered them was always quickly drowned out by the
beatings and whippings he doled out to any man who
dared to look at him too long to suit him.

Men like William Kelly.

Kelly's back had felt the lash of Old Bones more than any of the other men under his power, as the jailer chose to reserve his cruelest punishments for the papist scum he had hated so. He had offered Kelly a way out, of course; the same out he had offered to other prisoners, who had willingly taken it. To renounce the Church of Rome and accept the Church of England. Kelly had never been a very religious man, much to the sorrow of his poor mother, but he refused to relent. Not out of any love for the papacy, but because he knew it was what Old Bones wanted. Day after day, he whipped Kelly and demanded renunciation. Kelly responded by spitting blood on his boots. He had stopped praying to God to take him from all of this. Instead, he prayed that he might live long enough to give Old Bones a taste of his own medicine.

God seemed to find that wish easier to grant, for William Kelly did not die. He lived to endure more whippings, more beatings, more indignation than he had ever seen doled out on the beasts of burden back on his father's farm in Longford. He knew that if he was going to survive this ordeal, he could no longer think of himself as a man. He had to adopt the mindset of a beast, which is exactly what he did.

In this, his nightmare, the sea voyage to Fremantle was a blur of pain and blood and death. He remembered forgetting what the sun had looked like, much less how its blessed warmth felt on his skin. His world had shrunk to the dark, dank hell of the ship's hold.

His dreams of seeing the world, once lofty and romantic and exciting, had shriveled to prayers for any god that could hear him for the chance to live until he could kill Old Bones with his bare hands.

Kelly's mind jumped to those first blessed moments when he and the other prisoners had been pulled from the hold and led up to the deck of the prison ship. He cringed, not from fear of another blow from Old Bones's whip, but from the intense heat he felt on his skin. It took him more than a few moments to remember what all of this was. Sun. He drew clean, salty air deep into his lungs. Warmth. The salty ocean wind felt good against his skin, even against the countless welts that now crisscrossed his bare back.

He had not died. He was alive. And he would take his revenge one way or the other.

Not even the whip of Old Bones as he commanded him to get to his feet was enough to take that moment from him. And in that moment of his rebirth, he swore to himself that one day soon, he would take the whip from Old Bones and show him what true pain felt like.

But until that moment presented itself, Kelly knew he would have plenty more pain and horror in store.

At the penal colony, he endured the beatings and the toil of breaking rocks beneath the blazing sun in the place they called Fremantle. The name was a lie. There was nothing free about that place.

Months blurred into another year of pain and blood before Kelly finally saw his chance for the freedom he had dreamed of for so long.

The colony's guards were all drunk from their Christmas merriment and Old Bones himself was more than a bit of the worse for wear. His tormentor was hungover just enough to miss seeing that Kelly was holding a jagged piece of rock he had broken. Not a big rock, but big enough for Kelly to smash it against Old Bones's head and knock his tormentor cold.

The prisoners, led by a Spanish pirate Kelly had come to know as Xavier, used the same tools they had used for so long to break rocks in the quarry to break the chains that had bound them for so long. Now free, the prisoners rushed the drunken guards and used the tools as weapons.

The battle was over before it really started.

But William Kelly did not join in the violent blood lust that had descended on the prison colony. Instead, he picked up the whip Old Bones had dropped when he had fallen. He had never had the chance to see the whip clearly, but now that he held it, a feeling of power coursed through his veins.

The whip was made of kangaroo hide, which Old Bones had often boasted of as being the toughest hide on God's green earth. Much better and far more durable than leather. The countless wounds on Kelly's back could attest to that.

Yes, William Kelly took hold of the whip—the tanned handle feeling good in his hands—and loomed over his jailer. He waited until Old Bones began to stir and open his eyes, so he could see the punishment he was about to receive. The terror in the man's eyes was intoxicating as Kelly slowly set about delivering a fresh kind of horror of his own devising on his old tormentor.

The death screams of his jailer beneath his own lash still filled Kelly's ears during the quietest moments. The memory made the scars that filled his back and his soul ache a little less.

Screams that echoed long after Old Bones was dead. Screams from his nightmare that carried forth through the years to wake him now.

William Kelly bolted upright on his blanket and listened to the sound of screams over the thundering of his heart.

The next scream he heard was from this world, not from his mind.

It was quickly followed by a gunshot, then another and another.

He snatched up the old whip that lay coiled beside him and scrambled for the Morgan he had picketed close by.

And although it was too dark to be certain, William Kelly knew the reason for the gunshots. Bledsoe's vengeance had begun.

CHAPTER SEVENTEEN

ALTHOUGH KELLY'S YEARS on the trail had taught him to see better at night than most men, he knew the horse could see much better. He gave the big animal its head as he spurred her through the darkness and toward the sound of gunshots and pain.

The clouds had parted enough to allow the moon to reveal the scene before him. The bull Hell had just gored a horse with one of its long horns and run down a man who must have been its rider, trampling the animal beneath its hooves as it pursued another horseman. Kelly saw the man turn in the saddle and shoot wildly back at the charging animal, but the bull kept on coming until it slammed into the horse and rider broadside as they found themselves trapped against a wall of frightened cattle. Its large horns impaled the horse and the great animal fell into the herd, bringing its screaming rider down with it.

Kelly raced past the scene and toward the sound of

gunfire ahead. He had told his men to avoid a fight at all costs, but the screams he heard were undoubtedly coming from some of his own men, maybe even his sons.

He could not allow that to stand.

He shifted the whip and reins to his left hand and pulled the pistol from the sash around his chest. There might be cause to use the whip yet, but until he knew for certain, the pistol might prove to be the better option.

He found the first stranger in the middle of a cluster of cattle, firing his gun into the air in an attempt to get the herd to run the other way. But the animals, tired from a long day of travel, barely flinched at the shots he fired in the air.

Kelly reined Morgan to a dead stop just as the man's pistol clicked.

"You're empty," Kelly said as he took careful aim from the darkness. "I'm not."

Kelly fired and struck the man in the chest, sending him tumbling from the saddle. The cattle shuffled to avoid the fallen man, before they closed in around him and crushed him to death.

More gunfire erupted from the back of the herd and Kelly spurred Morgan on toward the fray. Cattle shuffled out of his way.

The clouds closed in over the moon once more, but not before Kelly could glimpse what was happening before him.

Bledsoe had a line of men riding through the heart of the herd, trying to push them south toward the Diamond B Ranch.

The bastards were trying to take his herd.

William Kelly may have ordered his men not to fight, but that order did not apply to him.

These were his cattle, gathered by his labor to secure his future. He had killed one man who had tried to end his life once before. He would not allow this attack to pass without a fight.

He pulled the Morgan to a stop, took careful aim at one of the rustlers, and fired. The shot went lower than Kelly had intended and hit the man in the hip. The rider turned his horse as he fired, but the bullet went wide. Kelly's second shot hit home and put the man down.

He brought about the Morgan and charged through the frightened livestock toward the others who sought to take what belonged to him.

Another shot rang out and he felt fire in his left shoulder. He tightened his grip on the whip and the reins and sped on. He snapped off a shot at the next man he saw, but the bullet missed its mark. Kelly's next shot hit the man in the face.

Kelly sped by as the dead man fell, and pressed on closer to the sound of the guns.

The next rider in front of him struggled to retain control of his horse while he tried to reload his pistol. Kelly fired twice at the man but had rushed the shot and missed badly. He kept on charging toward his target, anyway, flipping the gun so that he now held it by the barrel.

Ignoring the pain of the searing heat from the barrel, he slammed the butt of the pistol into the rider's face as he rode by.

The sound told Kelly the wound was fatal.

More shots rang out and he heard bullets passing by

him in all directions. Good. If they were firing at him, at least they were not firing at his men or his sons.

The next raider appeared closer than Kelly had expected him to be. He swung the pistol butt again, but it was a poorly timed blow and he missed altogether.

But the big Morgan buffaloed into the much smaller horse and sent it tumbling into the sea of cattle. His mare spun wildly as Kelly struggled to bring her back under his control as he moved the whip in his right hand.

The stricken horse scrambled to its feet and ran away, leaving its rider to the fate of the dozens of hooves that pummeled him down.

Kelly decided against ending the man's agony. He was as good as dead anyway and deserved the pain.

Instead, he spurred the Morgan deeper into the chaos of cattle and men and horses. He snapped the whip over their heads, hoping to turn a few of the cows back toward the rest of the herd. Fear of the lash overcame their fear of men and they ran back the way they had come.

The clouds thinned once more and now he saw three men at the far edge of the herd, near a lone tree that stood off in the distance. His eyesight might not have been what it once was, but even in the dim moonlight, Kelly knew he saw a man on horseback with a bandage around the left side of his face.

He knew that man could only be Bledsoe.

He felt the Morgan breathing heavily as he put the spurs to her flanks again, intent on closing the distance between him and Bledsoe and ending this nightmare on his own terms. His way, not Bledsoe's.

The big horse sidestepped the cattle rushing to re-join the herd as it galloped forward toward the tree, when Kelly caught a glimpse of something on the ground before him.

A cow that had fallen during the stampede.

Kelly tried in vain to steer the horse around it, but the horse's size, speed, and momentum continued to carry it forward. The big horse tripped over the trampled cow and Kelly felt himself flying through the darkness, end over end.

He landed on the back of one of his own cows. He felt the air that was forced from his lungs as he continued to tumble forward and hit the ground head-first.

Despite every ounce of his being willing him to get back to his feet, to rejoin this fight to save what was his, the inescapable darkness rose up once more to claim him for its own.

CHAPTER EIGHTEEN

WILLIAM KELLY OPENED his eyes.

The sunlight hurt his brain and he quickly closed them before an arc of pain webbed through his head. He kept them shut as he felt the pain spread through the rest of his body, his left shoulder burning most of all.

When the pain finally ebbed a bit, Kelly dared to slowly open his eyes once again and found that he was sitting propped up against something. He saw his boots were caked with mud and blood. He tried to move, but the fire in his left shoulder burned again and stopped him.

Pain is a good sign. Means I'm still alive.

Kelly looked around as much as he dared, lest he risk another bout of intense pain in his head.

He saw his herd spread out before him. A sizable number, near as he could figure from his current position. He wanted to stand so he could get a more accurate count but did not dare risk it. He knew another shot of pain might cause him to black out.

He spotted Hell standing in a clearing behind the herd. The big bull's longhorns and muzzle were caked in mud and blood, just like Kelly's boots. The bull locked eyes with him as it began scraping the ground with its front hoof.

Kelly knew the animal was not ready to charge yet, but he was certainly thinking about it. The bull knew his tormentor was on his back. Maybe now that he was awake it was finally the time to strike?

Just like Kelly had struck down Old Bones in a moment of weakness all those years before.

Realizing he still somehow held the whip in his right hand, Kelly feebly shot out the popper with a flick of his wrist. "I'm still alive, you big bastard."

The longhorn blinked and moved back among the rest of herd.

"You are awake, my friend," Concho said in Spanish as he knelt at Kelly's side. "This is good. This is very good." He nodded toward Hell. "That is the first time the bull has left your side since we placed you here. He was watching over you like a nurse. I think he gave you some of his strength so you could heal."

Kelly's mind was too scrambled to speak Spanish, so he answered his friend in English. "Probably watching to make sure I was dead. What happened?"

"What you said would happen," Concho replied to his old friend in English. "Bledsoe's men attacked us. They tried to stampede the entire herd. You are very lucky to be alive, William. You took a bad fall. We feared you were dead."

Kelly had not needed him to tell him that. He felt

as if he had died and been brought back all over again. "What's my damage?"

"You hit your head very badly," Concho told him. "You were sick many times. I tried to keep you from going to sleep, but it was impossible. When the fever came, I feared you might die. I am glad you did not. You were also shot in the left side, just below the shoulder. It was a clean wound, through and through. I have bandaged it and you will heal." He handed him a tin cup. "Drink this. It will make you feel better."

But Kelly pushed the cup away. He did not want to drink anything until he knew more. "I didn't mean about me. I meant the damage to our men. Our cattle."

"When the attack started," Concho said, "I made sure the men followed your orders. They ran away just like you told them, though they did not like it."

"They didn't have to like it," Kelly said. "How many head did Bledsoe get?"

"They split our herd in half before you came along and turned them," Concho said. "That was a very brave but a very foolish thing to do, my friend. Cattle are no good to you if you are dead."

Kelly was not interested in himself just then. "How many did we lose, damn it?"

"Between what Bledsoe took and what was killed in the stampede, we think we lost less than a third."

Kelly eased his head back against the tree. One third of three thousand was about one thousand cattle. His cattle. Gone.

But he would think about that later. "How long was I out for?"

"Three days," Concho told him. "I am glad you woke up, William."

The news struck him like a lightning bolt. "You mean you let me sleep for three days?"

"I had nothing to do with it," Concho said. "It was your body that made you sleep for so long. You needed it in order to heal properly." He offered the cup to Kelly again. "Drink this. It will help you get stronger still."

But Kelly felt more urgency now than ever and ignored the pain as he tried to get up. A good chunk of his cattle had been taken. He had to decide how to get them back. "I need my boys," he said. "I need my men. Tell Joshua and James I need to see them. Baxter, too."

But Concho kept his friend pinned against the tree with a gentle but firm hand. "Drink this first, William. You need your strength."

Kelly knew something was wrong. The two men had been together longer than he had been with his own blood. They had been at Fremantle together. They had stowed away on the ship that had taken them here to America. They had worked the mines together, then had ridden the trails together. He knew from his friend's tone that he was holding something back from him. Something that was terribly serious.

"Xavier," Kelly said, using Concho's given name, "I want to see my boys."

The Spaniard sat on the ground beside Kelly. "He took them from you, William. Bledsoe took them."

Kelly heard the words in his own tongue, but they did not make sense to him. "What do you mean he took them? All of them? Even James? How could he manage that? They might not be gunmen, but they're strong boys. Every damned one of them. They wouldn't let anyone just take them away. Not without putting up one hell of a fight first."

Xavier placed his hand once more on his friend's chest to keep him still. "And they did fight. They fought well, like their father would expect them to. They fought as well as a man could hope to fight. But Bledsoe and his men took them just the same. But he did not take them with him, William. He left them here with us."

Kelly knew his friend had a gift for being able to say two things at once. It was as much about what he said as what he did not say. The spaces in between his words often spoke volumes.

The same cold emptiness that had filled him the morning he had lost Mary filled him now.

William Kelly knew his boys were dead.

Kelly heard his voice crack as he asked, "All of them?"

Xavier's expression told him all he needed to know.

Kelly could feel himself begin to cry as Xavier's hand pressed harder against his chest. "They are still here, William. They are in a beautiful spot beneath the shade of this very tree that has protected you from the sun these past few days. This tree will protect them, too."

Kelly was too numb to feel the pain coursing through his body as he forced himself to stand. The world tilted and he braced himself against the tree to keep from falling over. Xavier grabbed on to him as

Kelly pitched forward and was sick to his stomach. He was surprised he still had anything in his stomach to expel after being asleep for so long.

Asleep while men killed his boys.

Asleep while another man buried them.

Asleep while his whole world died.

Kelly regained his senses and, with Xavier's help, slowly shuffled around to the other side of the tree. He saw five graves with branches tied into crosses held by twine. Beneath the rocks and dirt was all that was left of his family. Of his future. Of the men he had helped bring into this world.

The men he had left for long periods of time so they would have a life after he was gone.

The men he had wanted to give a future to away from Texas. A gift that had ultimately cost them the very life he had given them.

Jacob. James. Jeremiah. Joel. Joshua.

Their names had been biblical. That had been their mother's doing. Now they were all with her. At least she would not be alone anymore.

But he was alone. So very alone.

And yet he could not mourn, for he still had business to attend to. A dire debt to repay.

He wiped the tears from his eyes with the tattered cuff of his shirt. He was surprised by the strength of his voice when he asked, "We lose any other men?"

Xavier shook his head. "No, William. When the shooting started, they fled like you told us to. Baxter and I made sure of that. Bledsoe and several others came straight on for James. His brothers rode to his side to defend him. They were very brave. All five of them went down as well as a man could hope to."

Kelly knew he should take some comfort in how they had all gone down fighting, but he could not. He had already known his boys were not cowards. Their deaths had done nothing to change his mind. Their deaths only served to break his heart.

"Greenly alive, too?"

Xavier smiled. "He was the one who tended to you while I slept. Like your favorite bull, he hardly left your side. He even put your whip in your hand, hoping it might make you feel better sooner."

Kelly looked down at the five graves. "Not soon enough."

The Spaniard gripped his friend's arm. "I know you have lost many sons, my friend, but I feel you may have gained another. These men of the outfit may not be your blood, but they are your family now. All of them, even me."

But Kelly had lost too much to believe he had gained anything. His dreams for the future were now rotting in shallow graves beneath the Texas dirt and rock from which he had wanted to free them.

William Kelly had worked for so long to give them something he had never had. A chance for something beautiful. Something peaceful. Something free.

And now they were dead because of it. All five of them.

Not just because of Bledsoe, but because of him, too.

Yet, as he stood looking down at the graves of his dead sons, he felt as though he might have gained something after all. Something he had found after he thought he had lost it decades before.

Something he had hoped he had left behind in the rock yard down in Fremantle all of those years ago.

Something that had nestled deep within him in that London jail the moment the first set of chains had snapped shut on his wrists.

Something that had struggled out of its seed and taken root in the deepest part of him.

Something that fed on darkness and hunger and beatings.

Something as unholy as it was real, and something he had hoped to never feel again.

Something he had not left behind the prison walls of Fremantle after all.

Something that had stayed with him, burrowing deeper inside him like a spider, still and cool, waiting for just the right moment to emerge and feed. And that moment was right now.

It was rage.

Pure, unadulterated rage.

William Kelly fought off another wave of dizziness as he pulled himself as upright as his aches and pains would allow. His body told him to lie down. To rest and heal.

But his spirit told him there would be no rest until the man who had killed his sons was dead.

Xavier removed his hand from his friend's arm and looked away. "Please, William. Don't do it."

But William Kelly knew what he had to do.

His steps did not falter as he walked toward the place where Xavier had parked the chuck wagon. The ten remaining men of the Kelly outfit stood up when they saw him. Each one of them quickly removed his hat.

"Mr. Kelly!" exclaimed young Greenly. "You're awake!"

But the boy's enthusiasm faded as quickly as it had come when he saw the look in the eyes of the trail boss. He looked different somehow, though Greenly was too young to describe or understand just how much.

Kelly swallowed hard before speaking to his men. "Mr. Baxter. Do all of the boys still have their horses?"

"Yes, sir," Baxter said, answering for all of the men. "And a few extra left over from the men you killed. Why, we've even got your old Morgan ready for you, sir. She's just fine. She got right up after you were thrown. She even stood over you to keep the cows away from you. That's a right good mare you got there, Mr. Kelly."

Then the cowhand remembered himself. He gripped his hat a little tighter. "Of course, me and the boys are all sorry for your loss. Them were some fine boys you and your missus raised, sir. Jimmy always found a way to make me laugh."

But Kelly's mind was now in a place where neither condolences nor regret nor sentiment could reach him. He was in a place that was distant and cold enough to numb everything, even the pain of his body, but not his soul.

"Mr. Greenly," Kelly said, "I need you to saddle my Morgan. Then I want you to pull out one of the mules. I want you to load it up with enough food and water for a five-day ride. Xavier will give you what you need. I want you to do all of that as soon as you possibly can. Think you can do that for me?"

"Xavier?" Greenly looked confused. "Who's Xavier?"

But Kelly was in no condition to entertain questions from the boy and kept talking. "While Xavier is loading the supplies, I want you to pull out one of the horses you corralled from the Diamond B. I figure it could come in handy as a guide back to its ranch. Think you can remember all that, Mr. Greenly?"

The young man only looked even more confused. "Of course I can, boss, but why? Who's going to the Diamond B?"

Kelly looked at the young man but did not truly see him. "I am."

"You can't do that, boss," Greenly stammered. "Why, you just woke up and can't hardly walk. You're in no shape to be riding up against the likes of the Diamond B bunch alone. Why would you want to do that?"

Kelly appreciated the young man's sentiment but did not have time for it. "Why is not your concern, lad, and neither am I. Not anymore. But I am still paying your wages, so best go on and do as I told you."

The boy slowly backed away from the group and set about following the orders of William Kelly.

Xavier reluctantly headed over to the chuck wagon to begin gathering the supplies Kelly had requested.

Kelly spoke to the men of his outfit who had remained. "Xavier tells me we've managed to save about two thousand head of cattle more or less. I'm glad to hear it and I thank you for saving so many. That's why I want you boys to get this beef back on the trail as soon as possible. Today, even, if it's not too late. I want you to keep on driving all the way up to the market in Dodge City. I'm placing Xavier in charge of the outfit as soon as I leave here. You boys only know him as a cook, but he's a better ramrod than I ever was. I want you to obey his orders as if they were my own. When you get up to Kansas, you can trust him to broker an honest price for the entire herd. He knows just who to see and how to get top dollar for you. Your share will be greater, I guess, now that my boys . . ."

Kelly choked on the words before finding a way to continue. "Now that my boys are no longer part of the outfit. I think that's only fair, given the increased work all of you will have to put in to bring these cows to market. I'd wager that way your cut should add up to about the same as you would've gotten with all three thousand head. Maybe a little more."

Some of the men began to grumble their refusal, begging Kelly not to go, but Kelly would not hear of it. "That's the way my boys would have wanted it, men. What's more important is that it's the way I want it now. Don't think I'm doing any of you any favors, either. You'll earn every penny of what those cows bring, given how hard you'll have to work, seeing how shorthanded you'll be. It's only fair that you earn more from doing more."

Baxter surprised Kelly by stepping forward from the rest of the outfit. "The men and I were talking while you've been resting, Mr. Kelly. We've got a pretty good idea of what you're planning to do. We think you're riding out to the Diamond B to raise hell with those boys for what they did to us. All of us would be honored if you'd let us ride out there with you."

Kelly began to tell them that would not be necessary, but Baxter interrupted him.

"The only reason why me and the boys didn't fight Bledsoe when he came at us was because you ordered us not to. We own a piece of this herd, too, you know, and the boys might have been your blood, but they were also our friends. We want Bledsoe and his bunch to pay almost as much as you do. That's why we want to ride out with you."

At another time and another place, Kelly might have been touched by the sentiment. But sentiment could not reach him now. "And what if it goes wrong? What if Bledsoe didn't hit us with everything he's got? What if we ride up there and come up against a wall of gunmen? What'll happen to you? What'll happen to our cattle?" Kelly shook his head. The matter had been decided before and nothing Baxter had just said changed his mind. "We've already worked hard to bring the herd this far. I won't have it all thrown away on a noble gesture. I might have lost everything. But I don't expect all of you to lose anything. My boys would want some good to come from all of this and so do I."

Baxter seemed stumped by the trail boss's logic, then said, "Then how about at least letting us stay here until you get back. We'll stay here three days, and if you're not back by then, we can go on without you, hoping you catch up."

"Adding in the time I was out since the attack, that'd mean the herd will have been in one spot for six days," Kelly reminded him. "The grass is mighty thin now, Baxter, and these animals need to be on the move. They need the water that's a day's walk north of here and they need it now. Waiting for me to come back is just plain foolishness and I won't hear another word of it."

Kelly looked at all of the men again. "I told you boys before all of this that I hired you to drive cattle to market, not fight. I meant it before Bledsoe hit us and I mean it now. The best revenge we can have on Bledsoe is for you to bring these cattle to Dodge City. That's your job. That's your duty, men. My duty lies elsewhere now."

Another man from the outfit looked as if he was about to say something, but Kelly fixed him with a hard glare before he spoke. "That's all I have to say on the matter, lads. My mind is made up and my word is final."

Kelly decided it was best to walk away now while he could, before one of the men offered another idea for him to consider. The point of considering and talking had passed. The time for action had come. He adjusted his ruined hat to keep the sun from hitting his eyes and walked toward where Greenly had picketed the horses. He moved unsteadily at first but found that the more he walked, the steadier he grew. Not exactly strong yet, but a bit better with each step. Perhaps it was the blood beginning to pump through him again. Perhaps it was just wishful thinking on his part.

He realized he was still dragging the whip behind him and began to coil it before fixing it to his belt with the thong.

Greenly had already brought the Morgan to the wagon, along with a pack mule and a horse bearing the Diamond B brand on its right rear flank. Greenly was a good boy. He showed promise of growing up to be a good man someday. Kelly regretted he probably would not live long enough to see it, but he found himself past the point of regret now.

Kelly took the reins from the boy and winced as he

climbed up and into the saddle. The pain in his left shoulder was worse than ever and another wave of dizziness hit him. He was grateful his stomach was too empty for him to embarrass himself by being sick in front of the boy. He did not want Greenly's last memory of him to be one of an old man throwing up on his horse.

He watched Greenly help Xavier drape the sacks of provisions across the flanks of the mule. The sturdy animal barely seemed to notice the weight.

"I gave you more provisions than you asked for," Xavier said. "And the Diamond B horse has a Winchester in the scabbard, fully loaded. Lots more cartridges in the saddlebags, too. I know you don't like rifles, William, but I think it might come in handy."

Kelly thanked his friend by nodding but did not say anything. He did not want to risk his voice cracking, betraying emotion.

Xavier continued. "I think you will remain dizzy for a while. There is no medicine I can give you for that, except rest, which you refuse. Be sure to keep your bullet wound clean and to change the bandage on your shoulder once a day. Otherwise, it will get infected and the fever will return. If that happens, you will not be much good to anyone, least of all yourself."

Bull Kelly looked down at Greenly. The young man appeared more confused than ever. He also looked to be on the verge of tears.

Kelly said, "You be sure to listen to what Concho here tells you to do, Mr. Greenly. His real name is Xavier Ignacio Ramirez. He might be an old Spanish pirate now, but he's a good man, by God. He'll make you one, too, if you give him half a chance."

Young Greenly choked back tears as he said, "Please let me go with you, Mr. Kelly. At least to take care of you. That shoulder's mighty bad and you don't want to be alone if it acts up again."

Xavier eased the boy aside and spoke to him in English for the first time. "No one can go where William Kelly is going, young man. Some journeys can only be taken alone, if they must be taken at all."

The boy broke free from Xavier's grip and ran off before he dared cry in front of them.

Kelly watched the boy run away. A small part of him wished he could do something to ease the boy's suffering, but knew no one could do that. The best anyone could do was stave it off for a while. Maybe numb it a little bit. But everyone got a fair dose of pain in this world before it was done with you.

Kelly brought the Morgan around and held down his right hand to his old friend. "Never thought it would end like this, Xavier. Not after everything we've been through."

Xavier shook Kelly's hand eagerly. "This is not the end, my friend. Not for you. And not for me. We will see each other in Dodge City. I know it in my bones. I have no doubt of it."

Kelly was not so sure and had no choice but to take his friend at his word.

Their good-byes finished, Xavier slipped the rope to the mule and the rope of the Diamond B horse over Kelly's saddle horn but held on to the Morgan's bridle. "God hates vengeance and He hates waste. He does not go with you on this journey, my friend."

Kelly did not think He would. "I wonder if He ever has."

The Irishman brought the Morgan about and toward the south and began to ride toward his uncertain destiny.

Kelly chanced one final look back at the herd as he rode away. And not just any herd. His herd. The herd he had hoped would be a new beginning for his family, not the end of it.

He spotted Hell standing a good piece away from the rest of the cattle. The longhorn bull was looking at him with the same hatred in his eyes that he always seemed to have just for him.

The kind of hatred Kelly had forgotten long ago, but now remembered all too well.

The bull looked away first and slowly walked back to the herd.

Kelly let the Morgan and the animals he brought with him move at their own pace.

He knew he would reach the Diamond B Ranch—and whatever fate that awaited him there—soon enough.

CHAPTER NINETEEN

"C AN'T YOU ANSWER a simple question?" Andrew Bledsoe bellowed at Rance from his bed. "Is that Kelly bastard dead or not?"

Rance had a tough time looking at his boss. He had removed the bandages from his eye. The bloody spectacle of it was difficult to see for more than a second or two at a time. He had heard Rita retching out back.

Bledsoe's wound had not made his temper any less fearsome. He brought his fist down on his mattress. "Answer me, damn you."

"We think so," Rance admitted. "We think he's dead."

"I don't pay you to think," Bledsoe said. "You're not good at it. I pay you to do whatever I tell you to do and I told you to be sure that William Kelly is dead."

Rance knew his boss was suffering something awful. He could not imagine what it would be like to lose an eye, but he did not think that was a good enough reason for him to take the man's abuse. He tried to keep the anger out of his voice as he said, "Some of the boys tell me they saw his horse throw him in the middle of the stampede."

Rance knew the answer would not be good enough for Bledsoe, but it was the only information he had. Lying to him would only make it worse, so he tried to emphasize the probability of the situation. "Some of the boys saw his horse get up, but Kelly was still on the ground. Given how thick that herd was, I can't see how he could've kept from being stomped on. We haven't heard from him or his bunch in the three days since we hit him. I'd say that means he's either dead or as good as dead. I don't think we'll be hearing from him again."

"But did you see his body?" Bledsoe persisted. "Did you see him dead?"

Rance had lost count of how many times Bledsoe had asked him that question since they had returned from the raid. Bledsoe's fever had returned in force and seemed to have robbed him of some of his senses and his memory.

"No, sir," Rance admitted once again, "I didn't. All of us followed you out of there after we finished off the last of the Kelly boys, remember? We rode back here with about a thousand head of Kelly's cattle. Do you remember that, too?"

"Of course I remember." Bledsoe's hands shook as he pawed at the damp towel Rita had put across his forehead. His fever had burned it dry in a short amount of time. He folded it over and placed it against his gaping eye socket.

"I just bet you'd like for me not to remember, wouldn't you?" Bledsoe said. "Yes, that would make your life much easier, I'm sure. No accountability. No one to keep an eye on you." He seemed to remember something that gave him great joy. "I remember something else, too. I remember I told you to send a man to keep an eye on the Kelly camp. Bet you didn't think I remembered that, did you? Well? What did he see?"

"Tom Chase," Rance reminded him of the man's name.

"Yes, Chase. Of course. But what difference does it make to me who you sent?"

"It should make all the difference in the world," Rance told him, "because he's one of the last able-bodied men we've got in this outfit. Your two raids on Kelly's herd cost us dearly, Mr. Bledsoe. We're down to four men, including me, who can ride without infirmity. That's four men to tend to a herd of four thousand, sir."

Bledsoe waved off any discussion about the Diamond B. "We'll worry about that later. Tell me what Tom reported seeing at the Kelly camp."

Rance had already told him twice, but the fever seemed to have erased his memory. "He told me he saw that Mexican feller with the chuck wagon digging graves with the rest of the men from Kelly's outfit. They were the yellowbellies who ran away when we came up shooting. Don't exactly know where they got off to, but they cleared out right quick."

Bledsoe seemed to be encouraged by this news, forgetting that Rance had told it to him before. "And does Tom think one of the graves might have been for Kelly?"

Even though Bledsoe was in a foggy state, the foreman did not dare lie to him. "Tom said he thinks so, but he couldn't get close enough to be sure."

Bledsoe might have been out of his mind with fever, but his glare was still harsh enough to fix Rance in his place. The gaping wound in his skull made it even worse. "And why couldn't this Tom Chase of yours get close enough to know for sure?"

Rance shrugged. "Guess it's on account of the fact that Kelly might not be dead after all."

Bledsoe sneered. "Sounds like this Tom Chase is another one of your cowards, Stumpy."

Rance closed his eyes. That was about the tenth time since the previous day that Bledsoe had called him by the previous foreman's name. Stumpy had died ten winters before. There was no point in trying to correct him, so Rance just let it go.

"Sounds to me like Tom is being sensible," Rance said. "He was right there with us when we rode against Kelly that first time, sir. He saw what that crazy bastard can do with a whip against eleven men. He saw what Kelly had done during that stampede we started. Going up against a man like that, even if he is busted up and near death, would be suicide. So don't go expecting me to blame Tom for being careful with his life, considering those odds."

"I can blame him as much as I like when I pay him to do what I tell him." Bledsoe was suddenly racked by a coughing fit. Rance knew the infection that had started in his eye wound was quickly spreading. His fever was far too high to be normal. He was already fever-mad, the infection probably in his lungs by now. He only hoped nature took its course sooner rather than later, before the rancher's madness got them all killed.

"I paid Tom to tell me if William Kelly was dead, not to hide out in the woods like a frightened jackrabbit."

"And he's doing that," Rance reminded him. "It's just that he's not a gunman, same as none of the rest of our men are gunmen. Besides, Tom was still outnumbered by the men in Kelly's outfit. They might not have fought against us when we hit their camp, but ten against one ain't likely odds for a man alone."

Bledsoe was struck by another fit of coughing. This time, the coughing jag was severe enough to make him almost sit up in bed. Rance went to help him, but the rancher slapped his hand away. He might have lost his eye to Kelly's whip and his mind to sickness and fever, but Andrew Bledsoe was still a proud man.

"Fools," Bledsoe said as he wiped his mouth with the same towel Rita had draped across his forehead. "That's all I'm surrounded by. That's why I've got to do all your thinking for you."

He threw the bloody washcloth to the far corner of the room and let his head drop back into the damp pillow. "I guess I'll have to keep on telling you what you have to do next, then."

Rance had been afraid to tell him anything before, fearing that he had misjudged his employer's sickness, but he saw no point in hiding the truth from him any further. "There's no need for you to tell me to do anything, Mr. Bledsoe, on account of there being only one thing we can do. We've got a thousand head of Kelly's cattle running with the herd we've already got. We've lost a lot of men to death and injury, but if we're lucky, I think we just might stand a decent chance of making it through the summer. And as more of our men heal, things will begin to get easier. Hell, by the end of summer, we'll be catching the boys coming back south along the trail. We'll be able to hire some of them to see us through next winter. By then, we'll be able to drive north with a mighty herd that'll bring in more than you've ever dreamed."

Rance knew it was a naked appeal to Bledsoe's greed, but he was plumb out of options at that point. He needed to get the dying man's mind off the Kelly outfit and focused on his own brand. Rance knew the Diamond B was a brand worth saving and the ranch could make a pile of money if it was given half a chance. All Rance had to do was hold Bledsoe in check until nature took its course and the ranch naturally fell to him. Old Man Bledsoe had named Rance the beneficiary of the will if something happened to his son. He knew Bledsoe had not done anything to change the will. Mr. Bledsoe did not like to dwell on such things. All Rance needed to do was wait out the sickness coursing through Bledsoe's veins and he could set about undoing some of the damage the rancher had started.

Rance could see Bledsoe might be dying, but was still aware enough to need convincing. The notion of shooting him or smothering him right now had passed through Rance's mind several times since they had returned to the ranch. However, any sudden death would obviously point to him. That would give Rita and Miguel or some of the ranch hands something they could hold over him for the rest of his life.

Rance had lived too long under the Bledsoe thumb to have them haunt him in the afterlife. Sure, he could buy Rita, Miguel, and the others' silence by promising them a piece of everything once he brought all of this to market, but why go through all of the trouble?

No, he decided. Bledsoe would be dead soon anyway. Better to do whatever he needed to do to bide his time and let nature take its course. Bledsoe would be dead in a day or two, then all of this would be his.

Bledsoe had not realized it, but he had actually been working for Rance all along.

The rancher surprised Rance by saying, "You're talking about something that won't happen for a year or more. I don't have that kind of time. I need Kelly dead now."

"Kelly's long gone from here," Rance told him, "and you'll be on the mend soon enough. Why, this time next week, you'll be right back out on your porch watching the sun come up. For now, you just lie there and rest and let me run the ranch like I've always done. Everything will be back to normal before you know it."

"No," Bledsoe panted from his bed. He blinked his eyes as sweat from his fever beaded down his face. "You're talking about waiting me out. You're talking about giving up and hoping Kelly does the same."

Rance waved him off. "Kelly's got plenty of problems of his own, sir. He's got all of his sons in the ground and a third of his cattle is gone. Let him limp north with whatever men and beef he's got left. Trust me when I tell you that we won't be hearing from him again anytime soon."

"And just hope he leaves it at that?" Bledsoe's

words were already beginning to slur with fever. "Are we to rely on his good graces to just let the death of his sons and the theft of his cattle go without some kind of response?"

Rance found himself losing patience with the dying man and saw no reason to keep playing to his ego. "We don't have much of a choice, sir. We've barely got enough men to tend to the cattle. We can't spare anyone to ride after Kelly's herd, especially when there's no reason to do it."

"Which is why we're going to hire more," Bledsoe panted. "And not more ranch hands, either, but gunmen. I want you to spread the word far and wide, in every newspaper between here and Kansas. I want you to post a bounty of five thousand dollars on the head of Bull Kelly. The territory is bound to be littered with broken men he has left in his wake, men whose backs still sting from his whip." He patted the socket where his left eye had once been. "Yes, that ought to be enough to get it done. Five thousand it is. I want you to ride into town immediately and see to it. Ads in all the papers. I want his body dragged onto this ranch within a week. I want to lie here and watch the buzzards slowly pick him apart."

"Consider it done," Rance said, though he had absolutely no intention of doing anything of the sort. Five thousand was just about all of the cash the ranch had on hand. He had better use for that money after Andrew Bledsoe succumbed to his wounds. And wasting it on the head of a mad Irishman was not high on his list of priorities.

Rance stood up. "I'll saddle my horse and get to it immediately, sir. You can count on me."

"Yes, I know you will, Stumpy," Bledsoe said. "You always get it done. Pa always said you were the most capable man he knew. Best hand he had ever hired. That's saying something, because my pa was quite a rancher."

"Yes, he was," Rance agreed, meaning it. *And twice the man you would ever be even if you did manage to live long enough*, the ramrod thought.

The elder Bledsoe had been as tough as he was fair. A rare combination to have in the ranching business in general and in Texas in particular. It was a harsh and unforgiving land that needed men who had similar characteristics to make anything grow out there. Be it crops or cattle or corn, the odds were stacked against any man who sought to call that part of the world home.

That Mr. Bledsoe had been the man who had saved him all those years ago. That was a man Rance would have gone to the ends of the earth to protect. His son was a poor shadow of his father. A Bledsoe in name only. Rance owed Bledsoe's father his life and never saw anything his employer had as his own. But given Andrew Bledsoe's selfishness, Rance could not allow him to throw away his family's legacy on revenge. If that attitude benefited Rance, all the better. Rance had bled for this ranch. He deserved it.

Bledsoe shook him from his thoughts by shouting, "Are you deaf, damn you? I asked you if your man Tom is due to come back to the ranch."

Rance shrugged. He saw no reason why it should make any difference to Bledsoe now. "No, he hasn't come back yet, sir. I sent him back out to keep an eye on the Kelly outfit yesterday, but I expect him to come back here soon after sunrise."

Rance glanced out the window and saw the first light of dawn had already begun to spread across the sky. "I expect him back in a couple of hours or so at the most. We'll know more about the Kelly outfit then. Why you ask?"

Bledsoe winced as he swallowed hard. It was clear that even the mere act of swallowing had become an effort for him. "Because until he comes back and reports on what he saw at the Kelly camp, I want this house under constant guard. Forget what I said about hiring on more men. There's no time for that. We need to be ready for the Kelly outfit if they decide to come hit us."

Guard? Rance thought to himself as if he did not understand the word. *We've only got six men who are fit enough to tend to the cattle and that's being generous. We don't have the men to spare to post a guard on a dollhouse, much less the ranch.*

But Rance decided it would be easier to simply tell his boss what he wanted to hear. "That sounds like a good idea, sir. It's better to stay close now instead of splitting up and bringing strangers in. The men we've got are better off if we keep them here to watch over you. You'll be better off, too." He stood up and was glad at the prospect of getting out of the room for the first time in hours. It would be good to breathe in fresh, clean air rather than the stale sick air Bledsoe coughed up.

Bledsoe began breathing in short, labored spurts again. He was panting like a horse who had just run a couple of miles flat out. "I need men to guard me, Rance, because I need you to do something else. Something much more serious. Forget all of that nonsense I said about putting a price on Kelly's head. That would take days, maybe weeks we don't have and won't do us much good. I need you to do something else. A special assignment that comes directly from me."

Rance had no intention of doing it but saw no harm in listening to the dying man's dream. "Whatever you need, boss. You know that."

"Of course I know it," Bledsoe said. "What do you think is the only thing giving me comfort right now if not for your loyalty?"

Rance expected to feel a twinge of guilt at that but did not. Bledsoe's foolishness in health had erased any goodwill now that he was dying. "What do you want me to do?"

Bledsoe almost cried out in pain when he winced before saying, "I need to be sure that Kelly's dead right now. Today. Before lunch, as a matter of fact. I know you disagree with me, Rance, but every day that man walks aboveground is another day that puts all of what we have built in danger. I can't live like that. I'm prey waiting for him to decide to strike us like some viper stalking a field mouse."

Bledsoe looked at Rance. His remaining eye was red, possibly from infection. His brow was flecked with perspiration from the fever raging through his body. "You'll need to go after him, Rance. You know I'm right. You'll have to find him no matter the cost and bring him down. You don't need to bring him back here if you don't want to, but end it, Rance. End it today so we can live in peace. You know I'm right, don't you?"

Live in peace, Rance thought as he headed for the door. *Peace will only come for this ranch when you've drawn your last breath.* "You're right as usual, Mr. Bledsoe. You've always had a knack for finding the truth when you need to." He reached for the doorknob. "You need anything else before I get going?"

Bledsoe allowed himself to sink back into the bedclothes. "No, Stumpy. I think that'll be just what the doctor ordered. Leave him wherever you find him. Just end him, by God. End all of this."

You mean you want me to save your backside again, Rance thought. *Pull you out of another round of trouble you have gotten yourself into.* Rance pulled the bedroom door open and stepped out into the hall. This time, whatever he did, he'd do for himself and the ranch. And throwing away the lives of good men like Tommy over the fevered rantings of a dying man . . . did not qualify. "Get better, sir. I'll be sure to send in Rita to tend to you immediately."

If Bledsoe heard him, he did not show it. He simply muttered to himself as the fever grew even worse.

CHAPTER TWENTY

RITA MADE SURE to hide from Rance's view when the top hand came out of Mr. Bledsoe's bedroom. She did not fear him, for Mr. Rance had always been respectful to her and her family. Instead, she was afraid he might ask her to go back inside and attend to Mr. Bledsoe's wounds.

She had no intention of doing that, for she had been listening at the door. She knew that the loss of his eye had changed her employer. She did not know if was the infection or the hatred he held for this Mr. Kelly, but whatever the reason, he was a changed man. A man who now frightened her more than ever. A man she saw fit to stay as far away from as possible.

She watched Mr. Rance walk out the front door of the ranch house and not even bother to close the door behind him. Normally, she would have chastised him for such thoughtlessness, but under normal circumstances, Mr. Rance would not have left the door open in the first place. His mind was elsewhere, which meant she and her family needed to be elsewhere, too.

She ran out the back door and found Miguel in the barn, tending to the horses of the riders.

Miguel was not a stupid man, but he didn't like to concern himself with the matters of the ranch beyond the horses of his stable. At night, when they were home with their son, Rita would sometimes begin to speak to Miguel about some of the odd things she had seen and heard that day in the ranch house. Miguel never wanted to discuss them. "These are other people's lives," he would tell her. "Not fodder for gossip over our dinner table in front of our son. They pay us for our labor and our silence. I will not have our dinner spoiled over such nonsense."

As she was the one who always prepared the dinner, she thought she should at least have some say about what was spoken over the meal she had cooked. But then she reminded herself that Miguel was older than she was. He had seen more of the world than she had, though he rarely spoke about what he had done and where he had been. She knew he was a good husband and a good father and decided this was worth the price of dealing with his moods and odd ways.

But on that morning, as she sought him out among the horses in the barn, she did not wish to discuss something strange she had overheard. She wished to flee the ranch as quickly as possible in the hopes of saving her and her family's lives.

She found Miguel grooming one of the horses as little José sat on a stool beside him. The toddler brightened when he saw his mother and ran to her.

She scooped him up in her arms and held her little boy close.

"Rita!" Miguel said. He grew very nervous and looked around the barn to see if any of the ranch hands were there. "You're not supposed to be in here," he said in Spanish. "You're supposed to be in the house, tending to Mr. Bledsoe's wounds."

"His wounds are beyond tending," Rita told her husband, "at least in this world. His infection is too far gone. His fever will kill him soon enough. By mid-morning at the latest."

Miguel set his brush aside and quickly crossed himself. "God rest his soul, then."

"God will do nothing for him," Rita spat. "Not after he killed those Kelly men and took their cattle. There is a curse on this place, Miguel, and on us, too, if we are foolish enough to stay here. We must go back to our home now."

"But why?" Miguel asked. "The Kelly men are dead. You just said so yourself. What danger do they pose to us now?"

"That's just it!" She struggled to keep her voice down for the sake of José and to keep from being overheard. "We don't know that all of the Kelly men are dead. The father may be alive. The same man who took Bledsoe's eye may be alive, and if he is, it is only a matter of time before he comes here."

Miguel shook his head, disappointed in his wife. "How do you know that, Rita? Sometimes, a man can lose so much that he even loses the appetite for revenge."

Rita's dark eyes flashed as she pointed to their son. "Would you turn and run if you had to bury him,

Miguel? Would you let the men who put your little boy in the ground live while our son was in his grave?"

Miguel reached out and stroked the little boy's hair. She saw that strange look come over her husband sometimes when he was with their baby boy. A loving yet protective look that both warmed her heart and chilled it at the same time.

When she was growing up in Mexico, her mother had told her that men were easy to control. A good woman could have a good life. A smart woman could make a man give her the world, or at least the part of it her husband was capable of owning.

But from the moment Miguel had ridden into their village when she was a girl, she knew he was a different sort of man. She often got him to do whatever she needed him to do for her and for their son, but he never did it blindly. He always resisted a bit, like one of the stubborn mules he tended on the ranch. He eventually did what she asked, but in his own time and at his own pace.

Yes, her Miguel was a strange man, but a good one. The best she had ever known.

"We must leave," she repeated to her husband. "Now. A great darkness is falling over this place. I know you can feel it."

Miguel picked up his brush again but did not go back to grooming the horse right away. "We can't just leave, Rita. Mr. Bledsoe pays us and pays us well. He owns the house we live in. The house where we raise our son. He puts the food that we eat on the table."

"And he has lost his mind," Rita yelled, no longer trying to keep her voice down because she doubted anyone was listening. "The fabric of this ranch is being pulled apart before our eyes. Mr. Bledsoe is not the same man now as he was yesterday. He will be dead soon, either from fever or from the men who are coming to kill him."

She patted the flank of the horse her husband was grooming. "The men who ride these horses will not be able to protect us. Those who are not hurt are not fighters and those who are have been hurt."

"Mr. Rance is fine," Miguel offered.

"Compared to the others, perhaps," Rita said, "but the same darkness that fills this place is in him, too. He is not a well man anymore and we cannot count on him to help us."

She flinched as her husband's eyes narrowed and he threw the grooming brush away, making the horses in the barn skitter and neigh. "Do you think I remain here out of fear of Mr. Bledsoe or Mr. Rance?"

She reached out a hand and caressed her husband's face. "No, my love. I think you want to remain here because you are a good and loyal man. But I beg you to trust me when I tell you that I know the time for loyalty has passed. The only loyalty we must have now is to our son and each other."

When he leaned into her hand and closed his eyes, she knew she had taken the fire from his heart. Now she simply needed to get him to agree to leave.

"You know what I am saying is true, Miguel. Please, let us go home. At least for a few days. The fight that is coming is not our fight. Our only concern is for ourselves and José. Please."

Her husband kissed Rita's hand before lowering it

from his face. "Do you still remember how to ride a horse?"

"Better than you."

He went off to fetch a saddle. "We will take two horses and lead them back to our home tonight. We may need them to escape if trouble comes as you say. We must move now before it becomes bright enough for the men to notice we are missing."

CHAPTER TWENTY-ONE

WILLIAM KELLY HAD not slept well on his first night away from his herd. In fact, he wondered if he had slept at all.

He had found a flat enough spot in the dirt to make his bedroll, but sleep was the furthest thing from his mind that terrible evening. He only lay down because it had been too dark for him to do anything else and he knew his broken body needed rest. He would have preferred to have kept riding all night until he reached the Diamond B Ranch, but his animals needed to be tended to. He had no idea how hard or long the trail in front of him might be and pushing the horses to their limits so early in his journey would be foolish. Bull Kelly might be a grieving man, but he had never been a foolish man. He had no intention of using the death of his sons as an excuse for him to become foolish now.

He also did not have fancy illusions about being able to rejoin his herd farther up the trail to Kansas.

He was still dizzy from time to time in the saddle and had to keep himself from falling several times the previous day. Even now that he was flat on the ground, the world tilted and spun from time to time, making his stomach churn. He had somehow managed to keep down whatever food he had in his stomach. He had tried to eat before he rested for the evening, but all he could manage was a bit of coffee and half a biscuit before even that exhausted him.

In the weak light of his meager fire, Kelly did his best to clean the hole in his left shoulder. The wound was beginning to itch as bad as it ached, which he knew was a sign that it was beginning to heal. He doubted he would be alive long enough to see it heal completely, but such things were beyond his control.

William Kelly's instincts about the curious condition of life and death in the wilderness had served him well many times over the years, which was why he knew he would not live much longer. He knew he had run out his string of luck. His wife and boys were dead, leaving him with nothing else to live for. His dreams of building a cattle dynasty had died along with his family. Dreams that now lay broken and buried in five graves beneath a forgotten tree in the middle of a cattle trail in Texas. Although his exact age had always been a mystery to him, he knew he was at least fifty-five years old if he was a day. It was too late to start over and he was too old to live with the shame of the deaths he had been unable to stop. The deaths of his boys weighed heavily on him, for he knew they would still be alive had he been content to spend the rest of his days in Texas.

His own death at the Diamond B was as inevitable as his life was now meaningless.

But if William Kelly lived for anything now, it was for his refusal to die before he took Andrew Bledsoe's life. He owed his boys that much. He owed his dead future even more. He dared not risk meeting Mary in whatever afterlife awaited him without having settled that score. She would have expected that. She would have demanded a reckoning from her husband.

Kelly looked up to the coming dawn that spanned the heavens and thought about talking to his departed wife, but the urge to speak with her was no longer there. Perhaps it was his own shame that had caused it. Perhaps it was her shame of him that had ended their connection, too.

Mary had been a good woman, but a proud woman. Losing her sons to a man like Bledsoe would have caused her great shame as well as pain.

For the first time since that fateful day in Fremantle so long ago, William Kelly was truly alone in this world. It was just him against the world, just as it had been back in England. He had survived it before and would survive it again, just long enough to set things right.

At least long enough to see his vengeance come true.

He sat up slowly when he heard something moving amid the tall grass. The false dawn had since faded, and the sky was beginning to turn purple as another morning began to rouse itself over Texas.

Kelly grabbed the whip he had kept coiled beside him as he rested, got to his feet, and listened.

The sound he had heard in the distance did not stop. If anything, it only grew louder. It was the familiar sound of shod hooves pounding dirt. Someone was riding toward him. It was too light to be cattle, so he decided it must be a horse. A single rider, from Kelly's estimation, riding directly toward him.

Kelly knew there was a rider on this trail and there was an excellent chance that it would be one of Bledsoe's men on his way back to the ranch. Probably a spy the bastard had sent to keep an eye on the activities of the Kelly outfit and report back what he saw.

Kelly imagined the spy had probably been forced to bed down for the night but had risen before dawn, ready to ride back home and tell his boss that Bull Kelly was not only alive but coming their way.

William Kelly had no intention of allowing that to happen.

Whip in hand, Kelly crept forward in the near darkness, keeping to the high grass along the trail. He listened closely for the sound of horse and rider moving away from him. Kelly decided then and there that he would abandon his packhorse and ride straight on to the Diamond B if it came to that. If the spy reached the ranch, whatever small element of surprise he possessed would be gone and, with it, his only advantage. He would have no choice but to hit the ranch and hit it as hard as he could. With what, he had no idea.

But the horse did not ride away from him. If anything, the sound of its approach only grew louder as it got closer. The sound rid Kelly of any doubt he might have had about the identity of the stranger. The rider was heading straight for home.

And he would have to ride past William Kelly to get there.

A man who spends a good deal of his life on the cattle trail tends to develop senses that other men do not. Not only had Kelly learned to see better in the dark, but he also could estimate where something was simply by the sound it made. His whip had taken the life of many a jackrabbit for his supper that believed it could evade the human by crouching in the grass and remaining still.

That was why Kelly knew the horse and its rider were coming his way at a dead run in weak light. He doubted the rider could see him yet, but his horse had undoubtedly caught the scent of the human and the three animals on the wind.

Ignoring the growing ache in his left shoulder, Kelly ran at a stoop and crouched low beside the path, hoping the tall grass would be enough to hide his presence in the predawn moments.

The horse kept coming along the trail at top speed, so Kelly knew the rider had not spotted him yet.

He allowed his whip to uncoil and waited until the sound of the approaching rider grew loud enough to tell him the man was only a few yards away.

That was when he broke cover and, with a great shout, cracked the whip high in the air.

The whip had not come near the horse, but the sound of the popper snapping in the air—and the memory of the horrible pain that often followed it—

was enough to make the horse buck and descend into the confusion of a full-blown panic.

Kelly watched the horse rear up on its hind legs and the rider hang on for dear life in the saddle.

But when the horse bucked forward, the rider's grip faltered, and he was thrown over his mount's head. He landed on his back with a heavy thud that sent all the air out of his lungs.

The frightened horse turned and ran back the way it had just come, leaving Kelly and the man from the Diamond B alone on the dirt path.

"Don't move, boy," Kelly said as he walked toward the prone shadow before him. "I'll not hurt you unless I have to."

The man surprised him by sitting quickly, but not so fast that Kelly did not have time to dive to the other side of the road before a shot rang out in the darkness. The rider's bullet had missed its mark. So did the second shot that followed, as well as the third.

Kelly ignored the fire in his left shoulder from the dive and got to his feet, snapping the whip low at the fallen rider. The man cried out, and although it was still too dark for Kelly to know where his whip had struck him, the rider's screams told him that the hooked popper had done some damage.

Cautiously, Kelly crept toward the fallen rider, whip trailing behind him in the dirt, ready to strike again if necessary.

The sky slowly began to brighten as Kelly approached his victim. He saw the whip's popper had raked the man across the chest. As he drew closer still, Kelly could see the wound was very deep, and bone from his rib cage was showing. He figured the curved end of the popper must have hit an artery, because the amount of blood coming from the wound was significant.

He saw the man's pistol had fallen on the ground where he had dropped it. Kelly moved quickly and kicked it away. The injured man reached for it too late and Kelly pinned his arm to the road beneath his boot.

"Now, why did you go and do a damned fool thing like that?" Kelly asked without waiting for an answer. "I told you I wouldn't hurt you unless you made me. Now look at what you've gone and made me do."

Kelly sucked his teeth as if he was disappointed at one of his boys spilling a pail of milk back on their farm. "You could have walked away from this free and clear, but here you are, dying in the middle of a road like an old snake." The trail boss shook his head. "What a waste."

The dying man's breath was shallow and ragged. Kelly imagined the pain was likely so great, he probably could not feel anything at all.

"Why don't you finish what you started, old man? Get it over with, damn you!"

Kelly looked at the deep gash his whip had made in the man's chest. "Not before I get some answers from you."

"Go to hell."

Kelly put more pressure on the man's arm as he crouched to get a better look at the wound in his chest. "Looks like you'll be waiting for me by the time I get there. But not before you answer a few questions. How about you start by telling me your name?"

"My name?" The dying man laughed, coughing up blood. "What difference does my name make now?"

"Your name makes no difference to me," Kelly admitted, "but your friends back at the Diamond B might be curious about what happened to you. I could put their minds at ease when I get there."

"You're headed to the Diamond B?" The dying man laughed again and coughed up some blood in the process. "That's rich, mister. You're on the wrong road. The Diamond B is in the direction I rode from. I was just on my way to town this way. You know the town. Bledsoe? Same place where your no-account son got himself in trouble?"

"Don't do that to yourself, lad," Kelly said. "Don't go into the hereafter with a lie on your soul. You haven't been whipping that poor animal of yours into a lather to get to a fly-specked hellhole like Bledsoe, especially this early in the morning."

The dying man struggled to raise his head. "You don't know anything."

"You might be right," Kelly admitted, "but I've got one of the horses from your ranch with me, and given the trail he's been laying out for me, he tells me I'm on the right track. One of us might be lying, but that blessed animal is telling the truth."

The dying man let his head drop back into the packed dirt of the trail. His breath was coming faster now, and Kelly knew he was not long for this world. If he wanted answers from this man, he would have to get them quickly.

There was no time for games.

He let the popper of the whip drop next to the man's face. "I can make your last moments on this earth as

pleasant or as painful as you wish." He put most of his
weight on the man's wrist, causing the dying rider to
cry out. "Lie to me again and you'll feel more pain in
the next few moments than you've known in your entire life. Let's start by you telling me your name."

Kelly did not really care what the man's name was,
but it was a way of getting him talking so Kelly could
tell later if he was lying to him.

"My name's Tom," the man gasped, "and I ride for
the Diamond B."

But Kelly had already figured that. "You with that
murderous bunch who raided our camp in the dead
of night and killed my boys?"

"No," Tom said through gritted teeth. "I was
working at the ranch both times they went after you.
They only sent me to take a look at your outfit after
they hit you. I'm one of the only hands you didn't
shoot up."

Tom coughed deeply and it took a few anxious moments for him to regain his breath. "Or at least I was."

"Bledsoe sent you to spy on us, then?"

"Not Bledsoe," Tom told him. "He's too sick to do
anything but rant and rave in bed. The fever's got him
bad. You took more than his eye with that damned
whip of yours. It was Rance who sent me. He's our
foreman."

"Why? He was there when they hit the camp. He
knew what they had done. He knew how many cattle
he had taken. Why send you?"

"Because they wanted to make sure you were
dead, old man," Tom told him. "And I couldn't get
close enough to your camp to make sure one way or

the other. Anytime I tried to get close enough, that damned longhorn bull of yours would catch my scent and set to fussing. I didn't want it charging me while I was trying to see what you and your men were up to. That damned thing killed two of my friends that night. I didn't want it doing the same to me."

Old Hell, Kelly thought. At least the bull had treated every human it came across with the same amount of disdain it had always shown him. There was something to be said for consistency, especially in an animal with such a nasty disposition. "How long have you been out there watching my men?"

"On and off for two days," Tom said. "I rode back to the ranch, told them how your Mexican had buried your boys, but I couldn't tell if you were alive or dead. I told them I saw you propped up against the tree but couldn't tell if you were alive or dead."

Kelly was beginning to feel encouraged. "And you were on your way to tell them I'm alive when I stopped you, weren't you?"

"I didn't know myself until yesterday, and even then, I wasn't sure it was you," Tom admitted. "I was going to ride back and tell them what I saw, but by the time you let out of camp, it was already going on dark. I tracked you for a bit and bedded down for the night. But I got moving again at first light."

His breath was growing more shallow and quicker. Kelly imagined Tom's lungs were fast filling up with fluid. The end would not be long in coming now.

Tom continued, "I didn't think an old man like you could have covered so much ground, seeing as how out of it you were for so long."

"I'm full of surprises." Kelly felt a wave of dizziness come over him and he almost lost his balance.

The hole in his left shoulder bit into him something awful and he thought he might pass out. The constant ache in his head spiked into a sharp, blinding pain that rocked him where he stood.

Tom cried out when Kelly accidentally shifted too much weight onto his arm, and it was enough to snap Kelly back to his senses.

He took his foot off Tom's wrist. "My apologies, boy. I didn't mean that. But now that you know the disposition of my outfit, you might as well tell me the disposition of yours. You've already told me a lot of you are hurt. How many are able to ride and fire a gun?"

"Why should I tell you anything?" Tom spat.

Kelly crouched down beside the man from the Diamond B, ignoring the pain it caused in his side and ribs. "You're dying and you've only got a matter of minutes before that happens. We both know that. You've had a hand in murder, even if you weren't there when the killings happened. If I was in your position, I know I'd want to walk into whatever might be facing me with as clear a conscience as possible. That's why I know you'll tell me the truth now while you still can."

Kelly watched a tear streak down Tom's cheek. He had never met the young man before, but imagined that he had probably been an honest and loyal hand to the Diamond B. Maybe he was a favorite of the foreman, which was why he had held him back from the dangerous work of hitting the Kelly outfit. He had saved him for the relatively safe duty of watching them from afar after all the killing was done.

But Texas was not a safe place for anyone and running cattle was no place for the faint of heart.

Kelly imagined Tom had already learned that in his young life, which was why he began talking now. "Hell, I'm dead anyway and I'd wager I'm not telling you anything you haven't already figured out for yourself. The Diamond B's in bad shape thanks to you, mister. Mr. Bledsoe lost his eye and his mind. Most of the men you didn't kill are either too banged up to ride or too scared to go up against you. We're cowpunchers, not gunslingers. A dustup in a saloon or a bunkhouse is one thing. None of us signed on for anything like this and it doesn't come natural to any of us."

Kelly had seen his share of gunslingers in his time. He had seen these men of reputation and supposed skill bossing their way around cow towns like peacocks, bullying people in saloons and whorehouses by their reputations alone. Owners often charged extra to those who frequented an establishment just because they could brag that a dangerous gunfighter had chosen their place to rest himself for a while.

Kelly had never had use for gunslingers. He had always made it a point to give such braggards a wide berth. He knew he had developed a reputation with his whip and saw no reason to risk getting tangled up in a fight where there was little profit to be gained except furthering that reputation. He had never feared risking his life for the right reasons but saw no point in risking it based on the opinions other men had of him.

But what had happened on this drive north was different from a simple run-in with a gunfighter. His sons had been killed and a thousand head of his cattle were gone. It was a fight no one had seemed to want except Bledsoe, and for the life of him, Bull Kelly could not understand why. Both men had already lost so much, and Kelly intended on making him lose more still.

The sheer waste of it all would have angered him if his mind was not already filled by the grief of losing his boys.

But Kelly saw no point in regretting what had already happened. It was time to address the situation before him. "How many will stand and fight when the time comes?"

"You can count on Rance, mister," Tom said. "He won't back down from a fight, unless the order comes from Mr. Bledsoe, which it won't. He's all but dead himself. Might be dead already."

Tom shook with another coughing fit and gasped for breath. "He won't run from you, Kelly. And if you're smart, you'll ride out the other way and let this go. The men might back him, and they might not, but he's more than enough for you to handle."

Kelly wanted to feel pity for the dying young man, but the memory of his own dead boys robbed him of any compassion he might feel. "Any man who rides with Bledsoe deserves to die for what they did to my boys. Your friend Rance included."

Tom swallowed hard as he raised his head in defiance. "Guess that means me, don't it?"

"It does." Kelly stood up and backed away from the fallen man. "Death will be coming for you soon enough. It'll go easier on you if you just lie there and wait for it. Given those wounds of yours, you'll last longer if you do."

Kelly heard panic in the young man's voice as he walked away. "You can't just go off and leave me here like this? Lying here out in the open like a lame steer?"

Kelly kept walking back to where he had set out his bedroll and where he had picketed his animals. He trailed the whip behind him.

"You've got no call to do this to me, mister," Tom yelled after him. "I wasn't even there when your boys got killed! I was on the ranch, just like I said I was! I never did anything to you."

But Kelly did not allow himself to stop walking. He did not dare look back. He did not want to risk changing his mind and set to whipping the boy for riding for the Diamond B.

"You can't do this to me after everything I done told you," Tom yelled again, his voice growing quieter now as the effort of yelling only caused him to lose more blood. "It just ain't fair."

No, Kelly agreed to himself. It was not fair. Nothing about anything that had happened since he had left El Paso was fair. James going to the Golden Dream had not been fair. Ace Cutter dying in a bunkhouse for his son's whims was not fair. James riding to Bledsoe against his wishes was not fair. The death that had resulted for a few hours of fun was not fair. Neither was the loss of a third of his cattle to a man who had no earthly reason to pick a fight with him.

It was not fair to have lost his sons the way he had. He wondered if any of them had begged Bledsoe and his men for their lives the way Tom was begging for his now. He thought Joshua might have. After all, he was the baby. He could have been forgiven for going out with a whimper, no matter what Xavier had told him.

He doubted James went down without a fight, though. That boy had probably been the first to go down. If nothing else, he had grit in all the wrong places.

Bledsoe had not shown mercy to his sons beneath that tree in camp. Kelly could not afford to show mercy to young Tom now. For mercy, like violence, was a difficult thing to stop once it was set into motion, and now was not the time for mercy.

William Kelly could hear the faint sobs of the dying cowhand as he stowed his bedroll, saddled his Morgan, gathered the animals, and rode away up the trail he knew led to the Diamond B.

If Tom had died for anything, it was to prove to Kelly that he was on the right trail to the Bledsoe ranch. His herd was likely too far away on the trail north to Kansas for him to consider joining them now. The Diamond B was too close for him to risk turning his back on it.

Kelly tapped his spurs into the Morgan's sides and moved her along a bit faster. He had no time to waste.

CHAPTER TWENTY-TWO

Rance knew it was likely that Tom was not coming back. He felt it in his bones.

Despite the coolness of the dawn, he felt a thin sheen of sweat break out on his hands and across his back. He had ridden away from the house up to the highest point on the Bledsoe property to get a good look at the land around them. He often liked to go up there when he needed time to think, and he needed plenty of time to think right now.

It was good land, by God, with the best water and grass in that part of Texas. He could see everything the Diamond B was and what it could be all at the same time. He saw a thriving ranch that would be better had it not been for the complacency of Andrew Bledsoe.

Rance saw wells that had never been dug. Cows that were thinner than they should have been, with a thousand head more waiting to be fed. Fields planted with crops that had not been rotated properly and grass that was not as healthy as it should have been.

In the hands of a capable man, the Diamond B could be a world-class outfit. It could have been the best ranch in the area and maybe even the biggest ranch in Texas had the Bledsoe men been inclined to spend the money to make it that way.

But the Bledsoe men had never been cattlemen. They were ranchers and only saw the cows and the men who tended them as a means to an end. That end had always been more money. Cattle deserved more than that, as did the men who tended to them.

Rance did not know why money had always been so important to the Bledsoe men, for they did not spend their profits on women or clothes or fancy trips or other finery. They did not even use it to buy more land or more cows. It was as if money was just something to have in the bank, like seeing the balance itself was enough to satisfy them. The idea of simply having it was more important to them than the actual spending of it.

Rance knew thoughts of such things were beyond the grasp of a common cowhand like him, even if he happened to be the man in charge of the outfit. Mr. Bledsoe's top hand at the Diamond B.

But Rance had always known exactly who and what he was. The top hand of a third-rate outfit that had no interest in being more than that. He often wondered if he had ever wanted to be more than that. The idea that he had remained on such a ranch for so long spoke volumes. He could criticize the Bledsoe men for their complacency all he wanted, but in the long run, he was no better than they were.

Rance had not been able to understand Mr. Bledsoe's reasons for stirring up all of this trouble with
the Kelly outfit. Bledsoe had never taken much pride
in his family's name or his ranch. Why had he decided to start now, especially over a two-bit card
game involving two of the worst hands on the ranch?
A decision that had cost so many good men—friends
of his—their lives as they went up against the likes of
Bull Kelly.

All the old trail boss had wanted was to keep moving north in peace to bring his cows to market. He
had not even come near Diamond B land or used
their water.

The only thing Kelly was guilty of was having a
son whose mouth was bigger than he was. Kelly was
not the first man in Texas to have such problems and
he certainly would not be the last. Why had Bledsoe
decided to pick a fight with this man now? Because
of pride he did not have? Boredom? It certainly was
not out of a desire to grow his own herd. The herd
was already well on its way to being big enough to
take to market.

Rance shifted in his saddle, for no matter how
much he thought about it, he could not come up with
an answer. And with Bledsoe driven near mad from
fever, he doubted he would ever know.

About the only thing he would inherit from the
Bledsoe family was a head full of questions and a
ranch that would soon be disgraced from here clear
on up to Canada. The men he had already lost would
soon be forgotten and go without mourning.

Like it or not, Rance knew that Bledsoe's fight had
now become his own. He might not have wanted the

fight, but it was his now, and if he wanted to make the Diamond B stand for something, he was going to have to take it on.

And just as he knew in his bones that Tom was dead, he knew Bull Kelly was still alive. Tom had already reported his suspicions that the man had not been killed and the fact that Tom had not returned from seeing the camp meant the worst. Tom was not the kind of man to ignore a task or oversleep. There was only one reason why he had not returned to the Diamond B by now and it was because he was dead. And chances were, Bull Kelly had killed him.

Another good man sacrificed on the altar of stupidity. Of James Kelly's stupidity and Bledsoe's notions of honor or whatever had led him to attack the herd.

Rance realized there was a very real possibility that he would have no choice but to sacrifice his own life before the matter was settled once and for all. Things had come too far for words to be enough. Blood could only be repaid with blood and it was now up to Rance to finish what Bledsoe had started. Kelly would see to that. Rance would not enjoy killing the old man, but he knew he did not have a choice.

Rance sat atop his horse as he watched the sun rise high enough in the sky to bathe the landscape in clear light. He was now able to see for miles around the Diamond B spread in every direction. It all looked so majestic from this far up this far away. Why, even the buzzards he saw circling in the distance looked graceful as they caught the wind and rode in a circle high above the Texas prairie.

Buzzards.

Rance took off his hat and shielded his eyes

against the sun as he stood up in the stirrups. He saw the buzzards were not just flying. They had settled into a circle over something, which meant that they had found something that was either dead or dying. And given the direction he was facing, it did not take Rance long to understand that was the place where Tom was likely to be riding through to get back to the ranch. Especially if he was in a hurry to tell him something important.

And just about the only reason why Tom would be in a hurry so early in the morning was to tell him that William Kelly was still alive.

Rance sat back down in the saddle, cursing the feeling in his bones that never lied. Tom was most likely dead. He was as sure of it as if he had seen his body himself. And he was equally sure that Kelly had killed him.

The inevitable could not be put off any longer. The time for Kelly to die had come.

Rance put the spurs to his horse and raced back to the bunkhouse. He would grab a fresher, faster mount and find a rifle and as much ammunition as he could carry before he rode out to face Kelly on the trail.

It looked like Mr. Bledsoe was going to get the showdown he had wanted after all.

As he sped down the hill, Rance made sure to soak up as much of the majestic view as he could.

He imagined it would probably need to last him a good long while.

Maybe forever.

CHAPTER TWENTY-THREE

KELLY HAD BEEN pleased with the horse his men had captured from the Diamond B. He had kept the horse on a long lead rope with as much slack as possible. The animal eagerly led them along a well-trodden path that Kelly sensed could only lead back to the ranch. The amount of trail sign and horse scat among the hoofprints told him a large group of riders and cattle had used this trail recently. His cattle, stolen from his herd the night they killed his boys. The sight of it boiled his blood even hotter.

But Kelly pulled his small party of animals to a halt when he heard something coming from the brush that he had not heard in quite some time.

A baby's cry.

And it sounded as if it was coming from somewhere close by. Off to the right side, off the trail Kelly had been riding.

His aches burned as he slowly climbed down from

the saddle, looped the ropes of the pack animal and the Diamond B horse around the saddle horn of the Morgan and tethered the Morgan's reins to a sturdy shrub. As long as the big horse did not break away, the others would hold their ground, too.

His bullwhip in hand, Kelly stepped as lightly as he could manage through the overgrowth toward the sound of the crying baby. When he reached the clearing, he saw that it was not quite a baby, but a young Mexican boy of about three standing alone, clearly terrified and crying for his mother.

The reason why he was crying was the same reason why the little one had not run back home.

A coiled rattlesnake blocked his path.

Upon seeing another human enter its territory, the snake hissed and spat as Kelly inched closer and gently pulled the frightened little boy behind him. The child was so frightened of the snake, he barely noticed the stranger who had stepped in to protect him. He clung to Kelly's pants leg as if his life depended on it.

Kelly knew, where a rattlesnake was concerned, his leg would offer little protection from a bite. Rattlers were fast and cunning and could strike from almost any angle without warning save for the rattle in their tails. Kelly knew the only good rattlesnake was a dead rattlesnake. And he set about making this monster the best it could be.

The sound of the rattle picked up as the snake grew angrier over the two intruders who had wandered into its territory.

Kelly slowly let his whip uncoil. The baby cried out again as the snake spat and shook its rattle even louder. Kelly knew a strike was as inevitable as the snake's own death.

Kelly remained very still except for the quick flick of his wrist that sent the whip across the ten feet or so between him and his target. In that fraction of a second, the curved popper of the whip quickly sliced the head of the snake from the rest of its body.

The little boy cried out as the dead rattler's muscles, unaware that it was already dead, sprang at them, only to collapse in the parched Texas dirt. The blood that flowed from the animal caused the little boy to shriek uncontrollably.

Kelly moved the whip to his left hand as he rubbed the little one's head with his right. Since the little boy appeared to be Mexican, Kelly chose to try to speak to him in Spanish. "It's okay, little one. That snake won't bother you anymore. He was very scared of you. You were very brave."

The boy forgot about his fear as he heard his own language spoken to him with such a strange accent. He pulled away from Kelly's leg, but not from his reach. His big wet brown eyes looked up at him as he asked, "Is it dead?"

Kelly smiled. "Yes, little one. As dead as it could ever be. It won't hurt you or anyone else anymore."

"José!" came the combined cry of a man and woman who broke through the shrub brush where the rattler had been coiled up. Their carelessness would have cost them their lives had they gotten there only a few seconds sooner.

By the way the boy rushed to their embrace and buried his head in the shoulder of the man, Kelly knew they must be his mother and father. The ma-

chete in the man's hand would have been a great de-
fense against the snake had he lived long enough to
use it. Given his concern for his son, Kelly doubted
he would have had the chance. He would have
stepped on the snake's body without any regard for
his own life. The rattler probably would have bitten
him, and the wound would have been fatal.

But his son would have been alive, and to a father,
that was all that mattered. Kelly remembered what
that felt like.

Assured that his son was unharmed, the father
stood up, machete in hand, and eased the little boy to
the mother. He noticed the dead rattler at his feet and
kicked it away. Then he looked at Kelly. "You did
this?" he asked in halting English.

"I did," Kelly responded in Spanish. "Your son's
name is José?"

The Mexican man nodded, looking at the bullwhip
in Kelly's hand.

"You're raising a good boy there, mister. He was
very brave. He cried out but he didn't cry. He didn't
run, either, or he surely would've gotten bit. He stood
his ground and didn't run. That's a mighty good sign
in a boy so young."

But the man seemed to finally understand the
gravity of their situation. "You saved his life. You
saved us, too."

Kelly waved the praise away as he re-coiled his
whip. Although the father was right, there was no
point in thinking on it any further. It only would have
made him more fearful for his son's safety, and too
much fear in a land like this could paralyze a man.
"The snake was more scared of us than we were of

him. Probably would've just slithered away if I'd given it the chance, but I figured it was better to be safe than sorry."

"Where are my manners?" The father shifted the machete to his left hand and held out his right to Kelly. "My name is Miguel Ramirez. This is my wife, Rita, and my son, José."

"And I'm Kelly." He shook the man's hand, not surprised by the strength of his grip. "Glad to know you."

Kelly also accepted a hug from his wife, Rita. She surprised him by speaking in clear English. "Thank you for saving our boy, Mr. Kelly. He's all we have in this world."

Kelly remembered his own sons and how he had once thought of them the same way. How he still did. "Boys have their own unique way of winning you over, Mrs. Ramirez. Especially their mamas."

Miguel beckoned him toward the way they had come from. "Please join us for breakfast. We do not have much, but we would be honored to feed the brave man who saved our son's life."

Kelly had been in too much pain to be hungry and his run-in with Tom on the trail had not done much to improve his appetite. But now that he had the time to think of it, he realized he should probably eat something. The Diamond B was bound to be close and he would need all of the energy he could get. No sense in riding all this way only to pass out when he needed to be awake the most.

He decided to take up the family on their generous offer. They might even be able to give him some information about the ranch.

"That's awfully nice of you," Kelly said. "I accept."

The father began to lead the way as Rita scooped her son into her arms and carried him back to the house. Kelly tapped the father on the shoulder and gestured toward the snake's head. "You might want to bring that inside, get the venom from the fangs before it spoils. Put some cotton over a jar and squeeze them dry. A dab of it makes for a pretty good painkiller when the time comes."

"And the snake is good for roasting," Miguel said. "And the skin will make a nice belt for Rita. But the rattle is of no use to anyone."

"Nonsense." Kelly flicked the whip again and sliced the rattle clean off from the dead snake's body. "It makes for a fine toy for the little one."

The boy, now safely in his mother's arms, where he felt nothing in the world could hurt him, did not cry out when Kelly picked up the rattle and gave it to him. In fact, he took it gladly and shook it, laughing.

Kelly rubbed his head. "Something good can always come out of something scary, little one. You be sure to remember that."

But José was too interested in his new toy to listen to an old man's wisdom as Rita carried him back home.

With the dead snake over his shoulder, Miguel beckoned Kelly to follow them, which he gladly did.

WILLIAM KELLY COULD not remember the last time he had enjoyed a homecooked meal. His Mary had been quite a woman, God rest her soul, with many fine qualities. Alas, cooking had never

been one of them. But her food had been good enough
to keep him alive on the rare occasions while he was
home. And it had been good enough to raise healthy
sons, so there must have been something to it.

Still, Kelly doubted his Mary could have managed
such a feast as he was enjoying now even if she'd had
all the fixings. Warm tortillas and fresh cheese and
beans from the kettle in the fireplace along with some
kind of chicken that was mighty tasty. Kelly's stomach filled quickly.

"This is delicious, ma'am," Kelly told her. "Best
meal I can remember having in quite a while."

Rita seemed pleased that the stranger liked her
cooking. "Thank you. It is simple food, but good."

"It's better than good," Kelly said, meaning it. "It's
even better than the food my friend makes on the
trail. And that's a compliment on account of him being an excellent cook."

"Is he Mexican, too?" Miguel asked.

"In a fashion." Kelly saw no harm in telling them
the truth. "He's a Spaniard. An old pirate I met when
I was down in Australia a thousand years ago." Kelly
was not accustomed to talking so much about himself
even though he had not said much, and decided to
change the subject. "But enough about me. What
made you fine folks decide to live all the way out here
by yourselves? There's no one around for miles."

Miguel slowly pushed his plate away from him.

Rita frowned and looked down at the table.

Kelly knew he could be thoughtless at times, but
for the life of him, he could not understand what he
had said that had upset these people so.

"What's wrong?" he asked. "Was it something I said? Something I did?"

Miguel shook his head. "No. It is just that now we know who you are, and we know why you are here." He looked at his guest. "And where you must be going."

Kelly suddenly lost his appetite and was glad his whip was coiled on his hip. He laid his hand flat on the table. "Do you, now?"

"Oh, you have nothing to fear from us," Rita assured him. "It is just that we both work at the Diamond B Ranch. Miguel is the blacksmith there and tends their horses. I work in the ranch house for Mr. Bledsoe. That is why we know you must be William Kelly. Bull Kelly, as some of the men at the ranch call you. And you are on your way to kill Mr. Bledsoe."

Kelly felt the warm food turn cold in his stomach. He cursed himself for not thinking of this before. Being so close to the ranch, it stood to reason that they worked there. "You work for Bledsoe. Both of you."

Saying the name seemed only to make their shame grow worse. Kelly wondered if it had been the way he had said it. He had probably done a poor job of keeping the hate out of his voice and the shadow from his eyes.

"It used to be a nice place to work," Miguel offered. "That is, until a few days ago."

Rita talked over her husband as she said, "You have nothing to fear from us, Mr. Kelly. We should be at work now but fled from that place when we saw what was happening there. A great darkness has descended over the entire ranch. Men have been hurt. Men have died."

"I know," Kelly said. "I'm the one who killed them."

"We know that," Miguel admitted. "We have seen what you have done to the men of the ranch. We have been tending to their wounds for the past couple of days. My wife has been tending to Mr. Bledsoe's wounds. You must know that your whip has done more than take his eye, señor. You took his soul, if he ever had one to begin with. He is very sick with fever that makes him grow crazy as it makes him grow weaker."

Kelly did not see where Miguel had placed his machete, but since both of his hands were in plain view, he decided to keep his hands on the table as well. "Whatever my quarrel with the Bledsoe ranch might be, it does not involve you or your family."

"And you must know that we do not mean you any harm," Miguel said. "You must believe that."

Rita finally looked up at Kelly from her plate. "You mean to kill them—Mr. Bledsoe and Mr. Rance and the others?"

Kelly did not want to scare her by meeting her eyes, so he made a point of looking away as he spoke. "You know what he did to me? That he took my boys from me? That he stole my cattle?"

He sensed both of them nodding, so he continued. "Then you'll understand that Bledsoe has to die for what he's done. As for Rance and the rest of them, what happens next is up to them. I figure they've found themselves caught up in all of this the same as me. If they stay out of my way, then I'm inclined to let them go. I figure they've suffered enough already.

But anyone who gets between me and their boss won't be in my way for very long."

Miguel slowly looked at him. "How did you hear about these things? How do you know so much about the ranch?"

Kelly had never felt ashamed about killing a man before, but he found himself feeling ashamed now, for some reason. "I ran into one of the hands from the Diamond B on the trail just before dawn. He told me everything before he died."

"You mean Tom." Miguel's eyes narrowed. "You killed Tom?"

Kelly could not tell from Miguel's tone if the Mexican was glad Tom was dead or not. "I'd like to be able to say I didn't have a choice, but I like to steer clear of lying when I can."

He was not used to talking about the things he had done, but there was something about Miguel and Rita that made it easy. Maybe even necessary. "I guess I might've been able to knock him out and maybe tie him up, but things didn't work out that way." He looked at Miguel. "I didn't set out to kill him, but he's most likely dead by now just the same." Kelly looked at his empty plate. "And I guess his death doesn't bother me as much as it should."

Miguel glanced at the whip on Kelly's belt. "Did you shoot him or use that?"

"I prefer my whip to firearms," Kelly said. "I've always figured a gun is too easy to palm and use on a man. A whip requires a more deliberate application."

"That is a very special whip," Rita said, making no effort to conceal her awareness of it. "That is the whip that took Mr. Bledsoe's eye and made him mad with fever."

Kelly winced as he thought of the torment this poor woman must have gone through in tending to a lunatic like Bledsoe. "I swear to God it was necessary, ma'am. Bledsoe was going to shoot me dead if I didn't get him first. You've got no reason to believe me, but I hope you will."

"We know," Miguel said. "We were at the ranch when he and his men rode out to bother you and we were there when they came back bloody and broken. One man lost a hand. Many of them are so hurt they will be unable to ride for quite some time. Mr. Rance fears for the cows in the fields, especially now that he has more than he had expected. Your cows, Mr. Kelly. Tom was one of the few healthy men left to tend to them. But now?" The Mexican shrugged. "Well, I suppose none of that makes much difference now."

"Now"—Rita carried on the conversation for her husband—"we do not know what will happen to the ranch or to us. We only know that we want no part in it after what they have done to you and your family."

Kelly had not thought about that. He had not thought about how all of this might affect the people who relied on the ranch to make their living. He had not been able to think about much of anything since the moment he learned his boys had been killed. "I don't know either, Mrs. Ramirez, except that things have a way of working out."

"And not always for the best, señor," Rita added. "For any of us."

Kelly glanced at her, afraid he might frighten her.

He tried to keep the edge out of his voice when he spoke. "You said Bledsoe's in a bad way."

"I have never seen anyone with a fever burn as hot as he burns," Rita told him. "He has been ranting and raving for days. Poor Mr. Rance had been with him the entire time, more than I have. He has sat vigil over him, enduring the worst language and the darkest thoughts I have ever heard anyone say. It is unholy. Something is keeping him alive and I know it is not my bandages."

Kelly was secretly glad to hear the news about the fever. He made it a point to drag the popper along the trail and rarely cleaned it for precisely that reason. Even the slightest scrape from the jagged end could mean death to whoever he struck with it. That tended to make men more careful about risking him using it on them. Ace Cutter had learned that lesson the hard way back in El Paso. It sounded like Bledsoe was learning it, too.

"I'm sorry you had to go through all of that," Kelly said, meaning it. He imagined Rita's life on the Diamond B was hard enough without Bledsoe's suffering to make it worse. "I guess we all would have been better off if I had just killed that son of a bitch when I had the chance."

Kelly felt his throat begin to close in as a tear came to his eye and his voice grew thick. "Maybe then my boys would still be alive."

Rita gasped and held her apron up to her mouth.

Miguel reached out and touched Kelly's arm. "Then it's true. Your sons were the men Mr. Bledsoe boasted of killing when he came back to the ranch with the cows he took." His grip on Kelly's arm weakened a bit. "I had hoped these were simply boasts of a beaten man. I did not think he had actually done such a horrible thing."

Kelly felt the anger rising within him. He had figured a man like Bledsoe would be proud of killing his boys, but hearing he had boasted about it only served to make him feel worse. "Your boss owes me for five sons and a thousand head of cattle. Does he have any boys?"

Both of them shook their heads.

Kelly had thought not. "Then I guess his head and my cattle will have to suffice."

He did not know how long he had been sitting there in the brooding quiet of the small house, allowing the silence to settle around them in the tiny rooms they called a home. There did not seem to be anything more for anyone to say or do. What was more, there was no reason why he should not get back on the trail to the Diamond B and end this once and for all.

But despite his will, William Kelly found he was not able to move. His head hurt and his left shoulder ached and the gravity of all that he had suffered through in the past several days settled down upon him like a greater weight than he had ever known in his life. He found himself feeling something beyond tired that he could not describe.

More tired than he had been back on the prison ship to Fremantle.

More tired than after any of the endless, insufferable days he had spent breaking rock down in the quarry.

More tired than he had felt even after the longest trail he had ridden north and back again.

It was a crushing weariness unlike any he had ever known. A weariness that went deeper than his bones. Maybe deeper than his soul, if he still had one.

He felt a great emptiness open up inside of him, quickly filled by a profound darkness. There was something warm and welcoming about it as he felt it spiral through the core of him. Something inviting and new.

The only name Kelly dared to give it was hate. It was similar to the feeling he had felt before he had ridden away from the herd, but different in so many ways.

Kelly only snapped out of his trance when he heard the little boy begin to cry.

He looked up and saw José backing away from him only to run behind his mother. To the safety of where he believed nothing bad in his little world could reach him.

Far away from whatever he had sensed had come over this stranger in his home.

Kelly flinched when Miguel's grip on his arm tightened. "Our prayers are with you, William. No man should have to bury his children."

Kelly felt his mouth tremble at the memory of it, or rather, his lack of memory of it. "But I didn't bury them. My friend Xavier had to do it. Him and some of the other men in my outfit. I was lying under a tree, useless and asleep, while other men had to put my own boys in the ground."

José wailed and Rita scooped the boy up in her arms, holding him tighter than before. "I'm sorry for my son, Mr. Kelly. He is overly tired. I'll put him to bed and be right back."

But Kelly knew she would not be back. Not right away, anyway, and he could not blame her. Whatever had stirred within him had been enough to scare the little boy. It was almost enough to scare him, too, if he had still had any emotions left.

Kelly looked at Miguel and saw the man was crying. Crying over the loss Kelly had suffered and the thought of what losing his own son might do to him, too. The pain that only another father could feel.

Kelly did not recognize his own voice as he said, "I'm going to kill Bledsoe, Miguel. Raving or not, it makes no difference to me. I'm going to kill him just as sure as you and I are sitting here at your table right now. But I don't want you or your family to be part of what I have to do, so I think it's best if you leave. If one of his men were to find out that I was here, it would mean trouble for all of you after I'm gone. I wouldn't want that for you or your family."

But Miguel's grip on Kelly's arm did not weaken. "There is no one left to come for us, my friend. Most of the men are hurt, the good ones anyway. They have great lashes across their bodies. One of them is going to lose his hand. And those who are not hurt on the outside are hurt on the inside. The ranch is a different place now. Fear lives there. Fear and dread. They fear you are coming, and when you do, there will be no one to stand in your way. Except for Mr. Bledsoe, and he is half-mad with fever. The only man you need to fear is Rance."

The same void that had opened within Kelly only to grow warm grew warmer still. He sat back in the old wooden chair and welcomed the warmth that now coursed through his body. "I can handle him."

"Rance is a dangerous man, my friend, but I believe you have just enough anger in you to kill him," Miguel said. "But killing him and Bledsoe and anyone else who stands in your way will not help you. There is a great darkness within you. I can sense it and so could my wife. Little José most of all. Children are very good at seeing such things. Men can see them, too, if they are brave enough to look."

Kelly's eyes narrowed. "I've never been afraid to look at anything in my life."

"And you cannot afford to be afraid to look now," Miguel went on. "You must not be afraid to see this darkness within you for what it is. Evil. You must have the courage to face it so you can know how to walk away from it. No good can ever come from such darkness. Only more darkness."

Miguel folded his hands on the table. "I have not always been a simple blacksmith on a ranch. Like you, I have been many places and seen many things. Many terrible things, and I know how warm this darkness can be. That is why I know you must be brave enough to leave it behind. I know this because, not so long ago, I had to force myself to walk away from it, too."

Kelly regarded this quiet, unassuming-looking man as if he were seeing him for the first time. "You?"

"Blood cannot wash away blood, señor. Even when Bledsoe is dead, your sons will still be in their graves and nothing you can do will ever change that. The dead do not need the living and their spirts have no place here among us. I learned that lesson myself long ago. I only hope you can learn this lesson much easier than I did. And sooner, too. For your sake."

Kelly knew there was more meaning to Miguel's words than he could understand just then. But now was not the time for understanding.

Now was the time for something else. Something much more real.

Kelly eased his chair away from the table. "There is a time for understanding, my friend, but there is also a time for blood. And I won't be able to live with myself as long as Bledsoe is walking aboveground while my boys are in it."

He slowly stood up, almost afraid to make a sound in the quietness that had descended over the humble house. "I hope my being here hasn't caused you or Maria any hardship. I thank you for the meal and the kind words, but I think it's about time for me to be on my way and leave you be."

Miguel slumped back in his chair. "Then you are still going to the ranch."

"Where else would I be going?"

"Back to your men on the trail north of here," Miguel offered. "To the cows you still have. To this friend from Spain you speak of. To a new life up in Kansas." He looked at the bandage on Kelly's left shoulder. "Your wound is bleeding. At least let Rita give you a fresh one before you go."

But Kelly did not see much point in patching himself up. The way things were going, one hole would not make much of a difference anyway. "Thank you for the hospitality, Miguel. And the wisdom."

He extended his hand to his new friend, who slowly rose from his chair and shook it. "May God go with you, Mr. Kelly."

Kelly smiled as he remembered Xavier had told

him just the opposite before he rode away from the herd. "That'd be a nice feeling, for once."

The silence that had fallen over the house was pierced by a shrill yell that came from outside. "Kelly! Bull Kelly. You in there?"

Kelly turned to face it, but there were no windows in the house in that direction.

Miguel said, "That would be Rance. He is Mr. Bledsoe's foreman."

Kelly remembered seeing him when Bledsoe had first come to call on his herd. He remembered seeing him again riding next to Bledsoe that horrible night when his boys were cut down. "He was with Bledsoe when he rode against us, wasn't he?"

Miguel closed his eyes and nodded slowly. "He never leaves Mr. Bledsoe's side."

"That's what I thought." Kelly pulled the thong and removed the whip from his belt. Any doubt about his purpose melted away. "Wouldn't be polite of me to keep the man waiting, now, would it?"

CHAPTER TWENTY-FOUR

"COME ON OUT here and face me, Kelly," Rance called out once more. "I see your animals and I know you're in there. Don't go hiding behind poor Rita and Miguel. They're in enough trouble as it is on account of you."

Kelly stepped around the jagged adobe wall that surrounded the house, trailing the bullwhip behind him.

"Who said I was hiding?"

Rance was standing just beyond the low wooden fence that surrounded the Ramirezes property. Kelly recognized him immediately as the man who had always ridden beside Bledsoe whenever the men had come after him and the herd. He had seen him with Bledsoe beneath the tree where his boys were killed, before Kelly had fallen from his horse during the stampede.

"That's about far enough for you," Rance called

out. "I've seen what you can do with that whip, so I want you to stay right where you are."

Kelly watched Rance's right hand move toward the cracked leather holster on his right hip. He wondered how long it had been since the foreman had last worn it, much less used it. He wagered it must have been quite a while.

It was an expensive wager, for Kelly knew his own life was now at stake.

Kelly pushed his luck by stopping two steps after the warning. He judged the distance between them to be about ten feet. Maybe a bit more. But maybe would have to be good enough for what he had to do next.

"I'm not here to fight you," Rance said as his hand hovered near the gun on his hip. "There's been enough killing around here to suit me. Senseless killing on both sides. If I'd wanted a fight, I would've blasted you the second I laid eyes on you. I'm here to talk this thing out if you're willing to listen to reason."

Kelly gripped the handle of the whip tighter. "I've had just about all the talk I can take from men of the Diamond B. And so have my boys."

Kelly flicked the whip just as Rance reached down for his pistol. The popper slashed upward from the ground and cut a deep gash in the foreman's face. The popper caught the rim of his hat and sent it flying.

A single shot rang out as Rance fired wildly before falling backward, dropping the pistol in the process.

Kelly snapped the whip back and trailed it on the ground beside him as he slowly closed the distance between himself and the fallen man. Rance might be down and unarmed, but he was still alive.

The closer he got, the more Kelly saw his aim with the popper had been true. The cuts on Rance's face were bone-deep. His nose was gone, and a deep cut ran from his jaw to just above his right eye. Rance would be a mighty hard man to look at from now on, assuming he lived, but Bull Kelly planned on sparing him that indignity.

Rance covered his face and screamed into his arm as Kelly stooped to pick up the pistol from the ground. He knew a dying man was the most dangerous creature on God's green earth.

Kelly stood over the fallen man until he had screamed himself hoarse. It was a gory sight to behold, but Kelly had caused it and refused to allow himself to look away.

And he was not above taking a moment to gloat. "Guess you're not too good with judging distances. If you were looking to make me stop short, you were off by a good three feet or more."

Rance's litany of curses was muffled by the arm that tried in vain to cover his ruined face. "Damn you, Kelly! I just came here to talk!"

"Talk," Kelly repeated. "Talk long enough to get me distracted, maybe, before you pulled your gun. Or long enough until you realized I wouldn't change my mind about killing you. You had plenty of time to talk before today, Rance. Where was your talk when your boss decided to come after me and my men? Where were your words when your boss came to kill my sons and run off my cattle? Those were the time for words, boy. Words don't do any of us much good now."

"You and Bledsoe," Rance slurred through the

pain and the blood. "The two of you deserve each other. Why in the hell did you have to go and pull the rest of us into it with you? You should've just had at each other and been done with it."

"I wish that had been the case. That would've been just fine by me," Kelly said.

In fact, he realized he had probably never meant anything more in his entire life. But wishing a thing did not make it so. Things were the way they were. All a man could do was pick up the pieces afterward.

And, if he was lucky, get a little justice before a preacher read words over him.

His boys had not been that lucky.

He saw no reason why one of the men who had killed them should be that lucky, either.

Kelly felt the weight of Rance's gun in his hand. "You know, I never could understand the appeal a hunk of metal like this could have over a man. The damned things are heavy, expensive, and just as likely to miss a target as to hit one. Even after being shot, it can take a man a long time to die. Maybe even long enough to come around and kill you. Why, I remember reading somewhere that Abe Lincoln himself had laid in bed for hours before he went to his eternal reward. And that was from a bullet fired right against his skull." He tossed the pistol as far as he could.

Kelly looked down at Rance as he gripped the handle of his whip tighter. "No, sir. That's why I always stand by my whip. Works like a charm every time and a man isn't in much condition to do anything after it lays him low. That's why you're in the dirt right now with half your face gone while I'm standing over you. Guess that gun of yours didn't do you much good in the end, did it?"

Rance yelled at him through gritted teeth. "I thought you said you didn't come here to talk. If you're going to kill me, get to it, then."

"I plan on doing exactly that," Kelly said. "Right after you tell me how many men you have up at the ranch. Fighting men, I mean, not counting the ones I gelded on you. And if you lie, you'll feel my whip again."

"Why ask me?" Rance said through his arm. "Them two Mexes probably told you everything already."

"Because I'm asking you." He cut loose with the whip, close enough to make Rance flinch. "Last chance to answer the question before I set to plucking pieces off you like feathers off a Christmas goose."

"If we had any men, do you think I'd have come here by myself?" Rance screamed. "You've killed or hurt anyone we've got who's worth a damn. Most of them are set up in the bunkhouse, licking their wounds. The others are too scared to go outside, much less stand up to you. Mr. Bledsoe ordered me to round up some men and finish you off. You can see how many I got to come down here with me."

Kelly took that as good news. Very good news indeed. "Sounds to me like your boys aren't fighting men." Kelly moved the whip to his left hand and pulled out the gun with his right. "Neither were mine." He felt the rage begin to build up in him again. It was like an uncontrollable thing that threatened to get away if he did not hold on to it enough. "You remember my boys, don't you, Rance? Those young men you and Bledsoe cut down in cold blood?"

If Rance had any remorse, he hid it well. "I remember cornering the miserable varmint who had started all of this mess over a lousy card game. I remember putting him down, too, right alongside the damned fools who tried to protect him. I remember making sure every single one of them died for their trouble. If that varmint I killed was your son and those men with him were your other boys, I couldn't care less. I ride for the brand, mister. I ride for the Diamond B brand and I always will!"

Kelly decided a whipping was too good for the likes of Rance. He deserved to die the same way his boys had. His hand shook as he took the pistol from his sash and aimed it down at Rance's head. It was a shame the foreman would not see what was coming because his hands were covering his face.

Kelly thumbed back the hammer of the pistol. "You won't be riding for Bledsoe or anyone else. And you won't be killing anyone else's sons, either."

Rance pulled his hands away from his face and, with gore and all, roared up at Kelly, "I'll see you in—"

Kelly squeezed the trigger and silenced Rance forever.

"You might, lad." He tucked the gun back into his sash. "After all of this is over, you just might at that."

Kelly sensed someone standing behind him. He slowly turned to see Miguel near the low adobe wall, holding a shovel. The Irishman knew that his new friend had brought the shovel as a tool, not as a

weapon. He had met more than his share of enemies
that morning. It was good to have a friend around.

Kelly held out his hand and motioned toward
Miguel's shovel. "I'm the one who killed Rance. I
ought to be the one who buries him."

But Miguel held on to the shovel. "This is my land.
I will bury him, my friend. You have more important
things to do this day. Do them well and do them at
once. Bledsoe will miss Tom and Rance quickly.
When they do not return, he will know you are
coming."

Kelly figured Bledsoe already knew that. But he
did not mind passing on the burying duties. The hole
in his left shoulder was hurting something fierce and
he still had to face down Bledsoe and his men before
all of this was truly done. "How far is the ride to the
ranch from here?"

Miguel pointed in the direction Kelly had expected him to, the same one he had been riding all
this time. "Stay on this road and you will see the
main gate in about a mile. You will find the ranch
house and the bunkhouses and the stable another
mile after that. All of it is uphill, William. All of it is
open land, too. If you go in that way, there will be no
way to hide and Mr. Bledsoe will surely see you
coming. He will shoot you if he is healthy enough to
do so."

Kelly began to coil his whip and tied it to his belt.
"He already knows I'm on my way, Miguel. He knows
I don't have a choice. And I know neither does he."

Kelly walked out through the shrubs he had come
through to save José from the rattlesnake, mounted
his horse, and pulled the mule along. The spare horse

he had brought from the Diamond B was nowhere to be found. Either Rance had untethered it or it had broken free. Either way, it did not matter much anymore. The animal had served its purpose. It had helped lead him here to his destiny only a mile or two up the road.

Kelly pulled himself up into the saddle and spurred the big Morgan forward just as he heard Miguel's shovel take its first bite out of the ground.

Kelly wondered if Miguel would be kind enough to bury him, too, if it came to that. Kelly liked the idea of that. He had always thought Xavier would be the one who'd shovel the last spade of dirt on him when the time came. But Xavier had done more than his share of digging for now. If it had to be anyone, Kelly decided Miguel would be the best choice.

After all, he was the last one who had seen what William Kelly had become.

CHAPTER TWENTY-FIVE

"WHERE IN THE hell is everyone?" Bledsoe bellowed as he threw open his bedroom door.

He had just woken up only a few moments before, suffering from a sharp pain where his eye used to be. His fever had been hot enough to make it impossible for him to get back to sleep.

His sleep was plagued by nightmares that were so real, it was difficult to tell where the dreamworld ended, and the real world began.

It was terror and confusion that had forced Bledsoe from his bed to see the state of his ranch with the one good eye he had left. He had called out for Rita several times, but his housekeeper was nowhere to be found. He figured she was probably off somewhere cooing to that brat of hers. He would be sure to fire her the next time he saw her. Her husband, Miguel, too. The ranch could do without a blacksmith for a while. Hell, he could shoe and tend to the horses himself if it came to that. He had always prided himself on his ability at the forge.

"Rance!" he called out from the porch when he staggered outside. "Where are you?" His voice carried across the open front yard, echoing back on itself, making him feel even more alone. "Rance? Tom? Rita? Miguel?" The echo of his own voice was the only answer. "Where the hell *is* everybody?"

The only response was the dry wind that swept across his land.

Bledsoe quickly found that he was so weak that he had to hold on to the porch post to keep from falling over. His vision blurred and the land tilted back and forth quick enough to almost make him sick.

"God, boss," said a voice he did not recognize. "You look just plain awful."

He opened his eyes and saw Rance standing before him. "Rance! Where have you been? I've been calling for you for hours."

"I'm not Mr. Rance, Mr. Bledsoe," the man told him. "I'm Tisdale. Mr. Rance rode out of here more than an hour ago. Said he was going out to find Tommy somewhere."

Bledsoe vaguely remembered seeing Rance lurking about in his fever dreams, but had that only been a few hours before? It felt like he had not seen his foreman in years. He cursed himself for being foolish enough to confuse Tisdale with Rance. Rance was tall and lean, where Tisdale was dumpy and now walked with a limp thanks to Kelly's handiwork with that damnable whip of his.

Kelly, Bledsoe suddenly remembered. William "Bull" Kelly. Yes, he remembered everything now.

He had ordered Rance to go after Kelly. To face him down before the damnable old trail boss ever reached the Diamond B.

He realized Tisdale was still standing there. "How many men did you say Rance took with him?"

"I didn't say," Tisdale told him. "That's on account that he went by himself. He didn't ask for any of us to go with him, either. Said he could handle Kelly alone and ordered the rest of us to heal up right quick so we could tend to the herd as best we could as soon as we could manage."

Bledsoe gripped the porch post tighter. Rance, that insolent bastard! Bledsoe remembered telling Rance to raise as many men as he could and wipe out the Kelly outfit once and for all. Tisdale still being here at the ranch was just another example of Rance's defiance. Tisdale's bad leg made it nearly impossible for him to walk, but he could certainly ride. But Rance had decided to do things his way, not the way he had been told. His old foreman was finally spitting out the bit his father had placed there long ago when he rescued the boy from starvation.

Bledsoe wiped a sheen of sweat from his forehead and decided now was the time for him to take control. "To hell with Rance. Tisdale, I want you to pull the men from tending the cows, get a day's worth of rations from the stores, and saddle my horse. We're going to wipe out the Kelly outfit this very night!"

But Tisdale remained exactly where he was. "Sir, I don't mean to be disrespectful or nothing, but you're in no shape to crawl, much less ride. You look like you got a fever on you something fierce. Hell, I can feel the heat coming off you from all the way over here."

Bledsoe knew Tisdale might be right, but he refused to show weakness in front of his men. His father never had. His grandfather, either.

Andrew Bledsoe tried to stand on his own two feet, but another wave of weakness made him clutch the post again. "Don't worry about me, Tisdale. Just get yourself and the rest of the men ready to ride, loaded to kill. And saddle my horse while you're at it."

Tisdale still did not move. "We don't have any men left to ride, Mr. Bledsoe. We've been hearing you bellowing and hollering for the better part of an hour now over in the bunkhouse, but I'm the only man fit to stand up and come check on you. And getting out of bed on my own damned near killed me."

"Then ring the dinner bell and call the men in from the herd, damn you," Bledsoe ordered him. "They come awful quick to fill their bellies whenever Rita sets to banging on that damned bell of hers. Well, now they'll get a bellyful of lead if they don't do my bidding."

"Those men tending the herd have their hands full doing that, Mr. Bledsoe." Tisdale's shrug was almost a flinch. "I'm sorry, sir, but none of the rest of us are going to be able to go riding anywhere for a while."

Waves of heat and cold and pain and glory washed over Bledsoe all at once. He wondered if it was delirium from the pain and from the fever from his missing eye. That damned whip had taken more from him than just an eye. It had taken his life.

But Bledsoe men had always been masters of their

own bodies. They were above suffering from common illnesses. His father and his grandfather before him had fought their way through malaria and fever. Andrew Bledsoe had the same blood running through his veins. There was no reason why he would be any different. He would will himself into health, even if it was only to live long enough to kill William Kelly once and for all.

"Just saddle my horse, then, damn you. Or have someone else do it. I'll find Kelly on my own if I have to. I don't need help from anyone."

Now that he had said the words, he began almost to believe them. "That's right. I don't need you or Rance or anyone! I'll bring that old man to heel on my own if I have to, and it looks like I'll have to!"

Bledsoe closed his eyes and felt his mind begin to drift. "Tisdale. Do what I told you to do. What's wrong with you?"

But when Bledsoe opened his eyes, he realized he was sitting on the porch and Tisdale was nowhere in sight.

He tried to shake his mind clear. *How could he have gone so quickly? And without making a sound. Had I imagined the whole thing?*

He called out for Tisdale and looked around for where the ranch hand might have gone. It was not until he looked out onto the trail leading up to the ranch house that he saw a lone rider.

The man was still too far away to see him clearly, but he cut a familiar figure. The horse was huge—a Morgan, it appeared to his fever-addled brain—but the rider upon it commanded it as if it were a much smaller animal.

Kelly had ridden a Morgan, had he not? Bledsoe wondered if this might be Rance, returning home atop the horse of his fallen enemy.

But the closer the shape drew to the house, the more he realized that this was not Rance. The silhouette was too large and the way he sat in the saddle was different. But the man was still familiar to him and he wondered where he had seen him before. Was he one of his men coming back home? Maybe it was Tom upon Kelly's horse?

Then his memory cleared, and he remembered where he had seen the man before. It was years ago when he and Rance and the others rode out to put the fear of God into the man who had whipped his ranch hands half to death. He had seen that same, solitary figure crest a small rise in the valley as they blocked his trail. That had been the same black day he had lost his eye.

And the man that had taken it was William Kelly. Bull Kelly.

And through the fever that burned through him, he realized that this had not taken place years ago, but only a week or so at the most. What was happening to him? Was the infection so bad that it was eating his brain? He shook his head clear and almost fell over from the effort of it.

He grabbed on to the porch post again and looked out at the road to see where Kelly was. He was much closer now. Less than half a mile out, or so it appeared.

Bledsoe knew he did not need anyone to saddle his horse for him. He did not have to ride anywhere. His prey was coming to him.

All he needed was the right tool to do the job. And

it was somewhere inside his house. All he had to do was make it in there and back in time to set his trap and end the William Kelly menace once and for all.

He pushed himself off the beam and barreled through the front door of his home. He did not have a moment to lose.

CHAPTER TWENTY-SIX

KELLY HAD FELT a spark of hope when he saw the ranch hand hobble away from the porch and break toward the bunkhouse as soon as he saw Kelly coming. He watched Bledsoe hanging on to the porch post like the town drunk at closing time. He had heard the rancher's eye wound had left him in a bad way, but the man looked insane. He might have lost twenty pounds or more from the fever.

He watched the rancher slump against the post again before lunging back into his house to fetch only God knew what. Probably a gun, Kelly imagined. Or hoped. Aiming a gun at him would help Kelly justify a lot of what he planned to do to Bledsoe.

Kelly was glad Bledsoe was out of it enough to make it easy for Kelly to take him down. He was glad none of the men of the Diamond B appeared ready to die with him.

Kelly had ridden up this road expecting to meet

death waiting for him at the end of it. Now he was beginning to allow himself to believe the end he would be meeting might not be his own.

Kelly untethered his whip as he rode closer to the house, allowing it to drag along the ground as he got nearer. He was about ten feet away from the porch when the door was thrown open and Bledsoe came lumbering out with a rifle in his hand. Kelly had no idea if it was a Winchester or a Remington and cared even less.

He tensed as he watched Bledsoe stagger to the nearest post and fall against it, using it to prop himself up as much as he was using it for cover. The purple circles around his eyes and damp clothes told Kelly the rancher's fever was as bad as Miguel and Rita had told him. He had seen men suffer from such fevers before and had no idea what was keeping this man alive, much less on his feet.

"Stop right there, old man," Bledsoe slurred from the cover of the post.

Kelly doubted Bledsoe had the strength to cock the rifle, much less raise it.

"It's time for us to bring this miserable mess to an end."

Kelly gripped the handle of his whip tightly. "Yes, Mr. Bledsoe. I believe the time has surely come for that."

Kelly cut loose with the whip just as Bledsoe struggled to raise his rifle. The whip cracked against the porch post, and with two feet to spare, the popper arced around and punched Bledsoe in the temple.

The rancher had already crumpled to the floor before Kelly could bring back his whip for a second blow. When he did, he saw the rifle had skittered away from Bledsoe's grip, but was still within reach.

Another whack of the whip from Kelly laid the popper between the trigger guard and the stock, allowing Kelly to yank the rifle off the porch. It fell to the ground before he could grab it, but at least it was far enough away from Bledsoe's grasp to do anyone much harm.

The deep gash in Bledsoe's left temple said the rancher was no longer going to do anyone much harm, either.

Kelly had half re-coiled his whip when he heard a door open to his left. It was the bunkhouse. The same shape of the man he had seen hobbling away from Bledsoe while he was riding up here hobbled toward him now, hands in the air.

"Don't hurt me, mister," the man said. "I ain't armed and no one in there is armed, either."

Kelly moved the Morgan a few steps backward in case the injured man was trying to set him up to stop a bullet. He had fully expected that he and Bledsoe would probably end up killing each other, but as that had not happened, William Kelly found he had a renewed sense of survival. "What's your name, boy?"

"Tisdale," the man told him. "Don't hurt me."

"Quit saying that and state your case before I lose my patience with you."

Tisdale said, "We're all busted up pretty bad in there. We rode against you a couple of times, sure, but we didn't ride out this last time when Mr. Bledsoe wanted us to. Not even those men who were able. Some of us faked it so our wounds seemed worse than they were."

Kelly was not sure he believed him. "Why?"

"On account of what Mr. Bledsoe wanted us to do to you wasn't right. Scaring you that first day on account of what you'd done to Billy and Marty was one thing. But to go back after your cows and to gun down your boys like he did wasn't right. That's why none of us went back the third time like he wanted us to and none of us mean you any harm now."

Kelly had not been expecting this and admitted to himself that he did not know what to say or do next.

"Rance is dead," Kelly told him. "So is a boy named Tommy. That change your thinking any, lad?"

Tisdale appeared to swallow hard but kept his hands in the air. "Seems like you've lost some good people and we've lost some good people on account of a fight none of us wanted in the first place."

Tisdale glanced over at the porch. "The man who started all of this is dead and it looks like you're the one who killed him. The men who shot your boys are dead. If that's good enough for you to call even, it's good enough for all of us."

Kelly glanced toward the bunkhouse. "You speak for everyone in there?"

"Yes, sir," Tisdale said. "They told me I could."

Now was the real test. "How many of you are in there?"

"Ten now," Tisdale told them. "Another five working the horses in the pasture yonder."

"Bring your men out here," Kelly said. "One line, their hands up like yours. I see anyone come out of there with anything that even looks like it can shoot, I'll cut into the lot of you."

Tisdale relayed Kelly's demands into the bunkhouse and ten men filed out, each with his hands empty and raised in the air.

"Turn around slowly and let me see the backs of you."

The men followed his order, and other than a knife or two tucked into the back of their pants, they appeared to be unarmed. Since the knives were too big to be thrown effectively, Kelly decided to trust them. At least a little.

"All of you put your hands down."

All of the men did.

"This Tisdale fella says he speaks for you. Does he?"

All of the men said he did.

"He tells me you boys don't want any more trouble. That true?"

All of the men said it was.

Kelly gripped the handle of the whip tightly. Every single one of these men had ridden against him for Bledsoe. The busted arms or bandaged heads or missing hands or gimpy legs each of them suffered were because they had tried to kill him. They had been part of the murdering cowards who had killed his boys and stolen his herd. They had been counted with the man who had taken Kelly's beautiful dream and pulled it down before Bledsoe drove it into the earth.

Something deep inside William Kelly told him to kill every man he saw. If nothing of the Kelly name would last, then nothing of the Diamond B Ranch had the right to live after what it had done.

But something else inside him, something not as deep as rage but just as loud in its own way, told him he was wrong. It told him his fight was now over and all of his enemies were dead. Bledsoe and Rance had fallen under his whip. These men were as much caught up in all of this as he had been. As his boys had been. They were following orders to attack him the same as the men in his outfit had followed his orders to not fight and ride north with the rest of his herd. Their wounds were evidence that they had paid enough for the decisions of another.

Just as the graves of his boys were evidence that they had paid for his decision to ride north with the herd he had built for them.

Tears began to stream down William Kelly's cheeks.

His boys had not deserved death. Not even James.

And neither did these men.

The tears fell unabated and he made no attempt to wipe them away. The men were too far away to see them anyway, not that he cared what they thought.

Kelly cleared his throat and said, "I understand you boys are cowhands, not gunmen."

They all said that was true.

"Good, because if I wanted gunmen, I'd have hired gunmen and none of you would have the luxury of standing here now in whatever sorry state you find yourselves in. Well, despite what you might've heard or seen of me to the contrary, I'm a cattleman looking to be a rancher, so I'm in the market to hire myself cowhands. That's why I'd like to make a deal with each of you."

He watched the men shift uneasily. Some shifted because of the wounds they suffered. Some because they feared what Kelly might do with his whip.

He decided to not keep them in suspense any longer. "Any man here now or out in the pasture tending to cattle who wants a piece of something bigger than what he has now is welcome to help bring Bledsoe's herd and merge it with mine. When we get to Dodge City, you'll all get an equal cut."

Some of the men suddenly appeared not to be as injured as when they had first come out of the bunkhouse. Kelly's words seemed to have a healing effect on them. The power the idea of profit held over a man's disposition had never failed to amaze William Kelly.

"That might seem like a generous offer to you," Kelly said, "but that was the arrangement I had with my outfit before all this. That's the same arrangement I put to all of you right here and now. What do you say?"

The men traded glances, each one asking the other if they'd heard the man on the Morgan properly.

After a few moments, Tisdale took it upon himself to once again speak for the men. "You mean all of that, mister? Everything you just said? No bluffing? You'll forget and forgive all we done just like that?"

Kelly felt the old anger rise in him again, but that quiet voice in his ear helped him manage to keep it tamped down. "I never said anything about forgiving or forgetting, boy. I'm talking about needing you boys to take a herd to market and get a fair piece for your labors. You'll earn every penny of it, too. A herd of over six thousand cattle is big enough to make sure none of us need to see much of each other along the way. I'll have to get more provisions on credit, of course, but I figure it's worth the investment. A wise man once told me that time heals all wounds. It's a long way between here and Dodge City. Maybe that'll be time enough for all of us to do a little healing of our own. In mind and spirit and body, too."

William Kelly could not remember the last time he

had spoken so much and for so long. He was not usually that windy. He suddenly felt embarrassed by his behavior and shifted uneasily in the saddle. "That's about all I have to say on the matter. I'm willing to give it a try if you boys are."

They did not need Tisdale to tell Kelly they would all happily agree.

The men broke out into cheers and—those who could manage to do so—threw their hats up into the air in celebration. Working the Diamond B had lost its sheen for them long ago. Getting a piece of a cattle drive would be something that just might change all of their lives forever.

Tisdale held up a hand to momentarily stop their celebration. He motioned toward the ranch house. "I don't mean to throw a wet blanket on the bonfire, boys, but what'll we do about him? Looks like he's still alive if you ask me."

"Well, who asked you?" one of the men said to the immediate laughter of the others.

Kelly turned the great Morgan toward the porch and saw Bledsoe was beginning to struggle to get to his feet. He could not quite manage it, though, because the gash in his temple had served to scramble his brain. His feet gave out from under him whenever he tried to get his balance.

Kelly thought about taking mercy on the man and finishing him off once and for all.

But that's when that quiet voice returned to him with a better idea.

He looked back at Tisdale. "How soon do you think you and the boys could get that herd of yours moving?"

"Ain't my herd." Tisdale nodded toward Bledsoe, who had just collapsed back to the porch. "It's his for as long as he lives."

"Which won't be much longer," Kelly assured him. "Then ownership falls to his next of kin, which I know he doesn't have, so that leaves the foreman of the place to decide what happens to it."

Kelly was not sure if that was technically legal, but it was tradition as far as he knew it.

"And with Rance dead," Kelly went on, "I'd say that leaves you in charge, Tisdale. So, how long do you think it'll take?"

"Not long," Tisdale admitted as he thought it over. "But you know it ain't the gathering that's the problem. It's the getting them moving in the first place. A cow is a stubborn animal without the proper guidance."

But Kelly already had that figured. If there was one thing he knew about all too well in this life, it was how to move cattle. "You just get them headed this way. I'll take care of the rest."

Tisdale looked at Kelly crooked. "This way, Mr. Kelly? You sure? This is a mighty narrow passage for all of them cows at once."

But Kelly had already thought of that. "Let me worry about that, Mr. Tisdale. You just send them this way and I'll handle it from here."

Rejuvenated by the prospect of gold in their pockets and not being whipped to death, the men of the Diamond B hobbled and crept toward their horses, eager to saddle up and get the outfit moving. Eager to put the past behind them and go on to better things.

William Kelly was beginning to like the sound of that.

* * *

A S THE MEN began to lead the first group of cows from the pasture toward the ranch house, Kelly watched Bledsoe try to get to his feet.

He could tell the man was clearly dying, but he was glad he had not died just yet.

Not before he saw William Kelly leading his herd and his men past his home.

He saw Bledsoe raise a feeble hand as if to stop the cattle from leaving, but the crack of Kelly's whip and the encouraging yells from the cowboys kept the herd moving along.

Kelly turned in time to see Bledsoe slump against the porch post, trying to lift his head. To say something that might stop his legacy from passing him by.

But just as Kelly could do nothing to bring back his boys, Bledsoe was powerless to keep from being left behind. What's more, he had lived long enough to know it, which was the only kind of justice Kelly could expect from this horror. It would have to be enough because it was all he was going to get.

Kelly rode into the herd and rode out among the tide of cattle that passed the ranch and down the main road, beneath the gate that bore the Diamond B above it. He steered the big Morgan through the herd and broke free at the front, where he slowed down just enough for the herd to see him. To see the black Morgan and know who was really in charge.

He wanted to make twenty-five miles a day or more if he could. It was a big herd, but he figured Xavier would not drive his men as hard as he had. He would be content with twenty miles a day in the hope his friend might catch up. Kelly would be happy to grant his old friend his wish.

Kelly hoped the cattle were so pent up, he might get thirty miles a day out of them. The sooner he saw Xavier and Baxter and Greenly and the rest of the boys from the Kelly outfit, the better for them all.

Ready to find
your next great read?

Let us help.

Visit prh.com/nextread

Penguin
Random
House